Prai[se]

author of The Hometown Harbor Series and the Cooper Harrington Detective Novels

"This book was just as enchanting as the others. Hardships with the love of a special group of friends. I recommend the series as a must read. I loved every exciting moment. A new author for me. She's fabulous."
—*Maggie!, review of Pieces of Home: A Hometown Harbor Novel (Book 4)*

"Tammy is an amazing author, she reminds me of Debbie Macomber… Delightful, heartwarming… just down to earth."
— *Plee, review of A Promise of Home: A Hometown Harbor Novel (Book 3)*

"This was an entertaining and relaxing novel. Tammy Grace has a simple yet compelling way of drawing the reader into the lives of her characters. It was a pleasure to read a story that didn't rely on theatrical tricks, unrealistic events or steamy sex scenes to fill up the pages. Her characters and plot were strong enough to hold the reader's interest."
—*MrsQ125, review of Finding Home: A Hometown Harbor Novel (Book 1)*

"This is a beautifully written story of loss, grief, forgiveness and healing. I believe anyone could relate to the situations and feelings represented here. This is a read that will stay with you long after you've completed the book."
—*Cassidy Hop, review of Finally Home: A Hometown Harbor Novel (Book 5)*

Killer Music and Deadly Connection are award-winning novels, earning the 2016 & 2017 Mystery Gold Medal by the Global E-Book Awards

"Killer Music is a clever and well-crafted whodunit. The vivid and colorful characters shine as the author gradually reveals their hidden secrets—an absorbing page-turning read."
— *Jason Deas, bestselling author of Pushed and Birdsongs*

"I could not put this book down! It was so well written & a suspenseful read! This is definitely a 5-star story! I'm hoping there will be a sequel!"
—*Colleen, review of Killer Music*

"This is the best book yet by this author. The plot was well crafted with an unanticipated ending. I like to try to leap ahead and see if I can accurately guess the outcome. I was able to predict some of the plot but not the actual details which made reading the last several chapters quite engrossing."
—*0001PW, review of Deadly Connection*

Tammy L. Grace

Beach Haven

A Glass Beach Cottage Novel

Beach Haven is a work of fiction. Names, characters, places, and incidents either are products of the author's imagination or are used fictitiously. Any resemblance to actual events, locales, entities, or persons, living or dead, is entirely coincidental.

BEACH HAVEN Copyright © 2019 by Tammy L. Grace

All rights reserved. No part of this book may be reproduced or transmitted in any form or by any means, electronic or mechanical including photocopying, recording, or by any information storage and retrieval system without the written permission of the author, except for the use of brief quotations in a book review. For permissions contact the author directly via electronic mail: tammy@tammylgrace.com

www.tammylgrace.com
Facebook: https://www.facebook.com/tammylgrace.books
Twitter: @TammyLGrace

Published in the United States by Lone Mountain Press, Nevada

ISBN 978-1-945591-09-9 (paperback)
ISBN 978-1-945591-10-5 (eBook)
FIRST EDITION

Cover design by Elizabeth Mackey
Interior Formatting by Polgarus Studio
Printed in the United States of America

ALSO BY TAMMY L. GRACE

Cooper Harrington Detective Novels
Killer Music
Deadly Connection
Dead Wrong

Hometown Harbor Series
Hometown Harbor: The Beginning (FREE Prequel Novella)
Finding Home
Home Blooms
A Promise of Home
Pieces of Home
Finally Home

STAND-ALONE BOOKS
A Season for Hope: A Christmas Novella (stand-alone)

GLASS BEACH COTTAGE SERIES
Beach Haven

*"Our memories of the ocean will linger on,
long after our footprints in the sand are gone."*
—*Anonymous*

Chapter 1

The last year had been pure hell. Lily took another look in the hotel mirror. She straightened the flag pin she wore on her jacket lapel and moved a piece of hair from her eye, noticing the dark circles still visible after a healthy application of concealer.

The bathroom door opened, and a young man in a suit and tie smiled at her. "You look so handsome, Kev. Your dad would be proud." She wiped a tear from her eye.

"Aww, Mom, don't cry." He engulfed her in a long embrace. "We just have to get through today."

She nodded and brushed an invisible speck from his shoulder. "Okay, let's go." She reached for her handbag. "The hotel approved a late check-out for us, so we'll have time to come back after the service. We can change before we head out."

She flung a silky scarf, bright royal blue and emblazoned with gold badges, around her shoulders. "The car should be here by now." Kevin escorted her into the elevator, and they rode downstairs in silence.

They found their car waiting at the curb. The driver held the door, and they stepped into the sleek black sedan before it sped off into the traffic clogged streets of Washington, D.C.

Lily recognized the familiar buildings that made up the skyline of the nation's capital. Richmond was only a couple of hours away, but it seemed like a different world. She didn't venture into the city often. She and Kevin had spent some time at the National Mall yesterday, but their hearts weren't in it. All it did was churn up memories of happier times.

Their family of three had visited the capital and soaked in all the history the summer before Kevin's freshman year in high school. It had been a great trip and a fun time together. Now he was a junior in college, and they were a family of two. Yesterday's visit only emphasized Gary's absence.

Their route from the Mayflower Hotel took them by the massive Eisenhower Office Building and offered a glimpse of the White House. She took in the quiet green space of the Ellipse as the driver made the turn onto Constitution Avenue. The Washington Monument loomed above a steady stream of schoolchildren exploring the National Mall.

Traffic was heavy, but Lily was in no hurry. She took the time afforded her by the multiple red lights to gaze at the buildings. The look of awe and wonder on the faces of Kevin and Gary when they stepped into the Air and Space Museum all those years ago was still etched in her mind. She smiled, reflecting on the excitement and happiness of that day.

The thrill of seeing the Declaration of Independence and the Constitution in the National Archives was something she would never forget. Those documents housed in the dark, reverent space, encased in protective high-tech glass cases, signed by those brave founding fathers gave her chills. Lily's love for history had deep roots connected to her late father, a teacher.

As they passed near the National Gallery of Art, she gripped her son's hand. They had attended the candlelight vigil on the grassy area of the mall just north of the building on Sunday night. They had joined thousands of family members, survivors, and law enforcement officers as dusk settled over the city. Emotions ran high. Her eyes blurred with fresh tears as she recalled the beauty of the shining lights against the backdrop of the vast mall just a few blocks away from the memorial, where her husband's name joined over 21,000 others on a wall of marble.

Yesterday, she and Kevin had made a quick appearance at the conference put on for survivors of the fallen officers, but they'd escaped at the first opportunity. They wandered around the mall and the streets bordering it to pass the time. Last night, she and Kevin had visited the Law Enforcement Memorial in the early evening. They placed a rose near Gary's name in the curved marble wall. They sat on a bench for an hour and watched people visit the wall and make rubbings, as they had done, to capture the name of their loved one.

She could still feel the cool blue-gray marble against the hand she'd rested over Gary's name. She and Kevin read the inspirational inscriptions under the four bronzed adult lion sculptures at the ends of the memorial walls, positioned as protectors over their young cubs. That's how she always thought of Gary. The protector. Her protector. Kevin's protector. Now he was gone.

She forced her thoughts back to the task at hand as the driver pulled to a curb outside the U.S. Capitol. The ceremony was scheduled to take place on the West Front of the building, where inauguration ceremonies were held.

An escort officer met them at the curb and guided them to a path, explaining they would be seated in the front row. Senator Corwin of Virginia, a man Lily knew from his time in the Virginia General Assembly, had asked her to attend the ceremony and be one of the survivors chosen to go on stage during the event.

She knew it was an honor. She knew it was expected. It didn't lessen the feeling of dread in the pit of her stomach. Her position with the Virginia Capitol Police had been highlighted when Gary had been killed. They were both in law enforcement and had risen in the ranks in their respective departments. He on the streets of Richmond, she in the halls of the Capitol.

A young man greeted them as they made their way to the audience chairs. He extended his hand and introduced himself as Senator Corwin's assistant. He handed each of them a bottle of water and escorted them the rest of the way to their seats, in the middle of the front row. He explained that when the ceremony was over, he would return to help them find their way into the building for the luncheon organized by members of the Senate.

Flowers and greenery graced the stage set up at the bottom of the steps leading to the Capitol Building. The bright blue bunting fluttered in the breeze. Lily turned to look behind her and saw the thousands of chairs set up on the lawn. Law enforcement officers from all over the country were stationed around the area, and many of them escorted family members to their seats.

Both she and Gary had attended the memorial during their careers. They had been honored to be part of the officers chosen to represent the State of Virginia and escort family members to their seats. As she took in the somber faces of those filing into chairs, she knew how much easier it was to honor than to be honored.

She took in the vibrant blue banner that hung behind the stage, announcing National Police Week. The sun beat down and warmed her navy-blue suit jacket against her skin. Thankful for the bright day, she donned her sunglasses. The dark tint hid her sad eyes. She slipped a paper from her purse and looked at the pencil rubbing. His name, Gary E. Reed, stared back at her. She and Kevin made several pencil transfers at the wall. They were tucked away, secured in an envelope in her suitcase, save for the two they brought with them today.

The setting was surreal, as was the ceremony. Lily did her best to cast herself as an onlooker, not part of the service. She tried to observe, used her skill set to take in the crowd and remove herself from the pain of being one of them. The survivors. It was a funny word. She didn't feel like a survivor.

She focused on the lawmakers who stood on stage and welcomed the family, friends, and co-workers to the solemn service. The President of the United States was introduced and stepped onto the stage from behind a panel. The audience roared with welcoming applause.

President Clarkson, known for his staunch support of law enforcement, did not disappoint. He gave a heartfelt speech, acknowledging the sacrifices made by those who gave their lives in service. He lauded his praise on all those in law enforcement and touted their bravery and selflessness.

He expressed his sincere sympathy and sadness for those left behind. He then invited a few families onstage. Lily tightened her grip on Kevin's hand as they waited to hear their names.

Uniformed officers escorted them up the short set of stairs to the stage. She stood to the immediate left of President Clarkson. He turned and gripped Lily's hand in his and wrapped a strong arm around her shoulders. He did the same with Kevin, adding a pat on his back.

He bent and spoke in Lily's ear. "I know you will miss Gary forever, and I want you to know he will never be forgotten. I know you also serve, and you have my admiration and thanks. I appreciate you being here today. I know this isn't easy for you or Kevin. I also know this isn't the first time tragedy has touched your life. I'm sure you're thinking of your mother today as well as Gary. I'm honored to meet you and Kevin and will hold you in my prayers. If you ever need anything, don't hesitate to reach out to me."

His sincerity struck Lily. She'd served with politicians for her entire career and could detect artificial sentiments and platitudes in a heartbeat. He was the real thing. She saw the raw emotion in his eyes, and his heartfelt words had an impact. She was impressed he had taken the time to learn about her mother's death so many years ago, her career, and Kevin.

She watched as President Clarkson engaged in a conversation with Kevin, and she saw the glint in her son's eyes. She couldn't hold out any longer. Tears cascaded from underneath her sunglasses, down her cheeks.

The president consoled other family members and addressed the audience while they remained on stage behind him. She heard his words of comfort and gratitude. She heard him say Gary's name and recite his service record and date of death, the fifth of May, last year. A day she would never forget.

Like a leaf floating in a stream, she let herself be guided back to her seat, listened to more dignitaries speak kind words, and wept as a choir sang. The sound of "Taps" playing sent a chill through her. If she never heard another note from a bagpipe, it would be too soon.

The service concluded with the reading of names as each family approached a giant wreath and added a flower representing their loved one. Kevin placed Gary's flower in the wreath, and they made their way to the other side of the stage. An officer met them and guided them down a pathway that meandered to the building, where Senator Corwin's assistant led them to the luncheon.

He placed them at a table with four other chairs, not yet occupied. Lily downed the glass of water in front of her, and Kevin reached for the pitcher to refill it. She took off her sunglasses and dabbed at her eyes with a tissue, still clutching the paper with Gary's name on it.

Soon the room teemed with family members, and their table filled with the parents, wife, and young son of a fallen officer from Norfolk. A choir sang while waiters circled through the room delivering meals. As Lily picked at her plate, she felt a hand on her shoulder.

Senator Bruce Corwin stood before her. "Lily, Kevin." He gave them a nod. "How are you holding up?"

"Fine, sir. Just glad it's over." She gritted her teeth. "Sorry, that's not what I meant. It was a lovely service. It's just difficult."

"I understand, dear. I can't imagine." He glanced at Kevin. "One more year at William and Lee I understand? My alma mater."

"Yes, sir. I've decided to pursue a graduate degree in law."

"Wonderful. If you need anything, references or any help at all, just get in touch with my office. Maybe we'll see you in this wonderful building one day.

"And Lily, congratulations. I was surprised to hear you're retiring. I know you'll be missed. I'm sure it's bittersweet."

"Thank you, Senator Corwin. I'm on leave for a few weeks, but Thursday was my last official day on the job. I'm moving. I sold the house and am beginning a new adventure. It's been a tough year, and things sort of worked out to point me in a new direction."

"Sometimes change is a good thing, Lily. I know how hard this has been on you." He shook her hand and clasped Kevin on the shoulder. "You take care, young man."

She watched as the man she had known for most of her career ambled over to the others at the table and engaged them in conversation. She knew he meant well and that he cared, but it felt more like a duty. She'd become jaded serving with the Virginia Capitol Police and witnessing the hypocrisy that ran rampant through the halls.

After they finished eating, she tilted her head toward the door. "Ready?" she asked.

Kevin stood, and they both shook hands with the others at their table. The shell-shocked look on their faces advertised their devastation. Tears stained their cheeks as they said their goodbyes. They had suffered an unimaginable loss. Bonded forever by their shared experience of overwhelming sorrow, they were all members of the same club.

They could have asked for a car to return them to the hotel, but Lily wanted to be done with the whole ordeal. They took a walk through the grounds, enjoying the groomed beds and colorful flowers. They made a pass through the Library of Congress as an homage to Lily's mom. She had been a librarian and loved books. When they finished, she led the way to the escalator of the Metro station a block away.

Minutes later they emerged at the station near their hotel. As they strolled the few blocks, Lily chatted about summer plans. "I still feel bad about moving. I hate leaving you behind."

He grinned. "I'll be there with you for most of the summer. I don't come home that much nowadays anyway. I've got my apartment in Lexington, and school will start again before I know it. I'll be busy, so I think it's a good idea for you to do something new. Away from here."

Kevin put his arm around his mother's shoulders. "It's gonna be okay. Dad would be happy for you. You always talk about how much fun you had there as a kid."

Tears welled up again. "I just can't stay here. In our house. I can't go to work. I've tried, and I'm a wreck. I'm worn out from trying. I'm a bit unsure about moving across the country, but there's no time like the present." She shoved her shoulder into his. "Maybe you can find a law school out west."

He gave her a smile that reminded her of Gary. "It could happen."

She gripped him by both shoulders. "I just want you to be happy.

Safe and happy. I'm going to try to do the same, but I can't do it here. If things don't work, I can always come back, but it feels like this deal happened for a reason."

"I understand, Mom. I really do. I'm sort of set on staying here for school, but if you get too lonely, I can look at something out there."

She shook her head. "No, no. It's not about me. You do what you need to do and what's right for you. I know you have great connections at this school. Your roots are here. If you need me, I can be on the next plane. If you want to visit or stay with me, you're always welcome."

"Back at ya, Mom. We'll always have each other."

They hurried inside the hotel and gathered their bags. A car collected them and dropped Kevin at Union Station to head back to Lexington.

She held him in a long hug and fought back her tears. "Love you, Kev. I'll call you when I get there. I'll see you in a few days."

She waved goodbye as the driver sped away, steering for the airport and the flight that would transport Lily to her new life on the coast of Washington in Driftwood Bay.

Chapter 2

Exhaustion settled over Lily, gifting her with sleep on the nonstop evening flight. Due to the time change, her six-hour flight arrived only three hours later than she'd left. She retrieved her luggage and took a cab to her hotel.

The small coastal town she soon would be calling home was a couple of hours from the airport. She had a reservation on the shuttle tomorrow. Her room had a view of the water. She sat and took in the reflection of the lights on the inky surface. Her thoughts wandered to their home in Richmond, Kevin, her parents, the memorial service, and her job.

Lily's life had been her family and her work. The job hampered friendships, both for her and Gary. Most of their friends were fellow officers, and those friendships had faded after Gary's death. She had regular visitors from his department for the first few months, but as time marched on, their visits dwindled. She focused on work, even volunteering to work extra whenever it was needed. She was at the office more than she was at home.

Lily's parents had died over fifteen years ago, and Kevin was away at school. Gary's parents lived in Florida and had stayed with her after he was killed, but once she returned to work, they went home. She didn't have a large circle of girlfriends.

The people at work had been fantastic, but they weren't a

substitute for what she missed. Her partner and confidant. Her husband and best friend. Her everything. All of it, gone in an instant.

The house. Her office where she received the call that horrible day. Her car she had used to rush to the hospital to see Gary. The restaurants and stores she and Gary frequented, where the storekeepers still gave her sorrowful looks. Painful memories of all she had lost surrounded her.

She retired, sold the house, sold her car, and packed her belongings. She was pinning her hopes on a new start in a place that held comforting memories.

As she took in the beautiful skyline of Seattle, she whispered, "I hope I'm doing the right thing, Gary."

Lily enjoyed a hearty breakfast at the café on the corner. When she finished, she only had to wait a few minutes for the shuttle. As she watched the Seattle traffic swarm around the van, her thoughts drifted to the event that had spurred her to make a bold change. Uncle Leo had died five months ago. He had no children, and Lily had been his favorite niece. As a child and teenager, she had visited him and Aunt Maggie at their beach retreat. Summers at Glass Beach Cottage had been her reward for being a good student. As she got older, Uncle Leo gave her a summer job helping out around the property.

She knew from her trip a couple of months ago that the guest cottages needed attention. The main house had been maintained and modernized, but the quaint cottages were dilapidated and in need of an overhaul.

When she had met with her uncle's lawyer, he had given her a folder full of information and instructions from Uncle Leo. He'd hoped that Lily would move to beautiful Driftwood Bay and restore the cottages. He wanted her to discover a new purpose and happiness as the owner of one of the most sought-after vacation spots in the Pacific Northwest.

She had chatted with Uncle Leo by phone after Gary had died. He was too infirm to travel across the country for the funeral but had comforted Lily with his gentle words. He invited her to come "home" to the haven on the beach. She promised she would visit Glass Beach, but she didn't make the trip until Uncle Leo was gone.

The moving company had transported her possessions to Driftwood Bay. The lawyer had handled the minutiae and arranged for the unloading and placement of her items in the main house. She had taken a few days off two weeks ago, loaded their beloved golden retriever, Fritz, into Gary's truck, and driven three thousand miles to get him to Driftwood Bay.

Uncle Leo's longtime neighbor was delighted to look after Fritz until Lily returned. She had spent the night and taken a flight back to Virginia to finish her days at work and attend the memorial service.

Lily missed the comfort of her furry friend. Her lone companion now that Gary was gone. Fritz loved the water. The few times they made it to the beach in Virginia with him, he frolicked and played all day. Keeping him out of the ocean was going to be next to impossible. She smiled thinking of her sweet boy. Fritz would be beyond excited to see her and would be out of control when Kevin arrived.

She made a mental list as the shuttle made its way to the small town on the water that she would call home. Driftwood Bay sat on the edge of the Olympic Peninsula, affording it picturesque views of the San Juan Islands as well as the Olympic and Cascade Mountains. Accessible via bridges or ferries from the Seattle area and ferries from

Canada and the San Juan Islands, it took some effort to visit. The postcard-worthy vistas were worth the trouble though.

The shuttle driver pulled to a stop on Bay Street. A banner welcoming visitors to the annual Rhododendron Festival hung above the street. The beautiful flowers overflowed from pots and planters lining the streets. Deep fuchsias, crimsons, and violets caught her eye, along with the subtler pinks and peaches.

She retrieved her suitcase and headed for the lawyer's office on Jefferson Street. He had promised her a ride to her new home. It was a walkable distance, but with her suitcase, she was happy to accept the offer.

Mr. Landon was in his office and expecting her. He introduced his assistant, Nell, and led Lily through the back door to his car. He tossed her suitcase in the trunk and drove the short distance along the waterfront. He pointed out the ferry dock, marina, park, and City Hall.

Uncle Leo's property was almost two acres on Paradise Point, a private enclave with beach access within walking distance of the heart of downtown. The main house had been remodeled and updated but retained its beachy charm. Instead of the old wooden shingles that had sided the house, new wide horizontal lap vinyl siding in a serene blue-gray had been added. Portions of the house were covered with vinyl shingles to give it character. The white trim gleamed in the morning sunlight, and the grounds were bursting with colorful bushes and plants.

Mr. Landon carried her bag up the large ramp that had replaced the steps she remembered leading to the entry. She unlocked the set of glass double doors. He placed the bag inside and said, "I'll let you get settled. If you need anything at all, just let me know."

Lily thanked him and wheeled her bag to the large master suite on the main level. She marveled at the view from all the rooms as she made her way to the open living area. She loved the glassed-in outdoor deck off the kitchen and dining area with its close to year-round usability. The glass panels in the walls could be opened in the warm months and closed in the colder weather. She opened a few windows to let the fresh breeze in before hurrying next door to retrieve Fritz from the neighbors.

Mr. and Mrs. Mott insisted Lily return and join them for dinner. She tried to refuse but admitted she'd rather get the house set up than go to the grocery store. She put Fritz's leash on and promised to return that evening.

When they got home, she found Fritz's box of supplies and unearthed his food and water bowls. She placed a bowl of water outside on the deck and added another one in the large pantry and storage area niche off the kitchen.

She noted the sizeable old desk in the area with a view out to the deck and beyond. It made for an inviting workstation. She and Fritz explored the downstairs level in more detail. Guest bedrooms and bathrooms surrounded an area that had been outfitted with cabinets and countertops. Laundry machines took up part of the wall space, along with a sink, microwave, and ice machine. Aunt Maggie had used the cabinets and counters for her art projects.

Built-in shelves under the windows held stacks of nostalgic board games and puzzles. Wooden tables were situated around the room, allowing guests to spend their downtime playing cards or games. Lily smiled at the memory of walking by the table where her aunt always had a puzzle going and guests would take a few minutes to look for pieces.

The house sported three round windows, like portholes on a ship. Aunt Maggie had crafted beautiful stained-glass designs in each of them. She had been a talented artist, and several of her paintings graced the walls. She had passed away several years ago, but her supplies were still in the cupboards.

There were a couple of couches and a coffee table atop a thick area rug in front of an entertainment center, which housed a television and stereo equipment. Mr. Landon had left all of the furniture in the downstairs area. The garden level, as her aunt called it, made for a generous living space, separate and private from the main floor. Guests had use of the common area for watching television, doing laundry, and relaxing. Lily had been given the run of the downstairs when she had spent her summers on the coast.

Fritz gave the entire space a thorough sniffing before following Lily out the sliding glass doors. Benches were situated along the wall of the house, offering views of both the garden and the water. A fountain bubbled in the midst of a circle of plants donning vibrant flowers.

Concrete paths wove through the garden and to the three private cottages. Lily noticed the rotting wood siding, missing roof shingles, and broken windows. She'd have to get some contractors to take a look and give her some estimates.

Fritz romped through the grass and took off down a dirt path. She followed and stopped at the edge of the precipice overlooking the deep blue of the inlet. A rickety wooden rail fence ran along the bluff, and faded signs warned of danger. She bent down to Fritz and said, "No. Stay here."

She made a mental note to get the fence reinforced. She couldn't bear the thought of Fritz getting hurt, or worse, if his exploring led him through the generous gap between the sagging rails.

She took the leash from her pocket and snapped it back on his harness. "Come on, Fritzie, let's stay out of trouble today." She led him back to the main house, noting the firepit in a screened area of the garden. She sat on a bench and looked out to the water, knowing it would offer an amazing night view.

She and Fritz took the stairs up to the deck on the main level.

She made sure the glass door was secure and took off his leash. She opened the door to the dining room and went about exploring while Fritz rested on the deck.

She opened cupboards and ran her hand over the cool white and gray granite countertops. The modern stainless appliances blended with the more traditional white farmhouse style cabinets. She opened the refrigerator, designed to look like a cabinet, and found it stocked with a few essentials.

She smiled and said, "Mr. Landon thought of everything." She took out an apple and found a cutting board and knife set. As she sliced it, she looked out the window and saw Fritz sleeping on one of the cushioned chaise lounges.

It brought a smile to her face to see him content. He missed Gary and continued to search for him at their old house until the day she drove him across the country. She munched on her snack and went about unpacking the boxes stacked on the other side of the kitchen island. By mid-afternoon, she had the kitchen stocked with the items from her old kitchen. Several empty cupboards remained, and the large pantry had plenty of space for more things.

She plugged in the kettle and made a cup of tea before tackling her bedroom and bathroom. Fritz had tired of the outdoors and followed her into the master suite. The first thing she placed in the room was Gary's urn. He had traveled with her when she and Fritz drove across the country. Using a soft cloth, Lily dusted the cool black surface that looked like a night sky filled with stars. She ran her fingers over the engraving of his name as she placed it on the center shelf of a bookcase.

She unpacked her clothes and hung them in the huge walk-in closet. It had a built-in armoire and plenty of space for her meager wardrobe. She had turned in all her uniforms, which accounted for the bulk of her clothing.

Hugging a small group of clothes, she brought the collar of a worn leather jacket to her nose and inhaled. She closed her eyes and reveled in the scent of her husband. Relief flooded over her at the faint aroma she recognized. She embraced his favorite flannel shirt and hung it with a soft t-shirt she loved.

She had donated his other clothes but couldn't part with a handful of favorites. One of his t-shirts had been her sleeping companion for the better part of the last year. She had packed all of them for the move, thus ending the ritual.

The leather jacket had been her Christmas gift to him more than ten years ago. It had been well-loved, with its scuffed spots and softened sleeves. She dreaded the day when his scent would no longer be evident.

Next, she tackled the bathroom and stocked the cabinets and drawers. It took her a few minutes to decide which of the double sinks she would use. The subtle aqua color of sea glass highlighted the whites and beiges used in the space. A large cabinet with more storage and a lowered counter separated the sinks. Lily noted the antique chair in front of it. She knew this style was popular for putting on one's makeup, but she didn't see herself using it. High maintenance was not a term used to describe her.

The attractive clawfoot bathtub positioned under a window offered a beautiful view for a bath. The large walk-in shower was adjacent. The bathing area was separated from the toilet and bidet by a wall. It was a considerable space containing a table with a stained-glass lamp and another large dresser that would be great for storage.

A beautiful round mosaic of sea glass in turquoise, aqua, white, and seafoam decorated the wall above the table. Aunt Maggie could have opened a studio and made a fortune.

She went in search of the boxes of linens. Earth-tones had

dominated her old house, but this dwelling was all about the beach theme. She'd have to invest in some new towels to match the color scheme. Not to mention, she had only two bathrooms in the old house, and this one had three full baths and two powder rooms.

Before she found the boxes she wanted, she opened another and extracted a stack of framed family photos. With tender care, she wiped each one, becoming tearful when she brushed her hand over the glass above one of her favorite images of Gary.

She carried the frames to the living area and placed them on the shelves of the two large bookcases that flanked the fireplace. She rearranged them a few times until she was happy. The main level furnishings had been well worn, so Mr. Landon had sold or donated most of them, except for the hardwood bookcases, the dining set, and a few tables, plus a newer pair of leather chairs.

Her own comfortable leather living room set now filled the space. Her flat screen television occupied the area above the fireplace. Gary's recliner that she couldn't bring herself to discard rested at an angle. Her bedroom furniture was set up in the master suite.

She spied the large glass vase in the window sill. Her aunt had always used it to collect sea glass from the beach. It held a thin layer of the turquoise and green colored bits of glass. When the vase was almost full, her aunt would dump it out on the counter and sort it to make one of her creations. One of Lily's favorites incorporated deep cobalt and cornflower blue glass, with a few pieces of rare lavender sea glass. It still hung on the wall of the master bedroom.

She remembered when her aunt had held up a piece of sea glass next to Lily's face. She had told her the rare cornflower blue glass was a perfect match for Lily's eyes. Aunt Maggie had fashioned a piece into a necklace Lily wore all summer. She had been heartbroken when she lost it while playing in the water along the beach. She looked and looked but never found the necklace.

She positioned Fritz's two beds, one in the open living area and the other in the master suite near her bed. It was a spacious room with an inviting window seat, large enough for a nap, with a panoramic view. Even with her king size bed and two dressers, there was room to spare. She estimated the master suite took up about a third of the main level, with the open living and dining area in the middle, and the kitchen with its pantry and work area opposite the master suite. Everything she needed, except for the laundry facilities, was on the main floor.

As her aunt and uncle aged, they spent all their time on the main level. She thumbed through the notebook left on the desk. She recognized Uncle Leo's perfect block letters. She took it, made another cup of tea, and curled into Gary's recliner to peruse the information.

She found the name of the gardener, plumber, housekeeper, and a handyman. She wouldn't need a housekeeper but checked the time and put in a call to Wade Lewis, the handyman. She explained she was Leo's niece and set up a time for him to visit and take a look at the fence and the three cottages.

She rifled through her bag and found her tablet and plugged her phone in to charge. Mr. Landon had organized all the utilities, including phone and internet services. She remembered seeing the instructions to connect to the wireless and went about setting up her devices. Once connected, she searched for grocery stores, drugstores, gas stations, and other conveniences.

After penning a quick shopping list, she discovered a local store and knew she'd have to pay a visit to Driftwood Bay Mercantile. She chuckled at the name, reminding her of days long gone and a local general store. That was her only chance of finding towels and household goods. She found a chain grocery store but opted for the smaller market serving the region. They touted local products.

She and Fritz ventured outside to the deck. She spotted a gas grill under a heavy cover. A tear leaked out of her eye. Gary had done all the grilling. She wasn't known for her cooking and looked for easy dishes rather than gourmet meals. He had enjoyed making dinner and was home in the mid-afternoon, giving him time to prepare dinner. Since he'd been gone, she had become accustomed to eating at work or grabbing takeout. That would have to change.

"Well, Fritzie, it's time to go."

He heard the magic word and ran to her, tail wagging in anticipation of an adventure. She attached his leash, locked the house, and strolled down the street to dinner.

She made a short night of it and declined dessert, reminding them she was not adjusted to the time yet. Mrs. Mott gave her a container of leftovers. Lily thanked them for their kindness before trudging to her new home. The sky was darkening as she let herself in the front door.

She wasn't fearful staying alone in her new house, but her career instincts made her check all the doors and windows. She had become more cautious since Gary had been killed. She had brought all of their guns with her when she drove out with Fritz, and they were secure in a gun safe Mr. Landon had installed.

She and Gary had always had guns in the house throughout their time of policing, and she wasn't about to change. They had taught Kevin how to use a gun and the responsibility and safety measures that came with its use. They had always kept their weapons within reach, and now that she was alone, she intended to continue the habit.

She left the under cabinet lighting on in the kitchen and padded to bed. Fritz followed and flopped onto his bed while she snuggled under the blanket. She touched her fingers to the pad on the small gun safe on her nightstand, and it popped open. She felt the cold metal and secured the cover, taking comfort in knowing it was within reach.

She'd never been afraid to be alone, but since Gary's death, it had become harder. Her imagination ran wild at night now. His absence created a nervous tension when it was time to go to bed.

With a quiet sigh, she burrowed her head into the pillow and reached across to the empty space on Gary's side. She hadn't grown accustomed to the vacant spot where he had slept for almost thirty years. Her thoughts quieted, and she concentrated on listening to the sound of the water slapping against the bluff. The curtains fluttered in the breeze, and she heard the faint lull of the bay.

Determined to craft a new life filled with fresh memories and new friends, she shut her eyes for the first of what would be many nights to come at Glass Beach Cottage.

Chapter 3

Lily woke early, and Fritz followed her outside to the path leading to the beach. They wandered along the shore in solitude. Other than their soft steps, the rush of the water on the beach and the call of the gulls were the only sounds.

A fat piece of driftwood beckoned. She sat, with Fritz leaning against her. They watched as the soft glow of dawn rose above the blue band of water on the horizon. Gary had been the adventure seeker of the two. He would have jumped at the chance to move across the country and undertake a new vocation. That's what had urged her to make a move.

She had wavered as she contemplated the decision. Like an old film, the memories played through her mind. Late in the evening, she and Fritz had been sitting on the deck at their old house, a spot where she often talked to Gary. She voiced her doubts and unease into the dark night. She looked at his chair and swore he was there. Smiling at her. Telling her to go. Assuring her all would be well and it would make her happy. That's when she knew she could go.

As she watched nature's display from her perch on the driftwood, a shaft of golden light traveled across the expanse of water in a perfect line to them. A beautiful greeting from the morning sun. Fritz whined and took an interest in the space next to her. She sensed warmth, and a hint of Gary's spicy aftershave hit her nose. She turned but saw nothing.

She ran her hand over Fritz's soft neck. "He would have loved this." She sat and waited for the glow to intensify and morning to arrive. She took a deep breath and sensed the salt in the air. The rhythm of the waves comforted her.

Movement caught her eye, and she saw a lone figure and what looked like three dogs at the far end of the beach. She wasn't in the mood to see anyone or urge Fritz away from an impromptu playdate. She took his leash and said, "Come on, buddy. Let's go home."

She turned and led him back the way they had come, guaranteeing they wouldn't encounter the beach walker before they took the path to their property. She raced Fritz through the grass, and he beat her to the door. The aroma of fresh brewed coffee from the maker she had programmed last night filled the air. The welcoming scent prompted her to pour a cup after she filled Fritz's breakfast bowl.

A stack of papers and mail on the counter caught her eye. Most of the envelopes were junk mail that she tossed, but she saw a flyer for the festival and noticed a pet parade was taking place the next morning. "Hmm, what do you think about a dog parade?"

Fritz's ears perked, and his tail wagged. "Let's see what that's all about. It's too late to enter, but it should be fun to watch."

After a quick shower, she unpacked more boxes. She was stashing some things in the pantry and opened a cupboard to find dozens of old teacups with saucers and several teapots. She always admired such treasures but never had the space or time to collect them.

She emptied the cupboard and washed all of the teaware. As she surveyed the area, her eyes landed on a cabinet in the dining room with glass doors and shelves. She went about removing the books that were in it and relocated them to the bookcases. Soon she had all the cups displayed in the cabinet, surrounding the teapots.

She eyed the delicate cups, all different, adorned with floral designs. Fritz watched her from his bed. "We might have to organize a tea party in the garden," she said to the dog.

He thumped his tail in agreement. She laughed and shut the doors on the cabinet. She added her books to those left behind by Uncle Leo and filled the bookcases.

The clock chimed and reminded her of the time. She motioned to the dog and made for the garage. Intent on getting her shopping done early, she loaded Fritz into Gary's truck and headed downtown. The weather was perfect. It was sunny with a slight breeze and not quite seventy degrees. Fritz had his head out the window, enjoying the fresh air.

She left the windows down for Fritz and went into Driftwood Bay Mercantile. She found towels that would match each of the bathrooms and browsed their selection of clothing and shoes. The friendly store had a smidgen of everything, and she knew she'd be returning soon.

She drove on to the market. She found all the basics she needed, including some appetizing local produce, freshly baked bread, and a huge cinnamon roll she couldn't resist. She picked up a few bottles of wine for the Motts to thank them for dog-sitting and snagged a bag of homemade dog treats for Fritz.

She loaded the groceries in the back of the truck, let Fritz try his new pumpkin treat, which he accepted with eager enthusiasm, and made for home. She drove by a few restaurants and coffee shops, a bakery, chocolate shop, ice cream shop, tea room, gift stores, the drug store, and a bookstore. She found the post office, a hardware store, and a flower shop as she drove through the surrounding streets.

She saw the entrance to Glass Beach and turned to Fritz. "We had a fun walk there this morning, didn't we? We'll have to make a habit of walking down there each morning." Fritz's tongue hung out of his mouth, and she could swear he smiled.

She pulled back into her driveway and admired the colorful flowers. She let Fritz in and unloaded her provisions. After treating herself to the cinnamon roll and letting Fritz have another treat, they wandered down to the cottages. They were separated from each other by a bit of space and some kind of large evergreen hedges. They each had a private patio area with a view of the water and colorful flowering bushes.

According to an online map she had found, the trail that ran along the bluff where she and Fritz walked could be followed all the way to Glass Beach. They could also use the streets or the trail at the back of the property to get there.

Wade was due to arrive right after lunch. She tossed her new towels in the laundry and used the rest of her morning to empty the remaining boxes and flatten all the cardboard.

She opened one of the containers of homemade soup she had found at the market and paired it with a thick slice of bread. Fritz kept his eye on her and the floor in case any crumbs needed his attention. "Mmm," she said. "I think I could live on this." Fritz stared at her, willing her to share something.

Gary had been a stickler for not feeding Fritz from the table. After he was gone, Lily had caved when those gentle brown eyes pleaded with her for a bite. She had created a skilled beggar in a few short months.

With lunch over, she took Fritz into the backyard and scoped out an area that could be fenced in and used as a dog pen. She didn't want to risk leaving him alone to run the whole property without a proper fence. He wouldn't be on his own often, but she needed to create a safe and comfortable place for him outdoors.

While she was wandering, Fritz heard a noise and forced his master to follow him around the end of the house. They found a grey-haired man and a young man walking from their truck at the curb.

"Mrs. Reed," said the older man, "I'm Wade. This is my son, Andy." Andy smiled at Lily and extended his hand.

She introduced Fritz, and they led the men to the backyard. Lily explained she wanted the fence repaired, a fence installed along the end of the house and into the grassy area for Fritz, and a dog door installed downstairs along the wall where his new space would be constructed. That would give her the option to let Fritz come and go if she needed it. "That leaves the cottages. I'd like to get them refurbished and ready for guests. You'll have to check them out, but at a minimum, they need some windows, new roofing, and siding like what's on the house." During the conversation, she noticed Wade signing to Andy.

He turned to her and explained, "Andy's deaf. He has no problem working, but if you need to talk to him, you need to get his attention. He reads lips really well. He went deaf in his early teens. He's thirty now."

Lily nodded her understanding. "I'm sorry. That had to be tough."

Wade gave a slight nod. "It was devastating for all of us, but Andy's a trooper. He's adapted." He watched as his son set about measuring.

"I'll leave you to it. We'll be inside, so just come up on the deck when you're ready," said Lily. Much to Fritz's dismay, she led him away from the activity.

Less than an hour had passed when the two knocked on the glass door. Fritz slid across the floor, hurrying to greet them. Lily retrieved a pitcher of fresh iced tea and a plate of cookies.

She invited them to sit around the patio table. They took long swallows from their glasses, and Andy helped himself to a cookie.

Wade slid a piece of paper across the table. "The dog fence and the repair of that other fence are straightforward. I need to get some pricing on the cottages and get back to you on those."

She looked at the prices and gave him a nod. "This looks terrific. When can you start?"

"If you don't mind us squeezing you in between some jobs, we'll get started tomorrow. We're finishing up a couple of small jobs but could bounce back and forth. It won't take long. I'll send Andy over to start some of it on his own."

"Sounds good to me. I'll be home, so whenever you get here is fine. Don't worry about checking in, just come through to the back and get started."

Wade nodded and made sure Andy understood. Andy gave them a thumbs up sign and petted Fritz, who was glued to his thigh.

"Your uncle would be so happy to see you getting this place going again. He spoke of you often. I visited with him the week before he passed away, and he told me how much he hoped you'd live here."

"I regret not getting out here to see him in person. I was dealing with the death of my husband. Not very well, I might add. I just couldn't get things together in time. I loved this place as a kid though. I'm hoping I can live up to Uncle Leo's expectations."

Wade bowed his head. "Leo told me about your husband. I'm very sorry for your loss. I hope you find happiness here."

With a catch in her throat, Lily whispered, "Me too."

Andy smiled at her and said, "Thank you for the cookies, Miss Lily."

She offered him more with a warm smile. "My son loves these. Take a few more with you." She noticed Andy's voice was a bit monotone, but clear and easy to understand.

They chatted more, and she told them about Kevin's upcoming visit and his college journey. "Andy's younger brother, David, is graduating this weekend. He's in Seattle at UW." He turned at Andy's tap on his arm and watched him sign.

"Oh, yes, we're having a barbeque and party at our house on Sunday. You and Kevin should come. It's super casual, just pop in and have a bite to eat, meet my wife and David."

Andy's head nodded with enthusiasm. Lily hadn't been to a cookout since before Gary died. She smiled at Andy, unable to resist his sincere invitation. "That sounds terrific. We'll be there."

Wade gave her the details and explained where they lived. He motioned to Andy, and they made their way downstairs, promising she'd be seeing them in her yard starting tomorrow.

She and Fritz watched as they drove away. "How about a walk to the beach, Fritzie?" His tail went into full wag mode as he followed her upstairs to get his leash. This time they set out on the street. They walked the few short blocks to the sign they had seen and wandered past the long sea grass to the shoreline.

Lily found a hefty log that made for an ideal seat. She let Fritz off his leash, and he sprinted to the water. His antics made her chuckle, and at one point, she turned to say something to Gary. The empty spot beside her jolted her back to reality. She stood and slipped off her shoes and rolled up her pants to join Fritz in the water.

After a good romping and lots of splashing, she coaxed the wet furry guy away from the water and attached his leash. She made like she was in a hurry and jogged a bit, and Fritz became interested in going with her.

They took the path that led to the nearby park. Fritz needed a bit more air-drying, and Lily wanted to take a look at the park she remembered from her time at Glass Beach. They strolled along the footpaths and came upon a fenced area advertised as a dog park. Several dogs were running around the grass, playing with and toppling over each other.

Fritz watched. His tail speed announced his excitement. He'd never met a stranger, canine or human. He looked at the dogs and looked at Lily, his eyes begging her to let him go. She took a look at his wet fur, full of sand, and relented. She took him to the gate and unleashed him.

He was the life of the party, greeting small terriers and large shepherds with equal gusto. He got down on his front legs, his rear in the air, signaling he was ready to play. A golden mix took him up on his offer, and the two frolicked together.

Lily sat on a nearby bench and took in the view. A gentle breeze shuffled the branches of the shore pines. Picnic tables were scattered throughout the park. A bandstand sat on the edge, offering those who attended concerts a scenic view. A white gazebo stood near the middle of the park. There were a few young mothers with toddlers, but the majority of park goers on this weekday afternoon were retirees.

She wandered over to a glass encased bulletin board and saw flyers advertising upcoming events. Memorial Day would bring a pancake breakfast and a patriotic concert along the waterfront. Movies and plays in the park, concerts every weekend in July and August, and the occasional classic car show rounded out the calendar.

She made her way back to the gate at the dog park and hollered for Fritz. He came bounding over to her, tongue hanging out, prancing. She reached for his harness and said, "Let's go home."

She stopped on the path and let him drink from a bowl of water before they set off for the house. When they arrived, she rummaged in the garage for the oversized plastic tub that doubled as his bathtub and set it on the back lawn. Fritz needed a good scrubbing, and he hopped in without hesitation. Soon she had him lathered up and smelling like lavender instead of salty sea water.

She led him to a sunny spot on the grass and used a towel to dry him. He bit at the cloth, hoping for a game of tug-of-war, but let her finish the job. He would take forever to dry, but he was fit for the deck. She left him there while she took a shower to wash off the sand and dog hair.

She finished the last two boxes left from the move and organized the garbage and recycling at the curb. After a quick dinner of soup and fruit, she took her hair dryer and a brush to Fritz.

He wasn't the biggest fan of vacuums or hair dryers, but while Lily reassured him with her soft voice, he tolerated the procedure. Eyeing his fluffiness, she pronounced him done, and led him into the house.

He nestled into his dog bed, and she slipped under her sheets. She thumbed the remote and searched for something mindless to watch. She found an old movie and settled into her pillows.

Nighttime brought out the longing in her. She craved a conversation with Gary. She knew it made no logical sense, but she still talked to him. It made her feel connected. "We had a good day today. Fritzie had so much fun in the water. We're going to walk to the beach each morning. I think the park is going to be our favorite hangout."

She heard only the soft snores from Fritz. She had survived another day and looked forward to Kevin's arrival that weekend. She offered to pick him up at the airport, but he had already made a shuttle reservation. He'd be at the house in time for dinner.

"Only two more nights," she whispered.

Chapter 4

The next morning, after a walk to the beach and another breathtaking sunrise, she and Fritz drove to town to watch the parade. After finding a great parking spot under a shady tree, she opened the tailgate and retrieved Fritz. They were able to sit in the back of the truck and watch the procession of people and pets. Fritz had a hard time containing himself and whined a few times, pleading with Lily to let him join the fun.

Smiling young girls adorned with beautiful flowers led the parade. After they passed by, rows of owners with their dogs marched through the street. There were a few horses in the group, several goats, and even a pig. Some of the dogs wore colorful outfits, and almost all of them sported rhododendrons in their collars. The people waved and smiled at Lily and Fritz, and a few even tossed dog treats to the spectators.

Lily laughed as she watched a pint-sized girl try to control the baby goats she had on leashes. Next came a guy wearing a flower lei with a large, colorful bird on his shoulder. Several llamas with rhododendrons draped over them announced the end of the parade.

She waited for the crowd to disperse and loaded up Fritz. They arrived home to find work had begun on the fencing projects. Fritz elected to sit on the deck and supervise Andy's work while Lily made lunch.

Over the next two days, Andy worked at the house all day. Lily invited him to join her for lunch each day and did her best to communicate. She had looked online to learn the best way to talk to Andy. She thought she would need to use slow and exaggerated pronunciation, but she discovered it wasn't necessary and actually made it harder for Andy to understand.

While they shared some iced tea on the deck, she expressed an interest in learning to sign. He nodded and smiled and pulled out his phone. He showed her an app for her phone that would help her learn.

Wade stopped by in the afternoon and helped Andy until the end of the day. When they left on Friday night, Fritz had a new L-shaped fenced area along the house and into the grass where he could stay in a pinch. They used black steel fencing that allowed Fritz to see out, but would keep him contained. Plus, it presented an aesthetic element that didn't detract from the garden or require maintenance. She coaxed him through his new dog door that led into the garden level. His new space provided him some shade beneath the deck, and with a few toys and a water bowl, he'd be set.

They started on the fence by the bluff and were using metal posts to solve the rotting problem. As they finished installing the last post, the evening light began to fade. Wade called to Lily, who was stationed on the deck. "We'll be back on Monday. See you at the party Sunday."

"We'll be there." She waved at the pair as they loaded their tools.

She and Fritz ate dinner and then went downstairs to make sure Kevin's room was ready. She stocked the extra fridge with his favorite cold drinks and snacks. After a few tries, Lily was able to get the television set up for streaming. While Fritz lounged on the cool tile floor, she put together a batch of cookies.

She baked while she watched television and texted with Kevin.

She told him about the graduation barbeque on Sunday and sent him a few photos of the views from the deck. He signed off to get to bed for his early flight and told her he loved her.

She put the cooled cookies away and poured a glass of wine. She took it outside to the deck and chose the lounge. The noise woke Fritz, who was happy to join her and nestle into the space beside her legs.

The shades of violet and pink settling over the water took her breath away. She relaxed and took a sip. "Our boy will be here tomorrow, Fritzie."

The dog's ears perked, and he nuzzled closer, giving her finger a gentle lick. She stroked his soft ears and watched as the day slipped into night in Driftwood Bay.

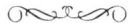

By the time Lily woke on Saturday, Kevin was flying over the middle of the country. After getting Fritz situated in his new outdoor space, she made a quick dash into town and bought a graduation gift for David's party. She also stopped at the bakery and picked up a pie to take to the gathering.

She stayed busy organizing and looking through the old reservation books her aunt and uncle had kept in the desk. History showed them booked solid throughout summer and into fall. She remembered they were closed for most of the winter but would sometimes let some of their regular guests stay downstairs if they were visiting family for the holidays.

As she flipped through the pages, it became clear that her aunt and uncle had provided more than just rooms to their guests. They had bundles of cards and letters from guests stashed in the drawers. The guests kept them informed of the milestones in their lives. Births, weddings, deaths. It was all there in the weathered paper and frayed ribbons.

The love for her aunt and uncle flowed through the words and photos. This had been their life. Never blessed with children, they had crafted their own family from those who'd call the Glass Beach Cottage home for a few weeks each year.

Maybe Lily would be lucky enough to create something similar. Perhaps she could find a circle of friends in the guests she would meet. She took great care in placing all the notes back into their bundles and returning them to the drawer.

She wasn't much of a cook but set about making some chicken salad. Kevin would be tired from his long day of travel, and she planned to spend their first night out on the deck, savoring the view.

Fritz's fine-tuned ears perked, and he zoomed to the front door. She watched as the dog spun in a circle. He only did that when he saw Kev. She opened the door and saw her son's smiling face. She wrapped him in a long hug, with Fritz circling both of them.

"I'm so glad you're here." She gestured to the dog. "Fritz barely noticed."

They both laughed, and she took his duffle bag while he maneuvered his suitcase. "I've got chicken salad for sandwiches and some cookies if you're hungry."

His eyebrows arched. "I'm starving. I didn't eat anything this morning, and the plane snacks didn't make a dent."

"Go on downstairs and get your stuff put away, and I'll get the food ready." Fritz hurried after Kevin as he lugged his bags down the stairs.

By the time he returned, Lily had things ready on the patio table. As they ate, she pointed out the cottages, Fritz's new fenced yard, and gave directions to Glass Beach and the park. "I thought we could explore the Olympic National Park while you're here."

"Sounds great, Mom. There's one thing though." His face saddened, and he hesitated. "Uh ... I got a message late Friday from my advisor."

He went on to explain that a summer internship had opened up at the last minute. "He wants me to do it. It's at the Capitol Building in Richmond."

Lily slid a smile over her disappointment. "That sounds terrific, Kev. When does it start?"

With a sheepish look, he said, "That's the bad news. I'd need to be there on June fifteenth." He explained how he'd be helping staff a critical interim committee and be working at the right hand of one of the most respected attorneys at the Division of Legislative Services.

Lily heard the excitement in his voice. "One of the paralegals has a room she rents to interns, and the program will cover the cost. It's all included. I even get a small stipend."

"Well, it sounds like we better squeeze all of our fun into the next few weeks." She rested her hand on his arm.

"I hated to tell you. I don't want to bail on you for the summer."

"This is a huge opportunity for you. Don't ever be sorry for making progress in your life. I don't ever want to hold you back from success. Fritzie and I will be fine here. It's a wonderful place, and there's plenty to keep us occupied."

Relief flooded over Kevin's face, and he let out a breath. "Thanks, Mom. I was dreading trying to decide what to do."

They spent the rest of the evening playing fetch with Fritz and sharing ideas for the cottages. Kevin finished looking at the last cottage and said, "These will be great when you get them fixed up and cleaned. You should think about advertising online. I could make your website while I'm here."

"That would be terrific. Only if we have time though. I want you to see as much of the area as possible."

Fritz elected to sleep in Kevin's room that night. As Lily's head hit the pillow, a tear drifted from her eye. She reached for Gary's side and said, "I was so much braver with you here. I'm trying to be okay with Kevin leaving, but I'm heartbroken."

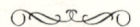

The next morning, they set out for the park. They opted for a late breakfast downtown. They found a great place with a deck, and Fritz was welcome too, as long as they stayed outside. After some initial excitement, he settled down and situated himself at their feet under the umbrella table.

After a delicious meal, they wandered the historic downtown corridor and admired the Victorian buildings. They took the long way home and walked along the beach. Lily kept Fritz on his leash this time. She didn't have time to give him another bath today.

When they got home, it was time to go to the party. She hadn't gotten Fritz accustomed to staying in his new area for an extended period, but knew they wouldn't be gone long. She made sure he had fresh water outside and filled his bowl she kept downstairs. They closed off the bedrooms, and she inspected the common area. "I don't think there's anything he can get into down here. I'll put a sheet over the couch in case he hops up there to sleep. That will keep the dog hair off of it." He was well exercised, and she suspected he would sleep while they were away. They left him on the grass in his new area, looking quite content.

Wade's place was a short drive away, near Fort Walden State Park. She pointed out the sign for the park and said, "That's on our list before you leave."

Wade welcomed them and introduced them to his wife, Barb, who was busy arranging dishes on a table. "Wonderful to meet you both," she said. "Please make yourselves at home. Cold drinks are over there." She pointed to another table with an assortment of beverages.

Lily presented the pink bakery box. "I had no idea what you would need but figured everyone loves pie."

Wade eyed the box. "We could always save it for later," he said with a wink.

Barb laughed and said, "That was very thoughtful of you. Wade and the boys could eat a pie a day."

Andy sidled up to his father and gave Lily a warm smile. "Hey, Andy. I'd like you to meet my son, Kevin," she said.

Kevin shook hands with Andy who said, "Nice to meet you." He pointed to a crowd of young men and women. "My brother, David, is over there."

Andy offered to help Kevin retrieve drinks, and the two made their way across the lawn. Wade motioned Lily to follow him and took her around to the various tables and groups and introduced her.

Barb was a retired school teacher, so the crowd was filled with many of her colleagues, as well as Wade's customers, and longtime friends. Wade made a point of presenting Lily to the Chief of Police, Jeff Evans. He added that she was a retired police officer and said, "You two might have something in common," leaving Lily with Jeff and his wife, Donna, the town's librarian.

She took the chair Jeff offered. "You look too young to be retired," he said. "Maybe we can entice you back into the uniform."

She shook her head as Kevin appeared at the table with a tall glass of lemonade. "Hey, Mom, I'm going to join the game of volleyball they started," he said, pointing to the action across the yard.

She nodded and said, "Kevin, this is Jeff Evans, the Chief of Police here, and Donna, his wife, who is the librarian." Kevin extended his hand and told them he was happy to meet them, before hurrying to join the other young people.

"Nice young man," said Jeff. "We were starting to talk about you joining our force," he smiled.

Lily shook her head. "No, I'm done with that chapter of my life. I had a wonderful career but need a change." She took a long sip from her glass. "I'll need to keep my retired law enforcement concealed carry permit up to date though."

Jeff nodded with enthusiasm. "Of course. That won't be a problem at all. We have monthly shoots at the range, and you can tag along whenever you want. Our training officer can qualify you each year." He slid her a business card and told her to get in touch and he'd add her to the email list.

Lily murmured her thanks and said, "I've carried a gun for so long, I think I'd feel lost without one. I'll call your office next week."

"What brings you to our little slice of heaven here in Driftwood Bay?" asked Donna.

Lily explained her family connection and the inheritance from her uncle. "My husband, Gary, was in law enforcement. He was killed last year. On the job."

Donna's hand went to her heart. "I'm so very sorry. I didn't know."

Jeff added, "You have my sincere sympathies. I've had a few friends lost in the line of duty. It's something I'll never get over."

Lily fought back tears. "I'm trying to start over here. A new adventure. A way to force myself to move on."

Donna put her hand on Lily's arm. "Grief never ends. It's a journey through a dark canyon in a horrid storm. The storm doesn't last forever, but it leaves you changed," she said, squeezing Lily's hand. "If we can do anything for you or if you just need to talk, please reach out."

Tears fell down Lily's cheeks. "That's kind of you. You're right about a dark journey. I took Uncle Leo's gift as a sign. I'd been miserable, just trudging through the days with too many reminders of our life. Gary. Everything."

"New scenery, new experiences, new people will make for a new normal, I'm sure," offered Donna.

They continued chatting, and Lily said, "My mother was a librarian. She adored books and stories." Donna responded with enthusiasm and described the programs they offered at the library.

Wade hollered that the food was ready and motioned them all to the line of buffet tables on the back patio. Lily looked for Kevin but saw the game was still going on, so she wandered over to fill her plate with Jeff and Donna.

She loaded a second plate for Kevin as she went through the line. Minutes after they returned to the table, Kevin jogged to her side. He thanked her for the plate and took the chair next to hers.

As they ate, Jeff and Donna told them about life in Driftwood Bay. "We moved up here about four years ago," said Jeff. "We lived in California and were looking for a slower pace and fewer people. Lucky for us, they were in the market for a Chief of Police and a librarian."

Donna said, "If you find yourself with some time on your hands, there are lots of volunteer opportunities here. The library, museum, arts center, Fort Walden, even the marina needs help. You'll love all the activities here."

The librarian turned her attention to Kevin and asked him about his studies and how long he would be in Driftwood Bay. With her encouraging questions, he explained about his upcoming internship and his plans for law school.

"You guys should stop by the Community Center downtown. They've got brochures and information on all the must-see activities in the area. You'll want to do Olympic National Park before Memorial Day to beat the tourists," suggested Jeff.

Jeff tipped them off to some points of interest in Olympic National Park and highlighted a few first-rate camping spots. "We're not much on camping. Gary was the adventurous one," said Lily. A hint of nostalgia glinted in her eyes. "We'll stick with day trips and look for a motel or something if we want to venture out longer."

She took the opportunity to ask for recommendations for life's necessities, like a hairdresser, doctors, and a vet for Fritz. Having to memorize all one hundred and forty members of the Virginia General Assembly had honed Lily's brain, and she filed the names and information away for future use.

Chapter 5

Monday morning, Wade dropped off the quote for the work on the cottages. Lily and Kevin skimmed it as they ate breakfast on the deck. "Do you think you should get another estimate?" he asked.

She eyed the figures and wrinkled her nose. "I don't think so. Uncle Leo used Wade for years and trusted him. I think this a fair price, and I know he does good work. There's plenty of money in the fund Uncle Leo left for maintenance. I'd like to get things started so I can open in July."

She called Wade and told him to move forward with the project. "Feel free to come and go as necessary. Kevin and I are going to explore the area and won't be home much while he's here."

She retrieved a map of the area from inside, along with a coffee refill, and they began to plot their first excursion, to Olympic National Park. They mapped their route and booked a beautiful dog-friendly lodge near Forks so they could explore the entire area before returning to Driftwood Bay.

They organized their supplies, made a trip to the market for snacks, and made sure they packed Fritz's portable water bowl along with the small pack Gary had bought him to use on hikes.

Fritz watched the activity and followed them back and forth to the truck as they loaded it with all their gear and luggage. He was always up for an outing and knew one was coming.

The next morning, they stopped for a filling breakfast on their way out of town. They drove past Port Angeles and straight into the park. Their first stop was Hurricane Ridge.

The views were worth the drive. Kevin held Fritz's leash while Lily took several photos of the dramatic vistas. Beautiful snowcapped mountains on one side and the ocean on the other made for a magnificent sight.

Bunnies, deer, and squirrels darted from among the trees and scampered along the paths. Fritz was itching to make new friends, but Kevin held onto him. They stood silent at an overlook marveling at the expanse before them. Hills and mountains, near and far, in tones of blue and green stood out against the backdrop of a perfect sky. The majestic panorama was breathtaking and seemed never ending.

There were few visitors, and the quiet sounds of the park offered a peaceful respite from life. Lily took more photos and said, "Your dad would have loved this. We always talked about coming out, but…"

Kevin put a hand on his mother's shoulder. They stood in silence, admiring the magnificence of nature. Kevin took photos of Lily against the striking backdrops and some with Fritz too. They posed for selfies together and wandered the many paths.

After they had their fill of the scenic views, they took off down the road for Lake Crescent. Kevin lugged the cooler to an area set up with picnic tables. A beautiful sapphire gem set in the midst of imposing mountains greeted them. The glass-like surface reflected the white clouds from above.

While they ate sandwiches, Fritz romped in the water, unbothered by its frigid temperature. Lily didn't want him soaked, so she captured him on one of his visits to their table, putting his leash on before walking him to the shore.

A black retriever mix and her owners hurried to greet them, and the two dogs dashed to the water. Her humans were an older couple from Oregon. They suggested Lily and Kevin visit a waterfall not far down the road.

Fritz lounged in a grassy area while Lily toweled him dry. They sat in Adirondack chairs and watched fishermen in boats atop the water. The crisp air, the fresh scent of pine, and the occasional splash from the lake were working their magic on Lily's mind.

Far away from the memories of her life in Virginia, the pristine water soothed Lily's broken heart. The gentle lap of it against the shoreline, the vast blue expanse of it below the majestic mountains, the stillness it summoned, lulled Lily's thoughts.

Kevin was resting with his eyes closed beneath his sunglasses. Fritz napped next to his favorite boy. Lily could have sat on the edge of the water with the two of them for the rest of her days.

When Kevin opened his eyes, he said, "Let's go take a look at those waterfalls." He stuffed the cooler into the truck bed, and Lily wiped Fritz's paws before loading him into the backseat.

They followed the road around the lake until they saw the sign for the falls. Pets weren't allowed at the falls, so they left the windows down for Fritz and locked him in the truck. They trekked down the path and were rewarded with a cascade of water flowing over the rocks. The roaring of the falls drowned out the world around them.

The heavy spray splattered them as they got closer. The splendor of the water crashing down from ninety feet above them forced them to gawk. The thundering noise rattled in Lily's chest while she captured photos of the rushing water. Convinced of the sheer power of nature, they gestured toward the trail. They made quick work of the loop back to the truck and Fritz, and then continued on their way to Forks.

The road snaked through the lush forests. Trees surrounded it, towering above them. Intermittent shafts of sunlight broke through the dense cover of trees every few miles. They wound their way through the woods for several miles before they found the lodge.

The reception desk was located in the main lodge. Lily stared up at the massive vaulted ceiling supported by stout beams. A gorgeous stone fireplace stood in the center of one wall across from the stairs that led to the guest rooms. The staff guided them to their cottage, away from the main building. It was pet-friendly and featured two bedrooms.

Dinner options in the small town were outlined in a brochure next to the coffeemaker. Lily handed Kevin the information, "You pick." She organized their belongings and retrieved Fritz's bed.

"This pizza place looks okay. I could call it in and go pick it up," he said.

"Perfect," she said. "Fritz and I will stay here and get settled."

The rustic cabin didn't offer television, but Lily was able to connect her tablet to the wireless internet. She moved the perishables from the cooler into the mini-fridge and fed Fritz while Kevin made the trip to town.

While they ate pizza at their outdoor picnic table, Lily showed Kevin her tablet. "I was looking at other guest houses and bed and breakfast places online to get some ideas for my website."

He scrolled through the sites and nodded, making faces at a few of them. "We need to make it simple and easy to use. You'll need lots of photos. We'll take some around town and add these from our trip. It'll be good to show people the surrounding area."

"I'll have to add photos of the cottages after they're remodeled." She finished her pizza and said, "Maybe I could find some historical photos in Uncle Leo's stuff."

"We could put a banner at the top boasting how long the cottages have been accommodating guests and incorporate some of the old stuff."

Her eyes sparkled with enthusiasm. "That would be fun. Maybe add a few of Aunt Maggie's mosaics."

"What are you going to do for the breakfast part of the deal? You're not going to cook, are you?" Kevin raised his brows.

She laughed and said, "No, I won't be subjecting anyone to my culinary skills. I thought I'd see about getting a local restaurant to provide it. I can include the cost in the room fee and get a deal from the restaurant."

"Good idea." Kevin continued to scan the sites while Lily shared more of her ideas.

"I thought it would be fun to do wine and beer with some light snacks in the evening outside by the firepit. I also wanted to have some cookies available along with coffee and tea, so if guests needed a snack, they could help themselves."

"We'll use a calendar that's easy for you to block out days you don't want guests." He made a note on her notepad. "This one looks good, and guests can book it themselves online."

"I'll have to research nightly prices and see what the going rates are. I'm sure it varies based on the season."

They chatted late into the night. Lily decided on using sea glass colors throughout the new website. She shared her ideas for the simple décor inside each cottage. "I found Aunt Maggie's old stepping stones she made using collected sea glass. They'll need a good cleaning, but then I can use them on the pathway to the cottages."

Kevin yawned and said, "I've got to get to sleep. I still haven't adjusted to the time out here." He kissed his mom's cheek and ambled off to the second bedroom.

She cleaned off the table and turned in, listening to the soft snores of Fritz from his bed in the corner. She lay in the darkened cottage and listened to the hoot of owls outside. The lonely whoo-whoo-whoo sounds eased her to sleep.

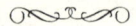

○～∾○

Lily and Kevin woke early and took Fritz on a long walk to explore his new surroundings. When they returned, they found a friendly staffer on the porch, delivering a basket of breakfast goodies.

Fresh pastries, yogurt, fruit, juice, a carafe of coffee, and some portable snacks were in the basket. Kevin retrieved plates and silverware, and they ate outside. "The Hoh Rainforest is about thirty miles from here," said Lily. "We can explore that area and hike a bit, have lunch, and then head to La Push on the way back."

They collected their supplies and Fritz jumped into the backseat. The drive took them along the edge of the park and ate up almost an hour. They parked and grabbed their raincoats before setting out on the trail. They walked, gazing at the jungle-like plants. Moss covered everything. The trunks and branches of the trees weren't even visible.

The shades of green were like nothing they had ever seen. Giant ferns in deep emerald were crowded amid plants and moss ranging from deep olive to vibrant lime. Kevin stood next to a giant trunk cloaked in a fluffy green pelt while Lily took his photo. "This is like being in a scene from *The Lord of the Rings*."

Moisture hung in the air and plants taller than humans flanked the edges of the trail. The soft sound of a gentle rain spattering the thriving foliage combined with their light footfalls. The air smelled fresh and clean, and in some spots, deep in the trees, it hung like a faint green net.

They made their way to the falls where an impressive display of white rushing water falling over a carpet of mossy rocks awaited them. "I could swear we were in some jungle in South America," said Lily, taking photos on her phone.

They spent time soaking up the view and followed the water to a stream where it bounced over worn and rounded rocks. The water gurgled and bubbled past them on its lazy journey. They stood gazing at the massive trees and the pristine surroundings that looked untouched by man.

They circled back to the truck and had lunch at a picnic spot near the entrance to the rainforest. Fritz enjoyed sharing a few bites of their food and slurping water from his bowl. "Shall we head to La Push and capture some photos on the beach at sunset?" asked Lily.

They drove the scenic byway to the tiny village of La Push at the mouth of the Quillayute River. They followed the signs and parked near the waterfront. Lily attached Fritz's leash, and the threesome set out for Second Beach.

The trail led them to a sandy crescent of beach. White bubbles of foam topped the small waves tumbling onto the shore. The sand was dark and saturated, making for a firm surface and effortless walking. Lily noticed her footprints next to Kevin's larger ones and the unmistakable paw patterns of Fritz. Only Gary's were missing.

She let the waves tickle her toes as she walked closer to the water. Fritz and Kevin ran ahead of her while she strolled and swished her feet back and forth in the fresh surge. At times, Gary's presence was intense. This was one of those times. She felt his hand on hers. She smelled him. She turned but saw only lingering mist from the ocean glinting in the sun.

A long plume of spray doused her. She squealed when the cold seawater hit her shirt. She laughed and said, "I know that was you, Gary."

Kevin turned at the sound of her voice. "You okay, Mom?"

She waved and hollered, "Fine, just got sprayed."

She watched as her son stopped at a sizeable pile of driftwood and sat. He pulled one of Fritz's favorite balls from his pocket and showed it to the dog before tossing it into a wave. Fritz took off like a rocket and returned with the plastic ball in his mouth, prancing to Lily to show her.

"Good boy, Fritzie." She took it from him and threw it again. She joined Kevin on their makeshift bench. "You've created a monster, you know?"

He smiled and laughed as Fritz bounded over to them. "I'll dry him off before we let him in the cottage tonight."

The columns of rock that rose from the ocean stood watch over the ripple of waves in the water. Kevin pointed and said, "I've never seen anything like that."

"They're called sea stacks. They're remnants of the coastal cliffs, battered for years by the sea until they eroded."

They stood ragged and worn, but still strong, defiant against the violent seawater. Trees poked out of many of them, while others remained jagged and bare. The tide swirled and thrashed against the rocky islets on its way to the soft sand. Lily shut her eyes and listened to the rush and surge. The advance and retreat. A rowdy arrival and a subtle goodbye.

She felt cold wet fur and gritty sand lean against her leg. She reached out and put her hand on Fritz's neck. She felt Kevin's arm around her shoulders. "It's beautiful here, Mom. I can see why you came. The sound or something just makes me feel calmer."

She opened her eyes and smiled at her son. "Yes, it does. The rhythm of the tide is comforting. People joke about beach therapy, but I think it's real. I feel more alive here and less frantic."

"I think Fritz agrees," said Kevin with a laugh. He pointed at the dog flopped on his back on the sand.

As the afternoon faded, Lily stood and said, "Let's head the other way and take a look at Rialto Beach. I want to get there before high tide." They trekked back to the truck, and Kevin gave Fritz a thorough toweling to get rid of the sand.

They backtracked and found the fork in the road that led north of La Push to the beach. Their timing was incredible. The line between the pinky peach sky and the deep blue water, broken by the dramatic dark sea stacks, made for perfect photos.

They sat on another hefty piece of driftwood and watched as the sky changed colors. As the sky dimmed, the dusky pastel light morphed into a vibrant pink. Faint clouds, illuminated by a vivid orange glow sitting atop the water, streaked across the horizon.

They captured several photos of their dark shapes in front of the impressive sunset, with a towering sea stack in the distance. Lily kept at it, not satisfied until she shouted, "That's it. It's perfect. All three of us against that stunner of a backdrop."

They tapped their phones until the last ribbon of orange slipped into the water. "That was awesome," said Kevin. "I've never seen a sunset so magnificent."

"The west coast is the premier spot for sunsets, and this is about as far west as we can get."

"I'm starving. Shall we stop for dinner somewhere on our way?"

Lily consulted her phone and found a casual burger place a few miles up the road. After stopping for a quick bite, they hit the road. Fritz rested in the back, tired after his long day of frolicking along the water. Gary had customized the backseat after they got Fritz. A thick mattress over a plywood base that ran the width of the space gave him a perfect spot for sleeping.

It was late by the time they got back to the lodge. Lily took Fritz's leash while Kevin unloaded the truck. She took the dog for a quick walk down a trail. The cool breeze stirred through the pines. While Fritz searched for a perfect bush, Lily looked up at the blanket of stars scattered across the indigo sky.

She'd never seen a sky this black living in Virginia. The lights from the clusters of cities and towns and the considerable population spoiled the dark skies. She marveled at the multitude of stars twinkling in the darkened heavens.

She took in a deep breath of fresh air and leaned back to gaze at the sky. One bright star caught her eye. She brought her fingers to her lips and blew a kiss high in the air.

They got home before the Memorial Day rush, did a bit of shopping, and admired the progress Wade and Andy had made on the cottages in their absence. Kevin got to work hanging the framed prints and photos Lily had brought with her in the move.

Once he finished, he wandered downstairs and found her going through the cupboards. "Got everything hung where you wanted it. What are you doing?"

"Just cleaning these cupboards and found a bunch of old sea glass Aunt Maggie had stashed in boxes in the back." She opened the lids to reveal collections of the frosted-looking colored pieces.

"Some of these were from trips they went on years ago. To the east coast and down the California coast, even some from Nova Scotia." She ran her fingers through the cool fragments, the remains of decades-old glass.

"Maybe I could find someone to help me make something out of all this." She shrugged and dusted the boxes. "I'm going to put all of this in that one cupboard with a lock. Just wanted to make sure there wasn't anything of value down here since guests will have access."

"Make sure you lock the door at the top of the stairs when you have people staying in the cottages. You never know what kind of weirdos are out there." Kevin's tone sounded like his father's.

Lily smiled and said, "I promise I'll be careful. I'm a pretty good judge of people. Most bad actors don't book this type of property. They want to be anonymous in a nondescript hotel or a dive motel. Trust me, I know what I'm doing."

"It's just a different time than when Uncle Leo had this place. Not as many creepsters back then."

She gave him a one-armed hug and said, "Got it. How about you fire up the grill, and we'll do something about dinner?" Fritz, who had been napping on the soft area rug, opened his eyes when he heard her mention dinner.

Chapter 6

Andy and Wade had reminded Lily and Kevin about the Memorial Day festivities before they left on Saturday. They promised to save two seats at their table since Wade would be one of the volunteers cooking breakfast in the park.

Monday morning ushered in a beautiful day. They walked to the park and found a crowd of people taking part in the fundraiser for local service clubs. As promised, Andy waved them over to a table, and Wade took a break from flipping pancakes to join them. A military band played patriotic music from the gazebo, and townsfolk visited as they ate and listened to the songs.

Fritz was well-behaved and rested under the table between Kevin and Lily, who slipped him a few bites of scrambled egg. After breakfast, they took Fritz to the dog park and let him play with a gang of fun-loving pups.

The park was swathed in red, white, and blue. Flags, bunting, balloons, and ribbons decorated the space. There were several wreath-laying ceremonies at cemeteries, but Lily couldn't bring herself to endure another rendition of "Taps" or the sound of a twenty-one-gun salute. Instead, they opted to take Fritz for a walk into town. There was a free concert on the dock in the late afternoon.

Fritz was excited to trek beyond their standard park and beach areas. He sniffed every bush and made new friends, human and furry, as they traveled the blocks to the waterfront pier. Flags flapped from porches surrounded by rhododendrons in vibrant colors. Residents waved hello as they wandered through the historic district close to downtown.

They reached the marina and stopped in the small park next to it. There was no dog park, so Fritz had to stay on his leash as they sat on a bench and took in the perfect day. The marina was busy with boats coming and going, vendors in booths set up along Bay Street, and people wandering around the area.

Kevin looked up the street and said, "How about we go to the pizza place with the deck? We can sit out there and listen to the concert, and Fritz can come with us."

Lily and Fritz followed him up the steps to a table with a good view of the concert area. The waitress brought Fritz a bowl of water and a treat. He was in love.

They watched the activity below and listened to the music, a mixture of patriotic and classical songs, while Fritz napped under the table. The place was busy, and it took longer than usual to get their pizza. "This is the best seat in the house," said Kevin.

They lingered over their pizza and drank a whole pitcher of iced tea. As the sky darkened and dusk settled in, they headed for home. The music played on as they made their way through the streets.

They reached the house and could still hear the faint sound of music coming from the concert. "It's a nice town. I had fun today," said Kevin.

Lily nodded. "Yes, and another day with no cooking. My favorite." She gave him a wink and a hug.

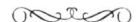

Lily forgot how much Kevin slept at the end of each school term. He always took a few weeks to recharge by sleeping in and lounging around the house. She had a list of places to visit and things to do, but it was clear he was content to snooze late, spend time on the deck, play with Fritz, venture to the park and the beach, and watch movies with her late into the evening.

Instead of long trips, they explored Driftwood Bay. They sampled breakfasts at the local cafes and chose two of them to approach as possible vendors for the guests at Glass Beach Cottage. The Busy Bee Café and Muffins & More offered Lily a considerable discount, and both were open seven days a week.

She purchased vouchers and had each of them send photos of their favorite meals to post on her website. Lily had Kevin add a section to the site to make it clear that each guest would receive a complimentary breakfast at a local cafe with their stay. "I know it might be unconventional, but it's less expensive than having the restaurants deliver breakfasts each day. Plus, it eliminates all the prep and cleanup associated with a meal."

"And it will get them moving in the morning," said Kevin with a wink. She watched the screen as he incorporated the breakfast photos and information. He scanned some of the old pictures Lily found and added those to the gallery. He and Fritz had made a trip to the beach and park one morning and taken several photos to use on the website. Lily wanted guests to know there was a dog on the property, in case they had allergies or issues with animals, so Fritz was prominent in many photos.

Wade and Andy found the old Glass Beach Cottage sign stashed in one of the cottages. Lily smiled when she remembered it stationed at the end of the driveway. She and Kevin cleaned it and repainted it. Wade and Andy installed it one morning and took a few photos of Lily, Kevin, and Fritz posing with it.

Lily called the housekeeper in Uncle Leo's book, and she recommended two sisters who cleaned guest properties. She negotiated a contract with them to provide cleaning services, and Kevin set up the system to alert them to reservations and checkouts.

He had researched the prices at similar lodgings and helped Lily decide on nightly rates for both the high and low seasons. He showed her how the calendar worked and how a reservation notification would be sent to her email.

He made sure her phone and tablet were set up to let her manage her bookings. Everything was automated, and in addition to showing Lily how to operate the software, Kevin made sure he could access it all from Virginia in case she got in a bind.

Within a week, the site was prepared. She needed to add the final photos, and then the site would be ready to publish. Wade assured her he would be done with the cottages by the third week in June. She hoped to have her first guests during the Fourth of July holiday week.

Andy was at the house early each morning working on the cottages. Wade stopped by several times a day to check on progress and lend a hand with the heavy tasks. Lily insisted Andy join them for lunch each day. They sat on the deck and visited while they ate.

Lily practiced her signing, and Andy provided gentle guidance when she made a mistake. He smiled as she signed how much she liked the new siding for the cottages. It retained the beachy look, like the main house, but the vinyl material would be maintenance-free. It took her forever to communicate with sign language, but each day she improved.

Fritz had taken to following Andy after lunch and spending the afternoons watching him from the shade of a tree. Lily signed to Andy to remind him to put Fritz in his new enclosure if he had to leave the gate open. "With the fence along the bluff fixed, I'm not as worried about him, but I don't want him to run off into the neighborhood. If he gets in your way, just put him in the house or his yard."

Andy petted Fritz's head and said, "Oh, he's a good boy. He won't be any trouble."

She picked up the dishes, refilled Andy's water bottle, and sent the two of them on their way. She hollered to Kevin, "I'm going to run downtown and do some shopping." He decided to stay behind and promised to barbeque something for dinner.

She had picked out new furnishings for the cottages, which would be delivered in mid-June, but she still needed some decorative elements for each of the interiors. She kept the same main colors for each so that she could buy items in bulk, and they would be interchangeable. However, she wanted to give each bungalow its own personality.

Her inspiration came from sea glass. She intended to use a different accent color in each cottage, keeping with the sea glass hues. She asked Wade to paint each entry door a different bright color to make it easy to direct guests.

She found beach inspired décor in several gift shops in Driftwood Bay. When Lily explained she was reopening the cottages and her connection to Leo, the shopkeepers offered her discounts in exchange for featuring their brochures in her cottages.

When Lily stepped through the door of Bayside Gifts, she knew she had hit the motherlode. Cyndy, who introduced herself as the owner, welcomed Lily. Each alcove of the shop overflowed with gorgeous items, and the whole place felt like a home rather than a store. It was clear Cyndy had a knack for decorating. Her displays invited visitors in and made them want to stay. It was Lily's last stop of the day. She had picked up a few items at other shops but hadn't yet found what she wanted.

Cyndy poured Lily a glass of tea. "If you don't see what you're looking for, I've got a load of catalogs, and we can search through them." Lily wandered through the shop and found the perfect items for the cottages, but not in all the colors she needed.

She explained her dilemma, and Cyndy offered to special order several items in Lily's colors. Lily sat on a stool at the counter and looked through Cyndy's catalogs.

The experienced decorator helped Lily choose items and wrote up the order. She handed Lily her copy and said, "These should be in next week. I'll hold them here in the back until you're ready for them. I'd love to help you put all this together. It'll be wonderful to have those cottages full again."

"That's such a kind offer. Unfortunately, my budget doesn't include anything for a designer." She handed Cyndy her credit card.

The woman shook her head. "Oh, no, I wouldn't charge you. I just enjoy decorating. I'd love to help you, and it would be fun to see the cottages."

"Wow," said Lily, her eyebrows raised. "I can't refuse that kind of an offer. I'd be thrilled to have your help. I can treat you to dinner as a thank-you." She laughed and added, "Not my cooking, but I could take you to dinner."

Cyndy chuckled. "Cooking's overrated. I'm happy to work for takeout and wine."

Lily shook her hand and said, "Deal. I'll get in touch when we can access them." Lily listened as Cyndy finished the transaction and spoke about growing up in Driftwood Bay. "My parents passed away a few years ago, but my younger brother lives here. It's nice to be near family and in our hometown. He's a veterinarian, like my dad."

Cyndy jotted her cell number on her card and handed it to Lily. "Leo and Maggie were two of our favorite residents. I'm so happy you decided to move here and not just sell the place. Give me a call anytime."

Lily glanced at the card and saw Cyndy's last name. "MacMillan? I asked about vets and was told Dr. MacMillan was the best. Is that the younger brother you mentioned?"

"Yep. He's a wonderful doctor. And brother. I'm divorced and alone. He's always watching out for me, helping me with anything I need around the house. He's a sweetheart." She wrinkled her brows and added, "Most of the time."

"I need to give him a call and get Fritz in to get established. He's my golden retriever."

"Jack is a huge fan of goldens. He has one of his own." She plucked the card from the counter and scribbled on it. "Here's his office number."

Lily took the card and said, "Wonderful. I'll get in touch and get something scheduled. My son is only here for ten more days, so I'm trying to spend time with him before he goes back to Virginia."

Lily explained Kevin's change of plans. "I'm sure you'll miss him," said Cyndy. "But I have a feeling you'll be so busy with the cottages, you won't have any spare time for moping."

Lily nodded her head. "I hope you're right." She glanced at the clock and hurried to her feet. "Speaking of time, I'm due back at the house." She extended her hand to Cyndy.

The woman stepped from behind the counter and embraced Lily in a long hug. "I'm delighted you came in today. It's been a pleasure to meet you. I hope you'll be as happy as Leo and Maggie were here on our bay."

Lily felt the sting of tears in her eyes. She thanked Cyndy and waved goodbye as she left.

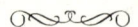

⁂

The smell of grilling meat greeted her when she pulled into the garage. She found Fritz keeping a watchful eye on the barbeque and Kevin in the kitchen. "Smells delicious."

"I'm making Dad's steaks and grilled potatoes." He gave her a smile that evoked memories of Gary.

Fritz scored several bites of apples and a few berries from Lily as she cut up fruit she had found at the farmer's market. When she finished, they carried the food out to the deck where they enjoyed their dinner with a gorgeous view of the bay.

After dinner, Kevin helped her put together an information binder for each cottage with the property's rules as well as local information related to shopping, dining, and sightseeing. They topped off the evening with another movie. Fritz positioned himself between them, close to the bowl of popcorn.

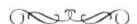

***

Lily crammed as much fun as she could into the days Kevin was in Driftwood Bay. They visited the lighthouse at Fort Warden Park and tried all the restaurants. Epic Ice Cream, with its homemade flavors and friendly staff, became a ritual. The couple who owned the shop and the teenaged girls who worked there loved Fritz. Each time they visited, they showered him with affection, a bowl of cold water, and a few doggie treats.

In addition to Kevin's favorite pizza place, they discovered a deli, three cafes that served a variety of food, a great seafood place, Bay Burgers, and Mexican and Chinese restaurants.

Lily savored every minute with Kevin and enjoyed their outings. She dreaded eating out alone and hadn't done it at all back in Virginia. She always chose takeout. Gary's absence was taxing, not to mention the sorrowful looks from the servers she and Gary had come to know. Enduring a whole meal that way was out of the question.

With word traveling fast and Driftwood Bay being such a small community, it didn't take long for the restaurateurs and other business owners to recognize Lily as Leo's niece and new owner of Glass Beach Cottage. Proprietors, servers, and townsfolk were friendly and greeted Lily like she had lived there all her life.

The baristas at the bakery and coffee shop knew her order and let her know when they had fresh cinnamon rolls. Waitresses knew she drank water or iced tea and remembered her favorite soups. She was on a first name basis with the local growers at the farmer's market.

She was finding her footing in Driftwood Bay. Not everyone knew of Gary's tragic death. Sad eyes and mournful looks didn't greet her at every turn. Cheerful smiles and a few happy hugs were dispensed by the generous people she had come to think of as friends in the tiny waterfront community where she began to feel at home.

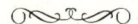

⁓⁂⁓

While Kevin was in town, they visited a few car dealers in the area. Selling her Toyota had been a spur of the moment decision. She hated the car that held so many sad memories of the day Gary had died. She was looking for a car that she could use for errands and trips to the city if needed. She wanted it roomy enough to carry Fritz in a pinch and needed something that was easy on gas.

She and Kevin test drove several cars and sports utility vehicles. They concentrated on the used sections of the car lots. One of the salesmen suggested a new SUV, and after driving it, Lily fell in love. It was small but would accommodate Fritz in the back. It was part of a huge sale, making it less than several of the used models they had driven. She suggested they go to lunch and asked the salesman to hold it for an hour.

Over sandwiches at a place down the street, she asked, "What do you think? Am I making a mistake?"

Kevin's brow furrowed. "No, it's great. Plus, it has a warranty, they'll service it for free, and you'll get roadside assistance. You won't have to worry about repairs or problems for years. I think it's a perfect choice. It's a great deal."

She nodded as she finished the last bite of her sandwich. "I thought so but was worried I loved the gorgeous red color so much, I'd overlooked something important." She ran over her finances in her mind and knew she could afford to buy it. It was only a couple thousand more than she had received for the Toyota.

They returned to the dealership, and less than an hour later, Kevin followed Lily home in her new metallic red SUV. They made the trip from Port Angeles in an hour and returned to find Wade and Andy still at work, with Fritz supervising.

"We're almost done with this one. Thought we'd surprise you with a finished cottage," said Wade as he adjusted the door on the cottage closest to the water. "How'd you make out car shopping?"

Lily admired the cottage and beamed when she told him about her cute red miniature SUV. Wade and Andy gathered their tools and walked to the driveway to admire her new purchase.

Andy sat in the passenger seat and looked over the interior, while Wade took in the shiny red paint. "She's a beauty," he said. They checked out all the features while Kevin sprang Fritz from his enclosure. The dog bounded over to the new car, sniffing each tire and all around it.

The dog started to get into the backseat, but Lily stopped him. "Not yet, big guy. I need to get a seat cover in there before you decorate it with your golden locks." Wade and Andy promised to return in the morning and thought they could finish another cottage. They waved goodbye as they drove away in their work truck.

Lily put her new car in the garage and met Kevin and Fritz in the kitchen. Kevin was gathering things for dinner and headed outside to light the grill. Lily saw her phone flashing. She answered it and held it to her ear.

She hurried to the deck. "The furniture is going to be delivered Friday, so I'll have to see if Wade and Andy can help with that.

Cyndy called and said all the stuff I ordered for the cottages arrived. Maybe you could help me pick it up before we start dinner? She said she'd be there late tonight."

"Sure. We could grab something to eat downtown, and I'll barbeque tomorrow." He closed the lid of the grill.

After they fed Fritz, they left him in his outdoor paddock and took Lily's new ride to meet Cyndy. Lily introduced Kevin, and Cyndy embraced him in a hug. She had Kevin pull the car to the back of the shop and left him to load the boxes.

"How's the work coming on the cottages?" she asked.

Lily explained one was already done and the others should be following in the next couple of days. "Kevin goes back to Virginia the day after tomorrow." Worry clouded Lily's eyes. "At least I'll have lots to keep me busy."

"How about I come over Friday night after work, and we can get started? I've got Saturday off, so we could get things finished up over the weekend."

"That would be terrific, but only if you're sure it's not a bother. I hate to take advantage of you."

Cyndy waved her hand at Lily. "It'll be fun. A bite to eat, lots of wine, and visiting. It'll be just what you need."

Lily's eyes watered as she understood what Cyndy was offering. Not just help with the cottages, but friendship. "Sounds perfect."

Chapter 7

While they ate pizza, Kevin updated the website with photos of the cottage exteriors, since they were close enough to completion to showcase. He showed Lily the steps to add pictures of the interiors, once she had them decorated. "Let's get this site up and running and see if you get some interest and reservations."

His fingers flew over the keyboard, and within the hour, he pronounced her open for business. Lily had already joined the local business group, and her site would be featured on the Driftwood Bay website as a lodging choice. Kevin helped her design postcards announcing the reopening, and they sent them to all the previous guests listed in Uncle Leo's ledger. They celebrated with some triple berry ripple they had stashed in the freezer from one of their outings to Epic Ice Cream.

They unloaded the boxes from Bayside Gifts and stationed them downstairs, so they'd be within easy reach. With that done, they locked up and plodded upstairs. Kevin looked for a movie, and Fritz flopped onto his bed.

"I can't believe tomorrow is your last day. Monday you'll be at your new job." Lily concentrated on keeping her comments about his new internship upbeat. "At least you know your way around from all the times you visited me there."

"Yeah, I'm excited about the new job." He smiled and then added, "Sorry to cut out on you."

"I know, sweetie. You'll like it. If you run into trouble and need anything, get in touch with Steve or Greg. They'll help you out." She reflected on the email she had sent both of them. Greg had taken her old position, and Steve was the Chief of Police. She trusted them both and asked them to look out for Kevin.

"I will, Mom. I promise."

"I can't convince you to let me take you to the airport, huh?"

"Nah, I ordered the shuttle. It's easier. That's a long day for you and Fritz. You need to be working on the cottages and stuff around here."

She nodded. "I guess that makes sense. I'll miss you, kiddo." She sat down on the couch next to him and put her arm around him.

"We can video chat after work, and I'll be back for Thanksgiving."

She nodded as tears clouded her eyes, thankful for the muted lighting and the diversion of a movie.

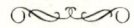

Lily was in the habit of walking along the beach to catch the sunrise each morning, and Friday was no exception. Kevin rose early to join her and Fritz on their excursion. They watched as the brilliant light broke over the dark water. "I'm gonna miss this, Mom. Can't beat the view you have here."

"I like it here. This probably sounds weird, but I feel close to your dad, here on the beach." She paused and added, "It's calm and peaceful. Relaxing."

"I think it's great that you're here. I think you're happier. Less stressed."

She nodded as the yellow orb rose and cast a band of light shimmering across the water. "It's easier without the memories."

"You can make new memories here. I'm excited to see how you do with the cottages. I bet they'll be busy."

"I know. I'm looking forward to it. I should have plenty of crazy guest stories for you by Thanksgiving. I'm going to try to come for the memorial in September."

"Don't stress about it. Grandma would understand if you miss it."

"I haven't missed one yet. Besides, I'll get to see you. I can't pass that up."

They made their way back down the beach to the trail that led to Glass Beach Cottage. Kevin kept hold of Fritz and steered him away from the water's edge. "How about we go to breakfast downtown before I catch the shuttle?"

"I'm game. I need a quick shower. Fritz and I can do our shopping while we're there. I need to grab some snacks and wine for the weekend with Cyndy."

"I'm all packed. Just need to load my stuff in the car."

They got ready and loaded Kevin's bags and Fritz into the truck. After a hearty breakfast, guaranteed to carry him through until he arrived in Virginia, Lily and Fritz waited with him at the shuttle stop.

Lily held Fritz's leash as Kevin bent down and gave him a thorough scratching behind his ears. He hugged the dog to him, and Fritz put a paw on Kevin's shoulder. "Take care of Mom, Fritzie."

Lily gripped her son in a long hug, tears streaming down her face. "Love you, Kev," she whispered. "Call me when you get in."

Kevin squeezed her tighter. "Everything's gonna be okay. Let me know when you get your first reservation."

She nodded and kissed him on the cheek before he stepped into the van. She and Fritz watched as the driver pulled away, and she waved at her son until the shuttle turned and disappeared. She loaded the dog and grabbed a handful of tissues to wipe her eyes.

"We're going to miss our boy, huh?" Fritz's gentle eyes met hers, and he lifted his paw to her.

She stopped at the market and picked up a few things for the weekend, including several bottles of wine for Cyndy. Fritz scored two bags of homemade dog treats at the bakery, and Lily picked up a quart of chocolate almond ice cream. She kept her eye on the time, not wanting to miss the furniture delivery.

When they returned home, Wade and Andy were working on the last cottage. She put all the groceries away and wandered outside to check on the progress. "We're just about done here. Should be right on time to get the furniture moved in," said Wade.

"They look terrific. Thanks for sticking around to help with the furniture. How about I make you guys lunch?"

Andy gave an enthusiastic nod. Wade smiled and said, "Sounds great. Did Kevin get off okay?"

Lily's throat tightened. She squeaked out a "Yep, on his way." She turned and took a few steps toward the house. "I'll have lunch ready in a few."

She concentrated on making a gigantic deli-style sandwich with a loaf of fresh from the oven bread. She chopped veggies and added meats and cheeses to her creation. She cut it in pieces, grabbed a bag of chips and a few bakery cookies, and delivered it all to the table on the deck.

She retrieved the pitcher of iced tea and glasses and called out to let them know lunch was ready. After washing up in the downstairs bathroom, the men made their way up the stairs and settled into the comfortable chairs.

"Whew, I'm starving, and this looks great," said Wade.

Andy helped himself and said, "Thanks, Miss Lily."

They chatted about the cottages, furniture, and Cyndy, who was due to help after work. Not Kevin. Fritz helped lighten Lily's mood with some begging antics and found the weakest link at the table—Andy.

They had started to clear the table when the furniture delivery arrived. Wade and Andy hurried to meet the driver and organized the placement of the beds, sofas, and tables. Lily had found small patio tables with mosaic tops that reminded her of Aunt Maggie's creations. She supervised their positioning in the patio space behind each cottage.

She smiled as she looked in the first cottage. It was fully furnished and looked inviting. She couldn't wait to add Cyndy's talents to the mix. Two hours later, the delivery truck was empty, and Andy went about collecting all the packing materials from the lawn.

"Looks terrific, guys. Thanks for all the help," said Lily, beaming as she inspected each of the cottages from their entries. "I can't believe you finished early."

"I'm glad you're happy with them. We're going to get a move on. If you run into any problems this weekend, just give me a call."

Andy gave Fritz a belly rub as he was leaving the yard. "Have fun decorating, Miss Lily."

She waved goodbye. "Stop by for a cookie and a visit sometime." Fritz watched them drive away through his fence and then hurried to Lily. She went to the back of the first cottage and sat at the new outdoor table.

Her cell phone rang, and she smiled when she saw Kevin's name. "Hey, sweetie." He had made it to Charlotte and had a layover, which would give him time to find some overpriced, underwhelming airport food. "We love you, Kev. Call when you get in tonight." She disconnected the call and gazed into Fritz's gentle eyes.

"It's just us now, Fritzie." The dog moved closer and rested his chin on her leg. "Yeah, we'll be okay."

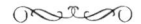

Lily moved all the boxes Kevin had helped stack downstairs to the cottages. She called in an order for Chinese food and made sure the wine was chilled. She and Fritz took the truck to town and picked up dinner.

Cyndy arrived, and Fritz welcomed her with several presses of his nose and a quick lick. "Oh, you're a sweet one, aren't you?" she said, petting Fritz.

"Come on in. I've got takeout and wine and some desserts for later." Lily motioned Cyndy to the kitchen. "I see you brought your own tools," she pointed at the tool caddy Cyndy held.

"Oh, yes. Have hammer, will travel." She laughed and added, "I've been looking forward to this all day. I'm so excited to see what you've done." She took the glass of wine Lily offered.

"The furniture arrived this afternoon. I just need your decorating expertise."

After they ate, Lily and Fritz led the way through the backyard and to the cottages. "I remember this yard. What a great spot and a wonderful view," said Cyndy as she took in the surroundings.

Lily opened the door, and Cyndy said, "Oh, this is terrific. I love it. Perfect choice on the paint colors." She surveyed the area and took in the scraped wood flooring and the soft sea glass colors on the accent walls.

The cottages had identical floor plans consisting of a living room with a window seat, one large bedroom, a bathroom, and a small alcove with built-in booth seating and a small table. A mini fridge, coffee maker, and a supply of cups and glasses were stashed in a cabinet near the booth.

Lily had chosen neutral beach colors of sand and white, along with distressed wood furnishings. To add color, she picked chairs for the living area in soft aqua, a dark turquoise cabinet for the wall across from each entry, and striped cushions in white and gray for the small booth and window seat.

Each cottage featured accent walls in soft beachy hues. Pretty sheets of glass tiles, resembling her aunt's sea glass mosaics, accented the white bathrooms. Cyndy nodded as she admired the space. "I'm itching to start." She smiled and went in search of the boxes she would need.

Over the next couple of hours, Lily took direction from Cyndy and fetched items for her to place throughout the quaint beach house. Cyndy asked Lily for her opinion on where pieces should be hung. After the third time of her asking, Lily said, "Just pretend this is your place. You decide. I trust you, and I'm a total amateur when it comes to decorating."

Cyndy smiled and quit asking. She had Lily help her hold and measure, and by the time it was dark, they had finished the first cottage. "It's gorgeous," said Lily, taking a seat in one of the chairs. "Better than I imagined."

Cyndy nodded and moved to the bookcase. She repositioned a starfish and took a seat on the couch. "I'm glad you like it." She yawned and added, "I'm beat."

Lily's cell phone sounded, and she held up a finger to Cyndy. "It's my son. I'll just be a minute." She stepped outside and took the call. Kevin had landed in Virginia and was on his way to his new room. A friend was helping him move over the weekend.

Lily returned and found Cyndy with her head resting against the back of the couch and her eyes closed. She opened her eyes when Lily took her seat. "Sorry, Kevin just called to let me know he landed. Get some rest and sleep in tomorrow. I'll pick up some pastries for breakfast and get all the items unboxed for the other cottages. That will save us some time tomorrow. Now that you've done this one, it should be easier to copy what you've done, right?"

She nodded. "That's the idea. Just the accent colors we're using will change. You're smart to do all white linens, towels, and duvet covers. Easy to accent and replace, if necessary."

"I'm trying to keep it simple. This just looks so inviting; I might sleep here."

Cyndy rose and said, "I need to get going, or I'll be sleeping here too." She pointed at Fritz, who had made himself comfortable and was snoozing on the pale aqua area rug.

Lily walked Cyndy to the house, told her she'd leave the door open and to come on in whenever she arrived in the morning. She waved goodbye from the gate before hurrying back to the cottages. Lily stacked the remaining boxes inside the other two cottages and locked them. "Time for bed," she said, motioning to Fritz to follow her.

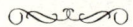

Despite the emptiness in the house and missing Kevin, Lily had a good night's sleep. Physical exhaustion had its benefits. She and Fritz took their customary morning walk on the beach. As the first light broke over the horizon, she petted Fritz and contemplated the work for the day.

The twosome headed home while the sun still sat atop the water. After feeding Fritz breakfast, she took a quick shower before popping down to take pictures of the first cottage. She had added the final exterior photos of all three cottages but needed the interior shots to complete the site. She uploaded them and reviewed the site one more time. Once she was satisfied, she hit the publish button and pushed her electronic presence out into the ether.

She and Fritz took Gary's truck and set off for the bakery. She selected an assortment of pastries and hurried home to get the boxes unpacked. Fritz amused himself with a new stuffie Lily had found at the mercantile. It took her the better part of an hour to organize the items.

While she was carting the empty boxes away, Fritz made a run for the house. Cyndy had arrived. She saw her waving from the deck. "Good morning, Lily."

Lily tossed the boxes and met her on the deck. "I didn't get very far," she said. "I've unpacked, but that's it. How about something to eat and some coffee?"

Cyndy followed her into the kitchen and selected a fresh bear claw dripping with icing. Lily poured coffee, and they sat at the island counter. Cyndy bit into her breakfast treat and said, "Nothing beats something from Sugar's."

"I took some photos this morning for the website. It turned out great." Lily refilled their cups. "Now I'm hoping for some reservations."

"I'm sure you'll get them." Cyndy took in the kitchen. "This is a great house. If we have time later, I'd love a tour."

"Of course. Let's get started, and with any luck, we'll be done before dinner."

The pair, followed by Fritz, got to work on the second cottage. Cyndy opened the bright purple door and saw Lily had the items organized and ready. The placement went quicker than last night's efforts. With only a break for a quick snack, they finished the third cottage that afternoon.

The things Cyndy had helped Lily pick out from her catalogs were the perfect touches. Glass bottles, lamps, pillows, throws, prints, shells, starfish, and driftwood made for a comfortable haven with echoes of the nearby beach.

The neutral foundation colors highlighted the soft sea glass tones woven throughout each of the cottages and made for a relaxing sanctuary. Lily and Cyndy sat in the cozy booth of the third cottage and admired their work. "I hate to toot my own horn, but the overall effect is quite charming," said Cyndy.

"You've done a terrific job of knitting my hodgepodge of

rambling ideas into something lovely. You've outdone yourself." Lily sighed and said, "They are magnificent."

"I'm pleased with them." Cyndy reached in her tote bag and pulled out tasteful tent cards advertising Bayside Gifts. "I'll pop these on the shelves. Might get some business from your guests."

"I hope you do. Feel free to place them anywhere." Lily stood and said, "I've got to run and get the last of the towels from the dryer, and then I think we're done."

Cyndy helped her break down all the cardboard and packing, and they carted it to Cyndy's car. She could recycle it through the store. "I'd love to take you somewhere for dinner. I know it's not much of a payment for all you've done."

"Oh, I enjoyed every minute. I need to run home and grab a shower but could meet you at the Bay Bistro right on the water. Does that work?"

"Sound great. I'll see you there." They agreed on a time, and Lily walked her to the driveway. "We can come back here after dinner, and I'll show you the house."

Chapter 8

After the most delicious salmon Lily had ever tasted and a piece of marionberry pie, shared with Cyndy, she led the way to her house. Knowing she wouldn't be gone long, she had left Fritz on the main floor, and he greeted them with several whooshes of his tail.

Lily offered Cyndy a glass of wine. "Sure, why not? I only had one at dinner. You were a good girl and didn't have any."

Lily poured two glasses. "Too many years in law enforcement. I don't drink a drop if I'm driving. We barely drank at all, since Gary was essentially on call every hour of the day."

"Your uncle told me he had been killed in the line of duty. I know it doesn't help, but I am very sorry."

Lily motioned her downstairs. "I appreciate that. Let's start down here, and you can see the area guests can use."

She showed her the open area and laundry facilities, plus the powder room. "These are guest bedrooms and two full bathrooms that will be locked when guests are here. It's where my son stayed when he came. I don't anticipate too many guests, so they won't get much use."

Cyndy took in the space and nodded as she strolled and sipped her wine.

"It's somewhat utilitarian, but it's comfortable. Lots of games and puzzles, movies, plus the fridge and microwave," said Lily.

Cyndy nodded. "Very functional and sort of like an old-fashioned rumpus room." Fritz followed the women as they made their way through the downstairs.

"Fritzie's doggie door is through this utility area. All the extra supplies are stored in here. Toiletries, towels, linens. I've still got to wash the rest of them."

She made sure the doors leading outside were locked and followed Cyndy upstairs. She closed the entrance to the stairs and turned the deadbolt. "Kevin insisted I have a sturdy lock."

"Smart kid. Living alone, you can't be too careful. Even in Driftwood Bay."

Lily took her through the kitchen and showed her the pantry and work area with the desk. "This gorgeous kitchen is wasted on me. I'm a rotten cook."

They toured the large living room and then made their way to the master suite. "Love all the art Maggie did," said Cyndy, taking in the pieces adorning the walls.

Lily smiled. "It's comforting." She ran a hand over Gary's urn.

"Tell me about Gary." Cyndy rested in the oversized window seat, and Lily joined her.

Lily's eyes twinkled. "He was my everything. A great husband, wonderful dad, dedicated officer, my best friend. We had a terrific life. It's been…well, overwhelming. I'm hoping I didn't make a mistake coming here. I felt like I was sinking deeper each day. Treading water, barely. I was lost and took this opportunity as a signal, maybe an excuse, to leave. Start again."

She took a sip from her glass. "I miss him. He wasn't supposed to be working when it happened. He was covering a shift for a few hours. As it turns out the call he went on was a ruse. A woman called in a suspicious vehicle, and Gary went with another officer."

"Gary approached the car first, no plates on it. It was an ambush.

A dirtbag with a long record shot him. Point blank. Wanted to kill some cops. The woman who called was his girlfriend. She claims he forced her to make the call."

Lily took a deep breath. "Gary's partner shot the bastard. Thank goodness. The girlfriend is in jail."

Cyndy placed her hand atop Lily's. "I can't imagine what you went through. What you're still going through."

Tears dampened Lily's cheeks. "Sometimes I still think it's a bad dream. A nightmare."

They sat together in silence watching nature's display from the window. A vibrant pink dominated the sky as the sun rested for the day. "Stunning view you have here," said Cyndy. "Makes you realize why it's called Paradise Point."

"It's soothing. This place. The beach. Reminds me of happier times when I was a kid. I'm hoping I can rebuild." She paused. "More than the cottages."

"Give yourself time to heal. I know how long it took me to adjust after my divorce, and that's a walk in the park compared to what you're dealing with."

Lily nodded and wiped her eyes. "How about a bit more wine?"

Cyndy laughed and said, "Once you know me better, you'll realize that is a ridiculous question." She led the way to the kitchen and refilled her new friend's glass.

The two sat on the deck and chatted into the night. Lily listened as Cyndy talked about growing up in Driftwood Bay. Cyndy, in her early fifties, had been divorced for the last fifteen years. She had left Driftwood Bay when she married and had lived outside of Seattle for a few years. When she divorced, she moved home and opened her gift shop. "We lost our mom and dad within three months of each other about two years ago, so now it's just Jack and me. Cancer took my mom, and I'm convinced my dad died from a broken heart.

It was awful." She blotted at the tears in her eyes.

"I can relate to that. My mom was on the plane that hit the Pentagon in 2001. It was her first year of retirement. She had been visiting us and left that morning. It was horrific. She was meeting my dad out in Los Angeles. He was at a work conference. A few months later he died from a massive heart attack. I didn't think I'd ever recover from their loss. Now Gary. Life can change in the blink of an eye."

Cyndy gasped at the revelation. "Oh, my gosh. I'm so sorry, Lily. You must have been devastated."

"It was utter chaos. I relied on Gary so much. He was the strong one throughout all of it." Tears dripped onto the table, and Lily used a napkin to wipe her eyes. "I wouldn't have survived without him."

They commiserated as they reflected on the impact of losing their parents. The utter despair they felt knowing they could never visit with them or ask their advice. "My dad was wise and kind. Always there to help and could solve any problem," said Cyndy. "Mom helped Dad with paperwork at the office but enjoyed cooking and gardening. She kept a beautiful home and had a knack for decorating."

"Must be where you got your talent," said Lily. "My dad was a high school teacher, and Mom was a school librarian. That's how they met."

"I'm fortunate to be close to Jack and enjoy living in the same town. I feel safe here. Growing up here was fun, but I remember thinking it was too small and full of nosy neighbors. Now I appreciate the idea of a close-knit community. I know I could call on loads of friends and neighbors to help me if I was in need."

Lily smiled and said, "That's a great feeling. I've never lived in a small town where everyone knows everyone. I like the sound of it though. Driftwood Bay gives off that kind of a vibe. Feels like home."

Lily nursed her glass of wine throughout the evening, but Cyndy had finished off the rest of the bottle. It was almost midnight. Lily said, "How about you stay in one of the cottages tonight? Sort of like a trial run. I need to make sure they're fit for guests."

Cyndy yawned and said, "Oh, my, I shouldn't have had so much wine. I didn't realize it was so late. I shouldn't drive, so might as well give it go."

Lily offered her some sweatpants and a t-shirt to sleep in and walked her to the first cottage. She made sure her guest was set and gave her a wave from the doorway. "If you need anything just call my cell. There's also an intercom at the back of the house."

Cyndy surprised her and hurried to the door, embracing her in a tight hug. "Thanks for letting me stay. Sorry to do this to you. I sort of forgot I had to drive home."

"Not a problem. It'll be fun. See ya in the morning." Lily made sure Cyndy locked the door and plodded to the house. Fritz, confused by all the activity, followed her like the faithful friend he was.

She doused the lights and realized the backyard was so dark it would be almost impossible to navigate the area without tripping. She made a mental note to get in touch with Wade and see if he could install some lighting. Lily glanced at Fritz's bed and saw him already curled up and snoozing. She chuckled as she turned off her bedside lamp.

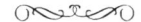

⁕

Sunday morning, Lily felt hot breath on her cheek and opened an eye to find Fritz's nose resting on the edge of her bed. "I'm tired, Fritzie." She groaned but flicked the covers off and slipped on her shoes.

"No beach walk this morning. Let's go out back." She led him through the door to the deck and downstairs. Fritz romped through the yard, sniffing and inspecting. They walked near the cottages but saw no activity.

"Come on," she whispered. "We'll let her sleep." Lily half-jogged so Fritz would follow.

She put his breakfast in his bowl and set about brewing a pot of coffee. After a quick shower and change of clothes, she rummaged in the fridge. She found the makings for breakfast, and while she was in the midst of scrambling eggs, Fritz bolted for the door.

Cyndy was climbing the stairs to the deck. Lily hollered, "Come on in. Breakfast is almost ready."

She came through the door, her hair in disarray, mascara stains under her eyes, and her t-shirt a rumpled mess of wrinkles. "I smell coffee, thank goodness." Lily gestured to the cupboard of mugs, and Cyndy poured herself a cup.

She took a few sips and sighed. "I am so sorry to be such an inconsiderate guest. I'm embarrassed that I drank so much wine."

"Aww, don't worry about it. It's not like I had any plans. And I got the bonus of having my first guest. How was the cottage?"

Cyndy's eyes brightened over the rim of her mug. "It was fabulous. Quiet and serene, but I could hear the faint sound of the waves on the beach. Comfy bed and linens. All our work looks great in the daylight. Love the colors."

"You'll have to test out the bathroom and take a shower. If anything can be improved, I want to know. I'll need to test the other two cottages this week. Fritz and I will have to spend the night and see what we think." She handed a plate to Cyndy and joined her at the island counter.

"As soon as I finish this, I'll hop down and take a shower and give you a full report."

They lingered over multiple cups of coffee. "I noticed last night

I'm going to need to get some lighting installed. If guests had to travel across the yard, they'd never make it without running into something or falling."

"Path lights would work well, and I love the look of strings of globe lights strung over a yard," offered Cyndy.

Lily nodded. "Oh, yes, those are pretty. That would make it look festive. I'll see what Wade can do."

Lily's cell phone rang, and she saw the screen. "It's Kevin. Excuse me for a minute. I need to take it." She connected the call on her way to the master bedroom.

Cyndy nodded her understanding and began clearing the dishes and loading the dishwasher. Fritz stood at attention at the edge of the dishwasher and was happy to lend a hand licking each plate she added. After things were tidy, she refilled her mug and headed downstairs to the cottage.

Lily listened as Kevin described his new living quarters. He was ready for his first day of work and excited to start. "Tomorrow I have orientation meetings and have to get my ID and parking permit." Enthusiasm radiated from his voice.

Lily laughed and smiled as she imparted her wisdom of the best coffee shops, lunch spots, and benches near the Capitol Square. After spending the last two decades serving with the Capitol Police, she knew every inch of the buildings, grounds, and streets surrounding the area.

Kevin's office would be in the Pocahontas Building, across the street from the Capitol. One of Lily's favorite restaurants was two blocks from his office. "Tell Sylvia and Mario I'm your mom, and you'll get great service."

Kevin promised to call and report on his first week at work. "I'm sure you'll have a reservation by then." They chatted for a few more minutes before he had to go.

"Love you, Kev. Talk to you soon." She disconnected and wandered back to the kitchen. She smiled when she saw the clean kitchen and made a detour to the work area to check the computer.

Her eyes widened when she saw the reservation screen. Her first reservation booked all three cottages. She looked at the notes and read that six girlfriends had booked the property for a getaway week. They were arriving at the end of June and taking in the Fourth of July in Driftwood Bay.

She verified the reservation and added a note to the automatic confirmation email. It included an offer to add extras such as wine, fruit baskets, or chocolates to their stay. The message also reminded them of the complimentary wine and beer social at the firepit on Friday and Saturday evenings. Kevin had suggested she limit this idea to weekends.

Cyndy came through the door as soon as she finished the email. "I just got my first booking for all three cottages. I've got about two weeks to work all the wrinkles out and get ready for them."

"You'll be ready. Everything was perfect in the bathroom. Nice bath products. I think you're set." She handed her the clothes she had borrowed. "I'm happy to take these and launder them."

"Ah, don't be silly. I'll toss them in the wash this week." She shoved them in the laundry chute. "I almost forgot, I have a little something to thank you for all your work." She retrieved a huge gift basket filled with wine and chocolates from the counter in the pantry.

"Oh, my goodness. That wasn't necessary." Cyndy admired the ribbon and read the thoughtful card. "This is lovely. It really wasn't work. It was fun. Not to mention, I feel like we connected as friends." She turned and hugged Lily.

"Me too. I'm so happy I wandered into your shop."

"I need to get going, but let's plan to meet for dinner soon. I can't really do lunch because of work but would love to get together."

"Sounds great. You could also crash my wine party on Friday and Saturday nights."

"You are a glutton for punishment. But, I never turn down free wine." She laughed and hugged her new friend again. "Give me a ring, and we'll do dinner this week before you get busy."

Lily and Fritz walked her to her car and helped her load the basket into the backseat. Cyndy tooted her horn and waved as she sped off and headed to town. Lily turned to Fritz and said, "Let's go wash some laundry and clean up Cyndy's cottage. Then we'll have a sleepover tonight and check out the next one."

Chapter 9

Lily and Fritz had no trouble getting settled in the second cottage. They tested all the furniture, opened all the cabinets, and tried all the lights. After a comfortable night's sleep, they made their usual early morning walk to the beach to welcome the first rays of sunlight.

Upon their return, the bathroom passed inspection, and Lily gathered all the dirty linens to cart to the house. She tossed them into the machine and started it before she dashed upstairs to dress.

She had an appointment for Fritz with Dr. MacMillan and kept her eye on the clock. She called Wade about the lighting, and he promised to get to it this week. She settled for a quick piece of toast and a few sips of coffee before loading Fritz in the truck.

They made their way out of town and turned into a driveway leading to a building that looked more like a farmhouse than a clinic. The gray clapboard house sat in the midst of green fields with white fencing. Corrals, a barn, and sheds dotted the property.

After checking in at the front desk and filling out paperwork, Lily took Fritz for a walk. She saw a sign with an arrow announcing a pond. They followed a walking path lined with flowers and shrubs to a tranquil area equipped with a few benches.

The woman at the desk told her they would find her when they were ready, so she didn't concern herself with the time. Fritz's ears twitched at the sound of a horse braying. After a few minutes, she heard her name called from the rear entrance.

"Come on, Fritzie, it's our turn." She hurried down the path and met a cheerful woman dressed in scrubs adorned with cats and dogs. Darlene was etched on her nametag. Another technician was holding a leash with a sweet looking golden retriever puppy on the end of it. The puppy hurried to Lily and Fritz, and the two dogs sniffed each other.

"Come here, Bodie. Be a good boy," said the technician. "Sorry about that, he's super friendly."

Lily bent and petted the soft puppy. "Aww, he's a sweetheart."

"This handsome boy must be Fritz," said Darlene, bending down to nuzzle his neck. "Let's get you on the scale and in a room."

Lily led him to the scale and then followed Darlene to the exam room. She asked a few questions, scribbled notes in a chart, and said, "Dr. Mac will be right in." After she left, Fritz proceeded to inspect every nook and cranny and give them all a good sniff.

Moments later the door opened, and a man with kind blue eyes, who reminded her a bit of Paul Newman, came through the door. He bent down and gave Fritz a thorough petting before extending his hand to Lily. "Hi there, I'm Dr. Mac. It's MacMillan, but everyone calls me Mac."

"I'm Lily Reed. I'm new to Driftwood Bay. My Uncle Leo had the Glass Beach Cottage, and I've moved here to reopen it."

"Oh, my sister mentioned you. Leo and Maggie were terrific. It's wonderful to have their place back in business." He glanced down at Fritz. "It looks like we're just doing a checkup today. Getting to know each other, right?"

Fritz's tail swished through the air at rapid speed. The doctor took his temperature, examined his ears and mouth, and listened to his heart and lungs. "We received his records by fax this morning, and it looks like he's all up to date on everything. Do you have any concerns?"

She shook her head, "No, just wanted to get established. Fritz has adapted to our new place. With our house near the beach, Fritz has found a new favorite activity. He loves to go for walks there and romp in the water."

"It's beautiful in that area. Just make sure he doesn't drink much saltwater. Take fresh water with you so he'll have access if he's thirsty. Another thing is to make sure and rinse him off after he goes in the water. The salt can irritate his skin. Keep him hydrated and out of the heat."

He slipped Fritz a treat from his pocket and made a lifelong friend.

"What about a good groomer? Anybody you recommend?" Lily asked.

"I have a golden and use a mobile groomer who is terrific. I'll get you her card." When he left, the door didn't quite close. Moments later a nose was visible through the crack, and then the opening widened. The puppy they had seen earlier, Bodie, came bounding into the room.

Fritz wiggled and wagged, and Bodie pawed at the bigger dog. Dr. Mac returned and said, "Oh, sorry, Bodie escaped his handler." The doctor picked up the puppy and held it on his lap as he took a seat.

"He is such a cutie. Reminds me of Fritz when he was a puppy. My husband got him. Fritz was a washout from a police training program. He was a tad too friendly and playful to be a canine officer, but he's a wonderful pet."

"Bodie here is also in training. He's going to be a hearing dog. I'm involved in a program that trains service dogs. This little guy was placed with a foster family for training, but they had a family medical emergency the day after Bodie arrived. I'm watching him." Fritz was now at the doctor's knee, nose to nose with the puppy.

"You know… I've been looking for a new foster home for him." He winked and added, "I'd sweeten the deal, and in addition to covering Bodie's care, I'll throw in Fritz's care. All his supplies are provided. He just needs to learn some basics and attend training sessions once a week starting at three months. Then you work with him on the weekly commands. He'd stay with you for about eighteen months to two years."

"Oh, wow, I haven't considered another dog." Lily smiled as Dr. Mac released Bodie to the floor and he scrambled on top of Fritz. She watched the two play with each other. "It's obvious Fritz is sold on the idea of a little brother. Could I give it some thought?"

"Of course. I've been keeping an eye out for the right fit. Bodie is a great fan of older brothers. He loves my dog, but I live alone. Widowed." The doctor looked down at the dogs. "I'm not home enough to work with Bodie, so I'm looking for someone that works from home or is home most of the day. You having a dog, and having people around to help socialize Bodie would be terrific. I don't have him at the clinic often because of sick animals, so he's been staying at home with my dog. He needs to be in a stable home."

"Sorry about your wife. I lost my husband a year ago, so I'm adjusting to being alone. With the new business, I'm just not sure how much free time I'll have."

"Very sorry to hear that, Lily. That first year is pure torture. All the firsts you have to endure. Birthdays, anniversary, holidays. I know that devastating feeling. All I can say is time lessens the intensity of the pain. It's been almost ten years for me." He ruffled Fritz's fur and ran a hand down his back. "I understand your hesitation, and I don't think Bodie will take a ton of your time. He's housebroken and is a quick study. You'll be teaching and reinforcing normal manners and then working on the exercises the trainer gives you to alert to sounds. The program even provides his food."

Lily picked up Bodie and held him to her. He nestled into the space between her neck and shoulder. "He sure is sweet." She breathed in the magical smell of puppy.

"I could bring him over for a visit and see how he does at your place."

Lily laughed and said, "You missed your calling as a car salesman." She glanced at the dogs again. "Okay, bring him by, and let's see how it goes." She held up her finger. "No promises, just an introduction."

He nodded and smiled, "Got it. You pick a night. I'll bring dinner and Bodie."

"Oh, you don't need to do that."

"I insist. All part of the package, ma'am." He chuckled. "Sherlock, my golden, would get along well with Fritz. They're a lot alike." He laughed as Fritz rolled on his back and let Bodie climb all over him.

"Sherlock?"

He shrugged. "I love mysteries."

"Bring Sherlock when you come. Fritz would love it. Does Friday work for you?"

"Sounds perfect. We'll be there with dinner around six-thirty."

Lily stood and attached Fritz's leash. "See you then. Come on Fritzie, time to go home."

Dr. Mac pulled Bodie away and held him while he opened the door for Lily. "Great to meet you, Lily. See you soon."

She stopped at the front desk to pay the bill. The woman behind the counter retrieved the chart and smiled up at her. "Dr. Mac says no charge today." She plucked a doggie treat from a bowl and handed it to Lily. "This is for Fritz. Come and see us again."

Lily thanked her and ushered Fritz to the truck. She turned onto the road and said, "How did you like Dr. Mac and Bodie?"

She glanced in the rearview mirror and saw Fritz smiling, the tip of his tongue visible.

༺━━༻

She and Fritz slept behind the bright teal door of the third cottage that night and found two defective light bulbs, but outside of that, it was ready for guests. The yard service was set to come on Thursdays to mow and groom all the plants. She made sure they would arrive after checkout time at ten, so as not to interrupt guests.

She and Fritz walked to the beach early each morning. She thought about the idea of fostering Bodie while she watched the waves and waited for the sun. It was the sort of decision she would have talked over with Gary. "We have a chance to train a puppy to be a hearing dog. It means more work for Fritz and me, but when I see Andy, I think it would be worthwhile."

She knew Gary wouldn't answer her, but it helped to talk to him. "Wish you were here." The first breath of daylight crept above the horizon. Lily smiled at the light. "Ah, there you are."

Fritz was her constant companion. His significance in her life had increased when Gary died. She knew how important a dog could be for someone in need and knew Bodie would grow up to help someone. Someone who needed him, like Andy.

She bent down and held Fritz's sweet face in her hands. "I think we should take Bodie. Will that be okay with you, buddy?" She looked into the gentle brown eyes that held only love.

"Let's get home," she tugged on the leash and slow-jogged along the water. Once back at the house, she hosed off Fritz's paws and threw the ball a few times to let him run off some energy.

She kept busy with laundering all the extra linens, stocking wine and beer, and setting up the coffee and tea station. The seat covers for her new car arrived, and she wrestled them over the seats. She cut some peonies from Aunt Maggie's bush and put them in vases around the house.

Wade and Andy installed solar lights along the walking paths and hung hundreds of globe lights across the yard, the sitting areas under the deck, and near the firepit. They added timers, so the lights came on at dusk.

It took some doing, but they finished it Friday afternoon. She fixed them lunch on the days they worked and caught up with Andy, practicing her signing. She told them she had received more reservations and was booked every weekend in July and had a few bookings into September.

She texted Kevin to check in and ask him his thoughts about fostering a service puppy. He thought Fritz would like having a playmate and encouraged her to do it. They set up a video chat for the weekend when he'd have more time.

Friday arrived, and Lily savored her accomplishments. Everything was shipshape in the cottages, the yard looked terrific, and the reservations kept coming. She had been thinking about surveillance cameras and had found and ordered a set online. She wanted to get them installed before the first guests arrived. With that done, she set about making cookies she could freeze.

She baked all day and had dozens of cookies and brownies stacked in containers in the spare freezer. She kept enough out for dessert. It was almost five when she finished cleaning the kitchen. She took a quick shower and changed clothes.

Her short, layered hair didn't require much time. She toweled it dry and ran some product through it before using the blow dryer. She had let her hair grow out since she was no longer working. As she tried to get the ends to cooperate, she remembered she needed to book an appointment with a hairdresser.

"Good enough." She pronounced her efforts complete and

headed for the kitchen. Fritz was lounging on the floor, his eyes closed. Lily had skipped lunch and was famished. She looked in the freezer and found some cranberry and cheese appetizers she had picked up at the market. She popped them in the oven.

The aroma of the baking pastry surrounding the savory and tart filling made her even hungrier. She worked on fixing a fresh pitcher of iced tea while she waited. Soon the timer sounded, and she removed the baking sheet from the oven.

She plucked one, still piping hot, and cut it open so it would cool faster. While she waited, she took Fritz out for a walk around the yard. He'd be thrilled to have furry visitors, and she knew the exercise would calm him.

After throwing the ball for about fifteen minutes, she led him upstairs. He slurped up a healthy amount of water and retired to the floor where he could watch out the door to the backyard. Lily took a bite of the appetizer and said, "Not bad." She took a few more bites and added, "In fact, pretty darn tasty." She ate one more and put the rest on a glass plate.

She bent to pet Fritz and rubbed his face with her thumbs. "I think we might be getting a new puppy friend to raise. Are you up for sharing the limelight with a new furry brother?" He put a paw on her arm and urged her to keep up the massage.

She slid onto the floor next to him, and he put his head on her leg. She rubbed each of his ears, and his eyes closed. Total relaxation. "I think your dad would have jumped at the chance to have another puppy in the house. You know we got you to fill our empty nest with Kev gone. That was your dad's doing. He had the best ideas."

She kissed the top of his warm head, and his tail thumped against the floor. She sat with him, content to run her hands over his soft fur as tears flowed down her face. Thoughts of Gary with Fritz as a puppy flooded her mind. She remembered the work involved in training him and keeping him out of trouble. Was she nuts to think about taking on something else while she was getting a new business launched?

Chapter 10

Fritz heard Dr. Mac arrive before Lily and sprinted from the kitchen to the front door. He gave a couple of low woofs, his signal to let Lily know someone was here. She hurried after him and opened the door.

Dr. Mac stood on the step, his hands full of bags. He looked less doctorly without the white coat. "Hi, Lily. The dogs are in the car. I wasn't sure if you wanted to start inside or outside."

"Oh, I haven't thought that far ahead. Come in, and we can stash the food in the kitchen." As she led him through, she said, "Maybe the backyard is the best idea."

He placed the bags on the counter and said, "Great house, by the way. I agree about outdoors. Less chance of an accident. You know how excited puppies sometimes spring a leak." Tiny crinkles appeared at the corners of his eyes when he smiled.

"Fritz and I were just discussing the work involved with a puppy." She moved the bag so she could read the logo. "Noni's? I haven't discovered that one yet."

"It's a tiny place. Doesn't advertise. Sort of a secret spot for locals."

"Shall I put it in the oven to keep warm while we let the hounds loose?"

He laughed and helped her put the boxes in the oven and stash the salad in the fridge. She slid the plate of appetizers to him. "Have one of these if you're hungry. I was starving."

He popped one in his mouth on his way to the front door. "Not bad. I'll grab the boys and meet you in the backyard."

She pointed to the side gate for access and told him she'd meet him there. "Come on, Fritz. Let's go."

He followed her down the stairs and around the corner. She opened the gate, and a beautiful golden poked his head into the yard. "This is Sherlock."

She knelt down and petted him. He leaned his head against her leg and soaked in the attention. Dr. Mac was holding Bodie, and Fritz was jumping a few inches off the ground in excitement.

He closed the gate, and they made their way to the back of the house. Fritz and Sherlock ran around in circles, chasing each other. Bodie weaseled his way into the fun and tumbled with the big dogs.

"You've got a lovely spot here, Lily. It looks terrific."

"I'll give you the grand tour after dinner. I've got my first guests booked starting at the end of June."

"I'm betting you'll have very few vacancies. Once word gets out." He glanced at the pile of dogs still romping together.

"We could eat out on the deck and keep an eye on the wild animals. I'll set us up, and you can stay here and make sure nothing crazy happens." She pointed at the chairs near the house. "I'll give you a shout when it's ready."

She hurried up the stairs and added the warm takeout containers to a tray, along with the crisp salad. She retrieved place settings for each of them, added the appetizers and desserts, and transported the lot to the outdoor table.

She made a second trip for glasses, a bottle of wine, and the iced tea. She leaned out the door and said, "Dinner's ready."

Not only did that get Dr. Mac's attention, but the two grown dogs made a run for the stairs, with Bodie following close behind. Dr. Mac scooped him up, since he hadn't quite mastered stairs and carried him to the deck. Fritz jumped onto the ottoman he liked to use, and Sherlock crowded onto it with him. The pup stood on his hind legs trying to reach the top of it.

Dr. Mac picked up Bodie and settled him between the other two. "Down, Sherlock. Down, Fritz. Down, Bodie." The two older dogs put their heads down. Bodie stayed where he was, looking between the humans and the dogs.

"Dr. Mac, this all looks delicious," said Lily, spooning samples of each of the pasta dishes onto her plate and adding a piece of chicken parmesan.

"Aww, please call me Mac. No need for the doctor title. My given name is Jack, but most everyone calls me Mac." He filled a plate and dug into the meal. "Looks like our three furry friends are tuckered out."

Bodie was asleep, resting most of his body on Sherlock, with his back legs atop Fritz's back. "We'll see how long it lasts," she said, reaching for the pitcher of tea.

He grabbed it and poured her a glass. She thanked him and said, "Would you like some wine? Cyndy helped me pick out a few bottles for guests. I'm not much of an aficionado."

"No, tea is perfect. I'm tired now, so wine would do me in for the night. My sister loves wine, so you're sure to have excellent choices if she helped."

"Cyndy is terrific. What an eye for decorating. Wait until you see what she did with the cottages. I paid her in wine. Not enough for what she did." She laughed and took a few more bites. "About Bodie. I think I'd like to foster him, but I'd like to see if there is any way to have him go to Andy Lewis when he's trained. Do you know Andy?"

He nodded and smiled. "I do. Terrific family and wonderful young man. He's had it tough. Have you mentioned it to him?"

She shook her head. "I just noticed how much he took to Fritz when he was working here. Fritz hung right by him and paid him special attention. I think Andy would benefit from having a service dog. Maybe become more independent and live on his own."

"I can do my best to encourage Bodie's placement with Andy but can't guarantee it. It would make sense to place him with someone nearby, and right now we don't have anyone in Driftwood Bay on the list to receive a dog."

Her brows rose. "So, it could work?"

He shrugged. "Not sure, but I'm happy to call the director and put in a request. We'll have to get Andy on board first."

"Leave that to me. I'll have him over to meet Bodie. I think that's all it will take." She pushed her plate away from the edge of the table. "That was wonderful food. I'm so glad you introduced me to Noni's."

"It's one of my favorite spots. Cooking for one is a royal pain. I end up eating takeout more than I should, but with my schedule, it works."

The new lights strung throughout the backyard turned on, giving the yard a festive vibe. "Wade and Andy just got those finished this morning. They make it look so cheerful." She moved to the edge and admired the view. "Shall we take a walk downstairs, and you can check out the cottages?"

He put down his napkin, picked up Bodie, and followed Lily down the stairs. The two older dogs shadowed him. Mac released Bodie, and he ran to catch up with the other two. Lily unlocked the bright pink door to the first cottage and ushered him into the entry. She pointed out all the touches Cyndy had added and showed him the small back patio with the lovely view over the bluff.

"I'm not much on décor, but even I can tell these are great. Nice that there's no television. Forces folks to talk to each other and get out and enjoy nature. Your setting is perfect." He gestured at the yard and the firepit niche.

He followed Lily and walked through the other two cottages. "I can see Cyndy was busy. She always does a great job. Her store is one of the most popular, and she has quite a clientele."

"I couldn't be happier." She locked the doors, and they wandered through the yard. "I haven't tried that firepit yet. I should do that before guests arrive."

Mac opened the door underneath and turned the valve to the open position. "Looks like you just push this button to ignite it." He pushed the button, and seconds later flames danced in the colorful blue glass stones.

"Looks easy," she said, as Mac showed her the valve to turn the gas on and off.

"I've got Bodie's things in the car. Do you want to give it a go and have him start staying here tonight?"

"Sure, I think it's best to start now. That way I'll have more time with him before my first set of guests check in."

"I'll run and get his stuff and meet you upstairs. And, if it doesn't work out, don't be afraid to tell me. I don't want you to be stressed out over it." He glanced at their feet and saw the pile of three dogs resting together. "He seems to have taken to Fritz."

"I bet Sherlock is going to be lonely."

"He goes with the flow. He comes to the office most days, so he gets his fill of friends and playdates."

She picked up Bodie, and the other two followed her upstairs and into the house. Mac came to the front door carrying a mountain of dog supplies. She helped him unload the beds, carrier, leashes and harnesses, toys, bowls, treats, and a file with his records and information. "Oh, one other thing. No beach, dog parks, or other dogs for Bodie until after his three-month immunizations."

Lily wrinkled her nose as he hurried back to the car. He returned with a large container that was cold from being in an ice chest.

"I've switched Sherlock to the same fresh food the program uses. Once Fritz gets a whiff of it, he'll want to eat it instead of regular food. The program pays for the food, and I've got a bunch of vouchers for you to use. You order it online, and they deliver each week. You can freeze it if you need to store it. I'll give you some extra vouchers because I know Fritz will like it."

"As you switch him, ease him into it. Twenty-five percent added to his regular food and then add a bit more every five days. He'll adjust to it, just go slow with the transition."

"Okay, looks like we're set," she said, after placing the container in the extra pantry fridge. "About the beach, I guess I'll leave Bodie in his crate when we take our walks in the morning. Seems so mean."

"He'll be fine. He needs to get used to amusing himself in the crate. Put him in there even when you're home to get him acclimated. He'll be fine while you walk for your hour or whatever. If he's whining, you won't hear it, because you won't be here."

"I just hate to think of him being sad, but I know you're right."

"I'll email you the training information. They offer it three days a week, at different times, so it's pretty flexible. Right now, they'll concentrate on manners, so basic stuff. They have videos online to help guide you. Again, he'll have to wait a few weeks until he has his shots to go to the training facility."

She positioned one of Bodie's beds next to Fritz's and set about organizing his other things. "I made some cookies today if you'd like some."

"How about one for the road? I'm beat and need to get home. Tomorrow is my Saturday at the clinic."

She put several cookies in a baggie and rewarded all three dogs with a treat of their own. "Thanks for bringing dinner. And, Bodie, of course."

He took out a card and wrote his cell and home numbers on the back. "Give me a ring if you have any problems. I'll check in with you in the next few days. I'll have some formal paperwork from the program for you to sign too. Thank you for giving Bodie a home."

"We'll take good care of him," Lily promised. Mac patted the puppy's head and stroked his ears. She held Bodie and watched as Sherlock and his owner made their way to his car parked on the street. Sherlock kept looking back at the house, searching for Bodie.

She watched as Mac knelt down and spoke to the dog while he nuzzled his head against his own. Then he loaded Sherlock in the car.

"Okay, Bodie. Let's see how we do tonight." She snuggled the bundle of squirmy fur close to her.

She let Bodie down and went about cleaning up the dinner mess. Once she had that done, she took both dogs outside. To avoid an accident in the middle of the night, she walked Bodie around the whole perimeter twice. Lily and her two furry companions made their way inside and buttoned up the house.

"Come on guys, let's go to bed." Lily led the way and smiled when she saw the strings of lights and their welcoming glow. They were programmed to turn off at midnight, and then the path lights would guide guests between the house and cottages.

After getting ready, she got the dogs situated on their beds. "Nightie night, boys."

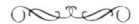

○~♈~○

Lily rose early and inched her head off the pillow to spy on her two charges. Bodie was in Fritz's bed, snuggled against him. She eyed the area around the beds and was pleased to find no puddles.

Fritz stirred and opened his eyes. "Hi, sweet boy." The sound of her voice woke Bodie, and he moved into a sitting position. "Let's go outside." She remembered from Fritz's puppy days how important it was to take a puppy outside the minute he woke in the morning.

She hurried them through the house and out the door to the backyard. As she carried Bodie, she knew mastering the stairs would have to happen this week. She set him on the second to last step and urged him down. He hesitated but put his front paws down. She eased his rear along, and he half tumbled down to the patio. "Fritz will teach you how it's done."

Fritz set about going to the area Lily had earmarked for him, and Bodie followed him. Lily hung back, ready to herd him if he wandered, but he was stuck to Fritz like a wad of chewing gum on a new pair of shoes. She praised his success and led him to the enclosure to see if he would go through the doggie door. Once she had them inside, she hurried up the outside stairs to unlock the door off the kitchen.

Praying they weren't tearing through the garden level as she scuttled down the stairs, she found they hadn't come through their door yet. She stuck her head through the opening to attract Bodie's interest. Moments later, he popped through the door, followed by Fritz.

Pointing at the door, she said, "Outside, Bodie." Fritz went through, and Bodie followed. They played this game for the better part of an hour, with Lily teaching Bodie commands for outside and house. Afterward, they followed her upstairs for breakfast. She added a measure of the new fresh food to Fritz's kibble and fed him outside in case he tried to help himself to Bodie's bowl.

Fritz ate the new food first and licked his bowl when he finished until it gleamed like new. Bodie gobbled his breakfast, and she put them both on the deck to rest. Fritz had the routine down and jumped onto the ottoman. Lily placed the puppy next to him.

"This is like having a baby again," she mumbled, as she dashed to the shower. Once she was dressed, she tiptoed to the kitchen and started the coffee. She peered out the window and saw both of the dogs still snuggled together.

Instead of the beach this morning, she ate a quick breakfast, loaded her pockets with training treats, and took the dogs outside again. After making sure they did their business in the designated area, she led them to the stairs inside the house.

For hours, she and Fritz went up and down and helped Bodie conquer his fears. Lily wanted him to master the stairs with a softer landing before they tackled the outside steps. That was the extent of her Sunday. Stairs. Stairs. Stairs.

By the evening, Bodie was going up and down them with ease and only faltered a few times. Tomorrow they'd tackle the ones outside. She fed the dogs and ate leftovers from last night while she waited for Kevin to call.

While the dogs rested, she gathered pens, business cards, keys to the cottages, and local maps and took them downstairs. She planned to welcome guests downstairs in the common area and keep them out of the main house. She matched the keyring colors to the cottage doors to minimize confusion. Kevin had helped her set up a credit card gizmo on her phone so that she wouldn't be tied to the computer upstairs.

She organized her supplies in one of the drawers with a lock. Her business cards had her cell phone number and a spot for her to write the code for the gate, which she planned to change on a weekly basis. There was plenty of parking along the side of the house, where the entrance was secured with the keypad lock. Guests could come and go as they pleased.

Soon she heard the sound of the dogs coming downstairs. "Hey, guys. Let's go outside and do your business." Leashes were hung by the door, and she grabbed one for Bodie, since that would be part of his next training topic.

She had checked online for leash tips, and several trainers recommended letting the puppy run around with the leash on his own to get accustomed to it. "Let's see how you do with it," she said, ushering the pair out the door.

She made sure to reward Bodie's good behaviors and praised him when he quit paying attention to the leash and focused on moving forward. Fritz was a good teacher, and Bodie was intent on following his lead.

After about thirty minutes, she picked up the leash and worked on leading Bodie and having him follow without pulling. The harness helped. They stayed outside working until the new lights lit up the yard. "Okay, I'm beat, you two."

"Kevin should be calling us soon. You can say hi to your human brother." She picked up Bodie and hugged him to her chest. He licked the bottom of her chin and made her laugh.

With the training done for the day, she locked up downstairs and shooed the furry friends up the stairs. They each got a reward of one more treat, and she pointed to Fritz's bed. Fritz went right to his bed, and Bodie followed.

She lounged on the couch, where she could see them and turned on the television. Within minutes she was asleep. The chime of her phone woke her, and she fumbled to find it. It was Kevin on video.

"Hey, Kev. How are you?"

"Great. Been super busy, but I really like it. I'm so glad I took the job." He went on to tell her all about his first week. While she listened to the excitement in his voice, she moved to the floor next to the dogs.

She held Bodie up to the screen on her phone. "Oh, what a cute little guy," said Kevin. "I guess you decided to foster him?"

"Yes, Fritz and I made the decision, and it's going well." She positioned the phone so he could watch the dogs together and told him about their training activities.

After hearing more about Kevin's work and telling him about the reservation activity for the cottages, she said, "I better get going. Talk to you soon, and I'm glad you're enjoying the work. Love you lots."

Bodie bumped into her as she was disconnecting the call. She almost dropped the phone and, in the process, activated her voicemail messages. "Hey, hon, I'm going to stay late for a few hours and cover a shift. I'll see you soon and call you when I'm on my way. Love ya, Lil."

Tears rolled down her cheeks as she heard Gary's voice. She had saved his last voicemail from the day he had been killed. She had played it over and over in those first few months.

Fritz's ears were perked, and he was looking for his buddy. He ran to the door and then hurried back to Lily, still sitting on his bed. He got as close as possible and placed his head on her lap, snuggling next to Bodie.

She whispered, "I thought I was doing better. Now I'm not so sure." Her body shook with sobs. She curled up on the bed with the dogs and wept.

Chapter 11

Lily stirred late in the evening and remembered she hadn't taken Bodie outside. She wriggled free from the two dogs and got up from the floor. Her back ached from the horrible position she had settled in for the last few hours.

She slipped a leash onto Bodie and motioned for Fritz to follow them outside. She jogged to the corner of the yard and urged Bodie to hurry. The puppy was rewarded with a treat when he finished. Fritz also got one for being a good sport.

After getting the dogs settled for the night, Lily fell into bed, exhausted from the emotional end to the day. Although Fritz's dog bed was thick and cushiony, it didn't compare to her bed. She concentrated on listening to the snores of the dogs and the soft waves from the bay and was asleep before the timer extinguished the new lights.

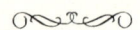

─✧─

Waking with a headache and a puffy face were Lily's rewards for her crying frenzy. She longed for a hot shower but took Bodie outside first. Fritz followed, and she chose to leave the two in the outdoor enclosure and see how they fared.

After a long shower and a cup of coffee, her headache diminished. She wandered downstairs to spy on the dogs. Fritz was lounging on the grass, and Bodie was jumping on him and nipping at him. Fritz was patient and put up with it but could only tolerate so much. She watched as Fritz placed his paw on Bodie's chest and, with the slightest bit of pressure, pushed him to the ground.

The puppy was helpless, on his back with a giant furry paw in the middle of his body. Fritz let him up, and he scampered away, sniffing the grass near the edge of the fencing. She tiptoed upstairs to get dressed and straighten her room.

As she took the container of fresh food from the fridge and went about portioning out breakfast for the two dogs, she made a note to use the vouchers to order more of it. Mac wasn't kidding when he said Fritz would love it, but it was expensive. She put their bowls on the deck and went downstairs to summon them. They used the outside stairs so Bodie could practice while she was there to catch him. All three made it to the deck unscathed.

After breakfast, she ordered the food and put it on automatic reorder status. Once done, she texted Andy and invited him to the house. She knew her cameras would arrive today and asked if he would have time to help her install them. She offered to supply dinner and didn't mention Bodie.

Her cell phone rang, and she was surprised to see a local number. "I'm trying to reach Lily Reed," said the voice on the phone. "This is Stacy from Paradise Spa and Salon."

Lily confirmed her identity and listened as Stacy explained her call. "Cyndy gave me your number. I heard you were reopening Glass Beach Cottage, and I was hoping to put my cards there for your guests. In exchange, I'm happy to have you come in and spend a day with us, having whatever treatments you'd like. It seems tourists and visitors sometimes like a relaxing escape, and I'd like to be the spa you recommend."

Lily remembered her hair needed a trim and the knots in her

neck could use some work. "That sounds wonderful. It will need to be this week if that works?"

They talked about timing and decided on Friday. "We'll do your spa treatments first and then finish up with your hair. See you at eleven."

She heard her phone chime as soon as she set it down. Andy texted back and said he could be there tomorrow to help and have dinner. He asked how Fritz was and said he missed him.

After a few more texts, she took her two roommates outside and praised Bodie for being a good boy. She provided treats each time he succeeded. She worked with him on the leash while Fritz urged him to follow his lead.

The box with the cameras was delivered right after lunch. Her work with the Capitol Police had convinced her of the importance of using them to protect an area. There were hundreds of them placed throughout the buildings and grounds, and they had been invaluable in deterring and solving crimes. She hooked up the equipment to her router and then went about charging the cameras.

She surveyed the area and found positions for all the cameras that offered her views of the entry points into the house and yard. She would need a ladder to install a few of them but would leave that to Andy.

By evening the cameras were charged, and she made sure the app on her phone worked and allowed her to view them. Satisfied they were all functioning; she elected to leave the installation until tomorrow when she'd have a helper.

Her cell phone rang after dinner, and she smiled when she saw Mac's name. "Hey, Lily, thought I'd call and check on Bodie. How are you getting on?"

"So far, so good. No accidents, and he's mastering the stairs and working on the leash."

"Excellent. Is Fritz adjusting?"

"He loves him. For the most part." She described the paw restraint and laughed.

"I thought it would be easier for you if I came by the house to give him his next set of shots. He's due next week."

"Oh, that would be terrific. I'll supply dinner this time." They chatted for a few minutes and made a plan so Bodie could get his shots before guests arrived, in case he needed extra attention.

Her phone beeped indicating another call as she was saying goodbye to Mac. She smiled and tapped the button to connect Cyndy.

Her cheerful voice made Lily smile. "I'm having a few people over this weekend and want to include you. Jack is coming and a couple of friends. Bring your dogs. Jack tells me he roped you into that sweet puppy."

She chattered on about her shop and Lily's cottages. "Did Stacy get in touch with you? She's terrific."

"Yes, I'm going on Friday. I'll tell you all about it." Lily noticed Bodie nosing around and said, "I need to run, but I'll think about the weekend. It depends on Bodie and how he reacts to his shots. I'll be there if I can but don't count on me."

She scooped Bodie up and hurried to the deck and down the stairs. He waited until he reached the spot, and she rewarded him with a treat and "Good boy, Bodie. You're such a smart dog."

⁎⁎⁎

Late in the afternoon the next day, Andy arrived. He greeted Fritz with a smile and got down on the grass to rub his belly. While he was busy with the dog, Lily hurried to the house and retrieved Bodie from his crate.

Her attempt to surprise Andy worked. She released Bodie

outside, and he made a beeline for Fritz. Andy laughed and pointed at the puppy. "Who is this?"

"Meet Bodie. We just agreed to foster him." She signed as she spoke, hoping she got it right.

Andy nodded. "Foster? He was abandoned?"

She shook her head and explained he was in a training program for hearing dogs. Too excited to share the news, she gave up signing and looked at him so he could read her lips.

"I wondered if you might be interested in having a service dog to help you. Bodie won't graduate until he's almost two, but I thought of you the moment I heard about the program. Have you ever considered a service dog?"

Bodie sprawled across Andy's lap, as the young man stroked his soft fur. He shook his head and put the puppy against his shoulder. Bodie buried his head in Andy's neck.

Andy smiled and said, "How does it work?"

She explained what she had learned from the program's materials and website. "Let's get the cameras installed, and then I'll show you what I found while we eat."

With the two of them working together and the dogs safe in their enclosure, they had the installation complete within a couple of hours. She grilled burgers to go with the potato salad she had picked up from the artisan food market. She had unearthed some cookies from the freezer to pair with the ice cream she had acquired on her trip to town.

While they ate on the deck and the dogs lounged on their ottoman, she showed him the information on Bodie's training and what hearing dogs could do for their owners.

"So, he'll be able to help alert you to the telephone, alarms, doorbells, your name being called, and lots of things. He can learn any repetitive sound that can be practiced with him. He would give you more freedom in public. You could watch him and see what he is reacting to and take your cues from him. Not to mention, he'd be a great friend and companion for you. You could take him to work with you and have all sorts of fun." She said all this as she signed, knowing she wasn't getting it one hundred percent correct.

Andy read more of the paperwork and pointed at the cost. "So, it's free?"

"Right. They require a deposit, and then once the dog is placed with you, they refund it. They just want to make sure only people who have a serious interest request a dog. They pay for all the training and care until the dog is placed with you."

He looked over at Bodie and Fritz and smiled. "I love Fritz. I love Bodie too."

"Why don't you talk to your parents and think about it?"

He smiled and nodded his head. "I'll talk to them and let you know." He continued to pet the dogs, talking to them in a soft voice.

"If you need help with the deposit, let me know."

He stood and hugged Lily in a long and unyielding embrace. "Thanks, Miss Lily. I love you too." He petted the dogs once more before waving goodbye.

She and Fritz had missed many of their morning walks on the beach but were able to get in a couple by leaving Bodie in his crate. As long as they weren't in view, he settled down and slept while they enjoyed watching the sunrise from their perch on the driftwood log.

Lily and Fritz worked with Bodie, and by Friday, he was walking on the leash without tugging and moving forward instead of sniffing every second. He had mastered the stairs and could go up and down without hesitating or falling.

During one of their training sessions, Wade stopped by the

house. He met Bodie and asked a few more questions about the program. Lily explained what she knew and gave him the website so he could do some research. "You could go by and talk to Dr. MacMillan. He's the one who told me about the program and said if Andy were interested, he would do all he could to make sure Bodie could go to him."

"Andy is excited about the idea. I just don't want to get his hopes up, if there's a chance it won't work. I'll go see Dr. Mac. If he's involved, I'm sure it's a reputable outfit. We think it would be great for Andy to have a companion like Bodie. He sure took to Fritz."

Wade petted Fritz and watched as Lily showed off what Bodie had learned. She walked along the perimeter of the yard, and he didn't falter or tug on his leash. Then she led him up and down the stairs a few times. "He's a smart one," said Wade.

After some lemonade and a few cookies, he stood and said, "I've got to get going. It means the world to us that you would think of Andy and take on Bodie to help him. You're as special as your uncle said you were."

He gave Fritz one last belly rub and petted Bodie before waving goodbye. "I'll be in touch when we make a decision."

They watched his truck rumble away, and Lily looked at Bodie and said, "That might be your grandpa soon. He's a good guy." She snuggled him close and whispered, "It's going to be hard to let you go."

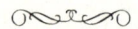

***

She put the furry friends in the outdoor enclosure when she left for the spa Friday. "You guys be good boys, and I'll see you soon." As she drove to town, she sensed a tinge of guilt. She convinced herself they would be fine and would play and sleep while she was gone for a few hours.

Stacy met her at the counter. "So happy you could come today, Lily. Follow me, and we'll get started." She led her to a sitting room and offered her a beverage. "I've got you set up for a massage and facial, then a mani-pedi, and then we'll do your hair, and we could play with some makeup if you're game."

"Sounds great. I don't wear much makeup, but I'll think about it."

Stacy provided her a fluffy robe and slippers and pointed to a door off the sitting room. "There's a closet for you to lock up any valuables. Then just come through the door when you're ready, and your therapist will meet you."

Lily followed her instructions and once enveloped in the soft robe, padded across the room and through the treatment door. A smiling woman introduced herself as Dee and led the way to another chamber. She explained the process and left Lily to get situated on the table. The aroma of citrus and peppermint lingered in the air of the room, lit only with soft mini lights draped around the walls. Lily slipped under the luxurious sheet on the table, face down, and let out a long breath. Minutes later, Dee returned and turned on some music.

"I like to use ocean sounds, but if you want something else, just let me know." She moved to her tray of oils. "I'm adding in some lemongrass oil. If you'd rather have a different fragrance, just speak up."

"Sounds perfect. I love the fragrance in the room and the sound of the ocean is so relaxing. It's what I love about living here. I can hear the waves from my bedroom at night."

Lily relaxed as Dee's skilled hands pressed into the knots in her shoulders and neck. As she worked, the tension in Lily's back eased. She tried to concentrate on the soft splash of the waves, but her thoughts drifted to Gary and Kevin.

All the kneading and the pressing released more than the physical aches in her body. Within a few minutes, she felt tears flowing and heard soft plops as they hit the rug under the table.

A wave of embarrassment raced through her. She opened her eyes and looked through the hole in the head cradle. She was powerless to control the flow. "I'm sorry," she whispered. "I'm not sure why I'm crying, but I need some tissues."

Lily lifted her head and plucked several from the box Dee held out to her. She wiped her eyes and blew her nose. "I'm so sorry."

"Not to worry. It happens quite often. Massage has a way of releasing not only tension in your muscles but also your emotions. There's a belief that repressed emotions get stuck and massage releases them." She patted Lily's arm. "Don't be embarrassed, just let it out. It's healing, trust me." She put the box of tissues on the floor where Lily could see them through the hole in the headrest.

Dee went back to work while Lily continued to cry. There was no sobbing, only an unrelenting cascade of tears. Dee made her way to Lily's feet and massaged each toe, along with every inch of her feet. She rubbed in a salt scrub, and the scent of peppermint reached Lily's nose. She felt the coarse crystals at work on the bottoms of her feet.

After Dee gave them a thorough scrubbing, she used a warm cloth to wipe off the residue. Next came a thick and cool masque. Once Dee applied it, she wrapped her feet in a warm towel.

She worked on Lily's legs and arms and then came back to her feet and wiped away the masque. She gave them another quick massage before holding the sheet and asking Lily to turn over and slide down the table. Dee removed the headrest and handed Lily a few more tissues.

Lily's feet tingled with coolness. Dee finished the massage with a scalp massage and worked a bit more on Lily's neck and shoulders.

She ran her fingers under her cheekbones and across her forehead several times. "All right, my dear. I think you're done. Felicia will be in to give you a facial. You can just relax here." She squeezed her foot as she moved to leave.

"Thank you. I can't believe how much better I feel."

"Hope to see you again, Lily." Dee shut the door with a soft click.

Lily was almost asleep when Felicia came into the room. She used a thick band to keep Lily's hair out of the way and began the process. Lily closed her eyes and listened to the gentle lap of the waves on the beach while Felicia applied gels and creams, using her strong fingers to massage her face.

Lily drifted between reality and a foggy dreamland. She had no idea how much time had elapsed when she heard Felicia say, "All done, Lily. You can get into your robe and just come through the door for your mani-pedi." She grabbed the doorknob and added, "Take your time, no rush."

Lily let out a long breath and swung her legs over the side of the table. She slipped into the robe and slippers. Dora met her in the hallway and ushered her into a room outfitted with pedicure chairs and nail stations. "We've got some salads or sandwiches if you need a snack."

Lily declined but took the water she offered. "Since Dee gave you a scrub, she's done all the hard work." After she helped Lily into the chair, she examined her feet. "They look pretty good. We'll do a quick soak, and you can pick out a polish color." She pointed to a wall with hundreds of bottles organized in acrylic racks.

Several colors winked at her as she soaked her feet in the warm bubbly water. She examined a few and settled on vibrant raspberry. Dora chatted as she worked on her nails and cuticles and slathered lotion on her feet and legs. "What about your nails, what color would you like?"

"Oh, just clear would be best. I'll be busy, and I'm not very careful."

Dora made quick work of both procedures, and before she knew it, Lily had shimmering fuchsia toes and shiny clean nails. "Let's get you back into your clothes. Stacy is going to do your hair, and she should be ready for you."

Lily changed and followed the hallway to the salon. Stacy waved her over and offered her a beverage. The cheerful owner of the spa and salon brewed her a cup of tea and placed it on the edge of the counter.

"So, what are we doing today? Add some color and a cut?" She ran her fingers through Lily's hair and studied it.

Lily nodded. "I've been letting it grow out a bit since I retired. I've noticed a few gray hairs making an appearance, so color would be great. I just need something easy. I don't want to waste a bunch of time on my hair each day."

Stacy mixed the color and used foil pieces to separate each section of hair. "We'll do some summery blondish highlights. That will help disguise any grays that want to sneak in there."

Stacy asked for feedback on Lily's treatments and smiled when she told her how much she enjoyed them. "I'd be happy to keep your cards or pamphlets on hand and put them in the cottages."

"That would be terrific. I have a bundle set aside for you."

"I'll be coming back for another massage. Dee is wonderful. I haven't felt this relaxed in a long time."

Stacy offered her a snack and magazines while she waited for the color to process. Lily declined the food but flipped through a few periodicals. One caught her eye as she read the features on travel in the area. They highlighted attractions, dining, and lodging. She retrieved her phone and took photos of the relevant pages.

Stacy returned and shampooed her hair and went about cutting it. She visited with Lily like she was an old friend. Snipping here and there as she talked. Stacy showed her how to add a bit of product and use a brush to blow it dry.

She called it a layered razor cut and used her fingers to arrange the layers as she wanted. The bangs and front were a bit longer than the other layers. The highlights added depth to her natural caramel blonde hair. Stacy gave her a mirror so she could look at it from all angles.

"It looks great and should be easy to manage." Lily smiled as she turned her head.

"How about a few more minutes, and we'll play with a bit of makeup? Nothing extreme."

Lily looked at the clock. "I need to get home to my dogs."

"Five minutes, I promise." She pulled a wheeled cart closer and pulled open a drawer.

Lily shut her eyes and let her work. Stacy used a silicone blender and applied a foundation. With quick movements, she used another sponge and dabbed at a few areas. She brushed on blush and lined her lips before filling them with a subtle plum color. After a brush of a neutral shadow on her eyelids, she said, "Open your eyes."

She applied a coat of mascara to her lashes and said, "Voila." She checked the clock and added, "With a second or two to spare."

Lily saw the surprise on her face from the huge mirror in front of her. "Wow, you are quick, and it looks great." I can't believe it made such a difference in those few minutes.

Stacy handed her a small gift bag. "I've got some samples in there for you to try and all the brochures for the spa and salon."

"It's been a wonderful and relaxing day. I can't thank you enough for the treat." She took the bag and flinched with surprise when Stacy gripped her in a hug.

"You look gorgeous. Come see us again soon and thanks for

agreeing to recommend us to your guests."

Lily smiled and waved goodbye as she left the salon. She caught a glimpse of her new look in the rearview mirror of her new SUV and smiled. "New house, new car, new job, new hair, new life."

Chapter 12

The dogs took no notice of her mini-makeover as they greeted her with enthusiastic wags and wiggles and a few licks. She let them in the house to relax while she did some work at her desk.

Reservations had been coming in at a steady pace, and she had few open slots in the calendar. Next week would be the beginning of a hectic season. She wouldn't have a real break until November. Her eyes widened as she studied the colorful online calendar. She mumbled, "Maybe I've gotten in over my head."

Butterflies fluttered in her stomach as she contemplated next week. It would be her first attempt at anything other than police work and a high school job at the library. Hints of doubt burrowed their way into her mind. She glanced at the photo she kept on her desk. Gary, smiling, with his arm around her on one of her favorite adventures he had planned. They had visited the George Washington National Forest and hiked several trails, but her favorite was this one—Crabtree Falls. The beautiful cascade of water was in the background of the photo. Happy times.

She noticed the time and hurried to change out of her ratty clothes before she went to pick up dinner. She chose a print blouse done in gorgeous teal and turquoise that reminded her of sea glass and a pair of white pants.

She knew how much Fritz liked to go for a ride. She loaded both the dogs into the back seat of her new car and headed to town. She used Bodie's crate since this would be his first ride, to make sure he didn't roam. Fritz had a seatbelt gizmo that clipped onto his harness to keep him safe.

Mac had said Noni's was a tiny place, and he wasn't kidding. It looked like a small house, and if she hadn't looked it up before she left, she would have driven right past it. A petite gold sign hung on a light post. That was the extent of the advertising.

She told both dogs to stay and made sure the windows were rolled down before hurrying up the steps. The inside was charming and evoked a feeling of bygone times. Victorian style furnishings and décor dominated the restaurant.

Her order was ready, and she was back in the car with a box of delicious smelling food within minutes. Fritz's nose was in the air. His interest in the package prompted her to put the food in the cargo area. She slid into her seat, and the aroma of garlic and tomato made her stomach rumble.

She left the dogs in the car when she got home and took the box into the kitchen. She put the hot items in the oven to stay warm and stowed the other things in the fridge. She unloaded Fritz and fed him on the deck. She withheld Bodie's dinner due to his upcoming shots.

Fritz gobbled his food while she retrieved Bodie. She stayed outside with him and let him run around and play, distracting him from his missing meal. Fritz bounded down the stairs and joined the game. She threw the ball, and he caught it and rushed to her to deposit it in her hand.

She praised him and threw it again. Bodie ran after Fritz, but his short legs couldn't triumph. Fritz nabbed the ball and was back with Lily before Bodie knew what happened. She laughed as the dogs romped through the grass, chasing each other in circles and play-biting.

Her phone chimed and showed the cameras had picked up activity at the front door. She hurried upstairs, and the two furry friends scampered after her.

Mac was at the door, holding his black medical bag and a colorful bunch of flowers wrapped in paper and tied with a ribbon. Lily opened the door to him. "Hello, please come in." The dogs greeted him and huddled around his legs.

He handed her the flowers. "For you." He considered her a moment and added, "You've done something different with your hair. It looks nice."

"I had a treat at the spa and salon today, thanks." She sniffed the flowers, "These are lovely and unexpected. Come on in and get something to drink while I get dinner out of the oven." She laughed and said, "Don't worry, I didn't cook it. I took a page out of your book and went to Noni's."

"We should probably do the immunizations first. Then we can keep an eye on him."

"Right, let's sit outside on the deck. They both like it out there, and Fritz can sit by me while I hold Bodie. He can distract him."

He followed her and went about retrieving items from his bag. He gave Bodie a good once over, listening to his heart and checking his mouth and ears. He took his temperature and pronounced him fit for the injection. Lily talked to Bodie and stroked him while Mac did the dirty work.

The sweet puppy twitched a bit, but that was the extent of his reaction. Mac bundled up his instruments and closed his bag. "I'll take them around the yard while you get dinner ready, and I'll meet you back here."

The dogs explored the yard and made their way to the area Lily had designated and been training Bodie to use for his business. Mac praised the pups and led them back to the house.

The aroma of Italian spices, tomatoes, and cheese mingled together. He saw the dog treat container on the counter and put a few in his hand. At that point, he was like the pied piper, with dogs trailing behind him to the deck. He pointed to the ottoman, and they assumed their positions. Tiny soft bits of yumminess were their rewards.

Lily added the tray of food to the table she had set and studied it. "I think we're all set."

They dug into the meal, passing dishes to each other. Lily took her first bite and moaned. "This is so yummy."

"Noni's never disappoints." He took another bite and said, "I'm glad you liked it enough to eat it again. It's a favorite, but I try to limit my intake. It's all fattening."

She glanced at the two dogs on their ottoman. Bodie, with his eyes closed, was snuggled next to Fritz. "I hope he tolerates the shots. I'd hate for anything to happen to him."

"He'll be tired and a bit lethargic for the next day or two. If you have any concerns, just call. Anytime, day or night. I'm used to it, trust me."

"Have you heard from Andy or Wade?"

His eyes flickered with excitement. "I meant to tell you first thing. Wade and Andy came by and talked to me this morning. Andy is eager to get a hearing dog. Wade wanted to make sure it was a sure thing."

"It does sound too good to be true."

"I know. It's a terrific program. I made some calls and have as much as a guarantee as I can get that if Andy is approved, Bodie will be placed with him. It's not something they like to do, but Bodie's circumstances are a bit special, and it makes sense to keep the dog in the area he's used to living."

"That's terrific news. It's easy to see Andy's affection for dogs, and Fritz was drawn to him, as if understanding Andy needed extra help and love. I got the feeling Wade wanted to check and make sure it was on the up and up, to insulate Andy from any disappointment."

"Exactly, he's a good dad and wants to protect him. Unless something crazy happens, I'm confident he'll get Bodie."

She felt the sting of tears in her eyes. Happy tears, for a change. She swallowed the lump in her throat and said, "That makes my heart happy."

They chatted about his work and her upcoming guests as they finished dinner. The sun drifted toward the horizon as the evening stretched later. Both dogs were sleeping. A gentle breeze complimented the perfect twilight weather. Lily's new lights provided the ideal ambiance for sunset conversations.

Mac's gaze drifted across the yard. "You've done an excellent job here, Lily. The place looks so inviting. Like a relaxing private retreat." He took a deep breath. "I can even hear the sound of the waves. Perfection."

The dim lighting hid the flush of color that rose from her neck. A proud smile filled the space between her rosy cheeks. "Thank you for the compliment. Next week will be the real test. I'm a bit nervous."

She took a sip from her glass. "My whole career, I've been a police officer, so this innkeeper role is a real switch."

She went on to explain her work at the Virginia State Capitol, highlighting some of her duties, including guarding the governor and keeping the legislators and the public safe.

"Well, you've had extensive training in pleasing tough customers if you've been surrounded by politicians for twenty years," said Mac, with a cynical chuckle.

She nodded with a smirk. "Fair point. Some of them are impossible. Others are the nicest folks you'll ever meet. You're right though, about the customer service aspect. You have to honor some bizarre requests and go above and beyond the normal call of duty." She pondered and added, "I hadn't thought of that part of my job. Keeping people happy was a large part of it, so that will translate to hosting guests."

"Should be much easier, hopefully," she thought aloud.

"My wife, her name was Jill. I know, Jack and Jill, but remember I'm Mac. Anyway, she was a natural at that hostess stuff. Great at decorating, finding junk and making it look pretty. She was an excellent cook and loved to host dinners and parties." He took a long swallow of his iced tea. "Quite the opposite of me. I lost the best part of me the day she died."

He talked more about Jill and the car accident that took her life when she was forty. "Somehow we survived. My daughter, Missy, she had a hard time without her mom. She moved away as soon as she could. I think there are too many memories here for her."

Lily nodded her understanding. "I can relate. That's what brought me out here. I was escaping memories." She shared about Gary's love of cooking and adventure, recounting some of their trips he'd organized. "He was full of life and always ready for whatever came." The sky glowed orange and pink as the day came to an end. Lily had emptied her glass as they talked.

The combination of wine and the cover of darkness granted Lily the courage to reveal more. "Gary was killed in the line of duty on May fifth last year. It was an ambush. A call set up by this punk and his girlfriend so he could kill cops." Her voice cracked, and she felt a tear slip down her cheek.

He reached for her and put his hand on top of hers and squeezed. As if he knew words were meaningless, he kept his hand over hers as they gazed at the sky. The fiery colors faded into the sea. They sat in silence, until the heavens turned to ink and filled with twinkling stars.

The dogs stirred, and Lily moved to them. "I better take these guys to the yard and get them to bed."

Mac gathered the remains of their dinner, boxed the leftovers, and had all the dishes put in the dishwasher when Lily returned with her charges. "Wow, you didn't have to do all that."

"No trouble. It's the least I can do for a wonderful evening." He moved to take Bodie from her arms. "Let me take a look at our friend."

She locked the door and motioned Fritz to his bed. "How's he doing?"

"He's doing well. Slight elevation in temperature, but nothing to be alarmed about." He placed him next to Fritz.

"They look so sweet together." She smiled and added, "I appreciate you taking the time to come and do that for him tonight."

"It was a welcome escape from my usual routine." He picked up his bag and said, "Best of luck to you this week on your new innkeeper role. I know you'll be fabulous."

She walked him to the door and said goodbye, promising to call him if she had any concerns about Bodie. After tidying the kitchen, she coaxed Fritz from his comfortable sleeping position. She carried the puppy, with Fritz following, to her bedroom where they snuggled together on Fritz's oversized bed.

She kissed Bodie on the head. "Feel better, little one." She turned and gave Fritz a neck rub and added a kiss on top of his head. "You're a good big brother."

She noticed the light blinking on her cell phone and found a text from Andy. A smile filled her face as she read it. *Miss Lily, I am so excited to get a hearing dog. We did all the paperwork, and Dr. Mac helped us. He says I should get Bodie. I understand, not 100%, but I already love him. Thank you. Love, Andy.*

Saturday, they skipped their walk to the beach and stayed behind to keep an eye on Bodie. He was more lethargic and seemed content to sleep on his bed in the living area. Kevin rang in on a video call, and Lily brought him up to date on the latest news.

"Your hair looks different, Mom. Good, different."

She thanked him and smiled as she listened to him recount his week. He had been working late each night but enjoying the challenges. Several new friends were in his circle, and he was joining them for dinner at a local brewpub.

She moved her phone so Fritz could get in the screen, which caused Bodie to stir from his slumber. Fritz pawed at the phone, and his tail thumped against the floor as he listened to Kevin talk to him. The pup became more animated at the sound of Kevin's voice and cocked his head when he looked at the screen.

"We're not doing much today. I've got a bit of shopping to do this weekend. Need to make sure I'm ready for the six guests arriving tomorrow night."

"I've been watching the reservations stack up. That's great, don't you think?"

"It is. I'm beginning to worry. I feel like one of those cartoons where there's a tiny snowball that rolls down the mountain and turns into a colossal wrecking ball. I don't want to be so busy that I end up hating it."

"I don't think it'll be that hectic. Just with checking people in and out, but they shouldn't bother you for anything. You've got it set up so they have access to everything they need. No cooking, you've got the cleaning covered. Should be easy."

She chuckled. "Sounds good when you say it. I found some ideas for a cheese board with a bit of fruit and olives. I'm going to try it out Friday night and see how it goes over."

They chatted for a few more minutes before Kevin disconnected with a promise to call next weekend and see how things were going with the cottages. Fritz got one more glimpse of Kevin when he said goodbye to him.

Outside of a quick trip to the market, she puttered around the house and the yard. She called Cyndy and begged off coming to her party, citing Bodie as an excuse. She didn't want to leave him alone so soon after his shots.

As she was sitting down to an early dinner of leftovers, her cell phone rang. Mac's name filled her screen.

"I wanted to check in on Bodie and see how he was doing."

"Not bad. He's been a bit sluggish. Not as much energy."

"He's drinking and eating?"

"Yes, all is normal in that regard." She glanced at him snuggled next to Fritz. "He's been hanging close to Fritzie, taking lots of naps."

"That's good. How are you?"

"Doing well. Had sort of a lazy day. Getting set for tomorrow."

"Did you know there's a Fourth of July Festival out at Fort Warden?"

"I saw something about it in the paper," she said. "Fritz isn't a huge fan of fireworks, so I'll have to keep an eye on him that night."

"Oh, yeah. It's the worst day of the year for dogs. I hate that aspect of it. So many dogs get scared and run away. The festival starts in the morning. It's sort of old-fashioned with games and miniature golf. Free root beer floats and lots of food vendors. Cyndy and I always go, and I thought you might be interested in venturing out for a few hours?"

"Hmm. You had me at root beer floats." She laughed and added, "As long as we're back well before time for fireworks. Seems like some idiots are always setting them off on their own, and I don't want to chance a problem."

"How about we pick you up around eleven, and we'll have you back no later than three?"

"You could bring Sherlock, and he could hang out with them in the yard. Bodie probably misses him."

"Sounds like a plan. He'll like that. We'll see you then."

She disconnected and smiled at the two dogs. "Dr. Mac is going to visit and bring Sherlock." Bodie lifted his head when he heard his friend's name.

Fritz's tail thumped against the ottoman and Bodie's wiggled. "You guys are right. It will be fun." She sat outside, enjoying the streaks of color in the evening sky.

As she soaked in the ambiance of the manicured yard and the soft lights leading to the three cottages, she smiled. Fritz, Bodie, Andy, Cyndy, and Mac. They all added to her life in Driftwood Bay. Today was the first day she'd had time to think and hadn't dwelled on her loss of Gary. Instead, she'd filled it with thoughts of the future and focused on her tiny circle of new friends and furry friends that brought her happiness.

As she gathered the dogs and made her way inside, something in the sky caught her eye. A bright streak of light with a concentrated glow at one end flashed in the dark sky. A shooting star. Gary always made her make a wish.

Lily closed her eyes and murmured her request. "Maybe dreams will come true," she whispered.

Chapter 13

Sunday morning Lily spent time in the yard with the dogs. Bodie's energy wasn't at full throttle yet, but he was making progress. The dogs played and followed her as she cut fresh flowers for the cottages. Her aunt's garden was gorgeous and healthy, with a variety of blooms.

She put together the ingredients for soup and started the slow cooker. She checked the downstairs common area and placed a vase of flowers on the table to give it a more welcoming look.

Along with filling the beverage station with lemon water, she made fresh iced tea. She added a plate of cookies to the welcome table downstairs and gave it all one last look.

A few minutes before three, her phone chimed with a camera notification, and she saw a large SUV in the driveway, following the signs for parking. She put Bodie in his crate, made sure the door to the downstairs was closed, promised Fritz she'd be right back, and hurried to greet her guests.

Women were climbing out of the oversized vehicle, when she waved and hollered, "Hello there."

The driver, dressed for an upscale lunch, waved at Lily and walked to meet her. "Hi, I'm Amy. I made the reservation for us."

Lily extended her hand. "Nice to meet you, Amy. If you'd like to follow me, we'll get you checked in and settled. Your friends are welcome to come with you or rest in the yard.

Amy relayed the message as the women wrestled their luggage from the cargo area. She followed Lily along the path to the downstairs door. "Oh, I love your yard. Beautiful flowers."

"Thank you. The credit goes to my late aunt. She had quite the eye for gardening." She guided Amy inside and offered her a cookie.

"Oh, no," she shook her head with a look of fear. "If I look at a cookie, I'll gain ten pounds."

Lily eyed her perfect figure, manicured nails, and her ombre colored hair. "Are you covering all three cottages?"

"Yes, it's my treat. A bit of girlfriend fun. We had our twenty-fifth high school reunion this weekend, and I organized this extended event to celebrate with my best friends."

"Sounds wonderful," Lily said, as she finished the credit card transaction. She handed Amy a small folio and offered to take the keys down and open the cottages for them.

They found the other five women sitting around the fire pit, their luggage parked on the pathway. "Girls," said Amy, "This is Lily. She's the owner."

The women introduced themselves. Lily committed them to memory using techniques she had practiced at work for twenty years. Sultry Sherry, Chubby Carrie, Barbie Bigmouth, Plain Pam, and Anxious Abby. She sized up people based on her initial impression and gave them a nickname designed to trigger her memory by association. Amy was the easiest. Awesome Amy.

"Welcome to Glass Beach Cottage. I hope you'll enjoy it here as much as we do. When I say we, I mean my golden retriever, Fritz, and my new puppy Bodie. You'll see them roaming around, and they're both super friendly. Anyone have any problems with dogs?"

She gazed at the group and noticed tears on Abby's cheeks. "I think we all love dogs, so no worries here," said Amy.

Lily pointed back to the house and said, "There's a television, small kitchen, with a fridge if you need to keep anything cold, ice machine, games, and puzzles. The Wi-Fi password is in your folio. The door is locked at ten o'clock, but there's an intercom outside if you need something after hours. The entry code for the gate near where you parked is also in the folio."

Lily led the way to the cottages and offered to help those who couldn't manage their luggage. They paraded down the path. Lily opened the door to the first cottage, and Amy said, "This is Barbie and Abby."

The two women walked through the entry followed by Amy. "This is lovely." The women uttered their approval as they peeked inside.

"All the cottages are set up the same. They just differ a bit in accent colors and pieces. The patios all have a view over the bluff to the water." She showed them the basics and said, "I recommend leaving your bedroom window open. You can hear the sound of the waves at night."

"Oooh, that sounds wonderful," said Amy.

She pointed out the brochures and highlighted the spa and Cyndy's store. She pointed at Amy's folio and added, "All your breakfast vouchers are in there. Each of you gets a voucher for the five days you are here. I've given you three days at one restaurant and two days at the other. They are both fabulous."

"On Fridays and Saturdays, we'll have beer and wine along with a snack by the firepit. I've got iced tea and water, plus a few cookies in the common area through the back door." Lily asked if anyone had questions, and they all shook their heads.

She took the next two, Carrie and Pam, to the second cottage. Amy and Sherrie were in the third one. "I'll leave you to get settled. If you need anything, just give me a call on the intercom."

Before going upstairs, Lily made sure the credit card gadget and paperwork were locked in the drawer. While she was doing that, Carrie and Pam came through the back door. They helped themselves to drinks, and Carrie put several cookies in a napkin. They gave Lily a small wave with their thanks and left.

Lily climbed the stairs and found Fritz waiting at the door. She sprung Bodie from the crate and attached their leashes before venturing outside. The women were in their cottages, but Fritz's nose was working overtime.

He tracked the new smells through the yard and down the pathway, along the front of each cottage. "Come on, boys, let's go."

As they made their way, Abby came out of the first cottage. "Oh, what sweet dogs," she gushed. On cue, the dogs made a beeline for her. She sat on the grass, and they commenced a licking assault.

"I'm so sorry. They believe everyone loves them," said Lily, as she tried to distract them from the woman.

Abby smiled and petted each of them, letting them cover her lap. "I don't mind. In fact, I love it." She scratched their ears and gave them belly rubs.

"The big one is Fritz, and the puppy is Bodie. I just got him a few weeks ago. I'm fostering him for a service dog program that trains hearing dogs."

"That's terrific. They're such wonderful dogs. I bet they have lots of fun here."

She chatted with Abby for a few minutes, until they were interrupted with Barbie's voice calling for her. "I better go." She stood and said goodbye to the twosome, who wagged their tails.

Lily hurried the dogs, so they could finish their excursion before any more distractions appeared. She led them up the stairs and to the deck. They slurped at their water bowls for several minutes and then went to their ottoman where they could watch over the yard.

As Lily snacked on her dinner, she watched the ladies leaving the cottages. They had changed clothes and looked like they were ready for an evening in town. Fritz lifted his head off the cushion. He quivered with curiosity. Lily said, "No, Fritz. Stay."

He watched the parade of women cross the yard. "They'll be back. You'll have to get used to strangers on our property," she said, kneeling in front of him and scratching under his chin. Bodie stretched out and put his head against Fritz and yawned.

"I'm tired too, little guy."

○~~~○

The first night with guests was uneventful. The camera notification chimed when they returned close to midnight. She heard them talking as they made their way down the path and to the cottages, but she went back to sleep.

After taking the dogs for their constitutional around the yard, she captured Bodie and put him in his crate in the house. She grabbed a leash, locked the door, and headed out past the bluff to go to the beach.

"Come on, Fritz. I think the ladies will be sleeping in this morning."

They reached their spot as the sun made its first appearance of the day. Fritz bounded along the shore, and Lily kept hold of the leash. "No time for a bath today, buddy."

They meandered today, rather than sit, and walked about a mile before turning back to the house. Fritz was prancing along with her, a smile on his face. They followed the trail to her property and made their way past the cottages. No activity. No aroma of coffee. All was still.

She whispered to Fritz, "Let's go find Bodie and let him out of his cage." She took off his leash and let him sprint up the stairs. They found Bodie with his body pressed against the door, waiting to be freed.

She made their breakfast and settled for some toast and coffee for herself. She got ready for the day, had another cup of coffee, and then let the dogs out to assume their position on the deck.

Close to nine, she glimpsed some activity at the cottages. She went about watering the potted flowers on the deck, and a few minutes later, the group emerged. They saw her, and she waved.

"We're heading out. See you this evening," shouted Amy.

After she finished her watering, she went downstairs with her cottage keys. She collected the dirty towels and replaced them with fresh ones. She only had to make two beds, as the other cottage had done their own. She replenished the used toiletries and hauled the dirty laundry to the house.

The maid service would come on Wednesday to change their linens and then again when they checked out on Saturday. She looked at the time and nodded. "That didn't take long to freshen the rooms."

She started a load in the washer before returning to the deck. Her cell phone rang and showed Cyndy on the screen. "Hey, Cyndy. How are you?"

"Wonderful. Just called to see how your first night went with guests?" They chatted for a few minutes, and Cyndy suggested they meet for lunch on Thursday when she'd have a helper who could cover for her.

"Sounds great. What time?"

"I'll meet you at the Busy Bee just before noon. Jack tells me you agreed to join us for the festivities on Friday. I'm so glad."

"I'm looking forward to it. It's been a long time since I had a friend call and invite me to lunch. It means more than you know," said Lily, as her eyes filled.

"Aww, that makes me happy. I've got to run, but I'll see you Thursday."

Lily's mood lightened after her conversation. The first day of business had proved to be rather dull and had left her disillusioned. Work had always been her escape, and she wasn't convinced there would be enough action at the Glass Beach Cottage to keep her mind occupied.

While the ladies were away, she used the time to continue training Bodie. Fritz kept nosing over to the cottages. "Fritzie, what are you doing?"

The door on the first cottage opened, and Abby waved at her. Fritz, full of wiggles, ran to his new friend. Lily and Bodie followed. "Sorry," she said, "I thought you were all gone for the day."

"I started out with them, but I told them I wasn't feeling well, and they dropped me at the corner after breakfast."

Lily noticed the spark in her eyes when she played with Fritz. "Are you feeling any better?"

Abby grimaced. "I'm fine. Physically. I just didn't want to spend another day with them. I should have never come."

"Let's go sit down and have some tea," suggested Lily.

Once in the common area downstairs, she let the dogs loose. She transferred the towels to the dryer and then retrieved two glasses. She filled them with ice and added tea. She took a chair, and Abby chose the couch. "So, you aren't having much fun on this trip, huh?"

Abby shrugged. "It's not the trip or the area. It's lovely here. It's the high school girls who haven't grown up yet." Fritz was sitting at her knees while she caressed his head. "I lost my dog a few weeks ago. Cancer. I miss her so much. I told them I didn't want to come, but like always, I got pressured into it."

"Oh, I'm so sorry about your dog. Tell me about her."

Abby smiled through her tears as she talked about Sophie, her golden retriever. Abby had her since she was a puppy, and Sophie had been her best friend. "I'm divorced and live alone, so she was my roommate. It's so quiet without her."

Fritz rested his chin on Abby's thigh, and she laughed. "My girlfriends don't understand. They keep telling me she was just a dog. They don't get it." She bent and touched her head to Fritz's. "This is better than any sightseeing they have planned."

"Fritz is my bestie. I understand how much they bring to your life. I'm on my own here, and I'm not sure what I'd do without this guy."

"Your place is gorgeous. You must have worked hard to get this done by yourself."

Lily chuckled. "It's a long story, but I inherited this place from my late aunt and uncle. I just moved here in May. I've had a lot of help and have hired some people to help me."

She refilled their teas and said, "It's a healing place. You might be glad you came. I find my mornings at the beach and evenings here on the deck bring a serenity I haven't felt for a long time."

"I can see that they would. I don't have the energy to carry on meaningless conversations with the rest of them. I'm a divorced teacher. My dog was my best friend. I'm depressed, I know it. It's too hard to pretend to be happy. I'd rather stay here and pet Fritz and play with Bodie."

She hefted the puppy onto her lap. "You don't mind, do you? I don't want to be a pain."

"Of course not. You're welcome to hang out here or in the yard, whatever you feel like doing. The walk to the beach is short, and you can even get to town that way. You need some time to heal."

Abby leaned against the back of the couch and let out a long sigh. "Thank you. I've been dreading trying to hide here each day. Carrie and Pam try to be understanding, but the other three are oblivious. They're a bit self-absorbed. I don't want to ruin their fun, but I'm not going to go and be miserable."

"It's your time. I say spend it how you enjoy it most." Lily stood and called Fritz. Bodie hopped from Abby's lap and made a clumsy landing. "Feel free to use the television, wireless, fridge, whatever you like."

"I appreciate you being so understanding."

"Come on boys, upstairs. See you later, Abby." Lily herded the two into the kitchen and rummaged in the fridge for some lunch.

She spent the afternoon doing some housework and her own laundry. When she checked her email, she saw more reservations had arrived. Once she had her computer work handled, she went downstairs to fold the towels.

She and her two furry sidekicks found Abby asleep on the couch, with her aunt's quilt over her. The sound from the television masked their entrance. Lily tiptoed to the door and led the dogs through it, closing it with a soft click.

They followed her away from the house and played in the yard, out of earshot of Abby. Fritz was fetching a ball. She hoped his skills would rub off onto Bodie, but at the moment, he was chasing and playing. They worked on a few commands, and he was getting the hang of sitting. He needed to work on staying.

She was leading them back toward the house when Abby emerged. "Hey there. Hope we didn't wake you from your nap."

"Oh, no. I'm embarrassed I fell asleep." The dogs ran to greet her, and a smile filled her face.

"I'm going to run in and fold some towels. Do you mind staying out here with these two hooligans for a few minutes?"

"Not at all." She sat, cross-legged, on the grass and let the dogs cover her.

Lily chuckled as she folded the laundry and watched out the window. "Dogs are the best therapy for a broken heart."

Chapter 14

The next day, Abby refused to yield to the pressure Amy exerted and stayed behind at Glass Beach Cottage. She feigned headaches and told the others she felt better just lounging around the cottage.

Lily overheard their conversation while she was in the yard tending to the plants. After listening to the whining voices of Amy, Sherry, and Barbie, her head hurt. When pleading didn't work, the mouthy women badgered Abby and belittled her. Abby stood her ground.

Fury bubbled inside Lily as she listened to the offensive remarks. Her assessment of the women upon their arrival proved to be spot-on. A few more piercing adjectives rolled through her mind as she watched Amy, Sherry, and Barbie exit the cottage.

She stuck her head further into the plant she was inspecting, not wanting to engage with them. They stomped back to their cottages, muttering about Abby. Once the group hit the road on Tuesday, Lily offered to give her a ride to town so she could eat breakfast and do some shopping at the market.

Lily joined her for breakfast at Muffins and More. Abby was five years younger than Lily, but her mannerisms made her appear much more youthful. As she talked about her work and the kids in her classroom, her face brightened. It was evident she was an ideal teacher.

She teared up when she talked about taking Sophie to her classroom each week and how much the students enjoyed her. "Have you considered looking for another dog?" With a gentle voice, Lily added, "I know you can't replace her, but it's clear you enjoyed having a dog, and so many dogs need loving homes."

Abby swiped at her eyes with a napkin. "I've thought about it, but it seems...disloyal." She shook her head. "I know it doesn't make sense. I know Sophie would want me to be happy."

Lily eyes stung. "I understand that feeling. My husband was killed last year and lots of people suggested I needed to move on when I wasn't ready. I'm not trying to do that to you."

Abby gasped and put her hand to her mouth. "I'm so sorry. I had no idea. Here I am blubbering about Sophie, and you lost your husband."

"Someone described grief as a journey. I've learned that the hard way. Not everyone follows the same path, and our experiences will be different. I moved here to run Glass Beach Cottage. It was unexpected, but I took it as a sign. I wasn't making much progress where I was, so I thought a new beginning was in order."

"Do you think you'll marry again?" asked Abby. As soon as the words left her mouth, her face fell. "What a stupid thing to say. I'm sorry."

Lily chuckled. "I haven't given it much thought. It's not something I'm seeking. After what I've been through, I'm not going to say it will never happen, but it would have to be someone extraordinary." She paused and said, "It's like what you said. Disloyal. Right now, it seems too fresh to me. Gary was my everything. I can't imagine someone else."

Abby sucked in a long breath. "If you can get through losing your husband, I can get through this. I know I will. It's just going to take some time."

"Of course, you will. When the time is right, I hope you'll open your heart to another dog. They are great at rescuing us." She finished her coffee and said, "Shall we go?"

After breakfast, they walked down the street to the market. Once that chore was done, they headed back home. The dogs, who had been left outside, were eager to see them. They inspected each item, as Abby unpacked her groceries and put them in the refrigerator.

By Tuesday evening, the ladies had accepted Abby's decision to spend her days at the cottage. From her perch on the deck, Lily listened to Amy's sanctimonious speech. She told Abby they were tired of begging her to spend time with them. "It's crystal clear you don't want to be part of the group, and we're not going to plead with you to come with us. You're free to do whatever you want. Join us or don't."

"Glad we see eye to eye," said Abby. "I'll plan to join you for dinner, but I enjoy staying here at the cottage during the day. I appreciate your understanding." Not giving them a chance to respond, she turned and went to her cottage.

Lily wanted to give her a high-five. Carrie and Pam were quiet. Probably beaten into submission by the other three, whose mouths never seemed to shut. Less than an hour later, the six of them went to dinner, leaving Lily on her own.

She watched a movie and shared a bit of her popcorn with the dogs. Abby had been a good distraction and kept her occupied. She felt for the poor thing. She couldn't imagine her despair if she lost Fritz.

Despite the guests, she felt a pang of loneliness. She put her hand on the empty pillow next to her. "Good night, sweetie. I sure miss you."

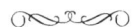

―――※―――

The housekeepers arrived on Wednesday after the five ladies left for the day. They made quick work of cleaning the three cottages. Most of Lily's day was consumed with laundry. Abby was content to play with the dogs, read, and hang out in the common area downstairs.

Amy had scheduled spa treatments for the afternoon, and Lily did her best to convince Abby to join them. "You'll be alone for most of the treatments. I think you could use some relaxation. Trust me, you'll feel better when you're done."

Abby surrendered when Lily described how great the massage was and how her feet felt brand new when she was done. Lily waved goodbye as the caravan set off for town before noon.

Soon after the guests left, Andy surprised her with a visit, and they sat on the deck and sipped iced tea. She knew his love for cookies and plated up a variety. With Bodie on his lap, happiness radiated from Andy. He stroked the puppy's soft fur and talked to him in a gentle voice. Bodie basked in the attention, stretching out and closing his eyes.

He reported that he should hear something about his application for the hearing dog program by September. "I'm excited to get Bodie. I know it will take time and there's a chance it won't be him."

She nodded. "Even if it's not him, and I hope it is, the important thing is for you to get a hearing dog. It will be wonderful." She looked down at Fritz, who had his chin resting on her foot. "Fritz hopes you get Bodie so he can still come over and play."

After a short nap, Bodie's eyes opened, and he bounced with energy. Lily showed Andy how she had been training him to use a designated area in the yard, making it easy for her to clean up after the dogs. They went downstairs, with Bodie mastering each step, and the dogs led the way.

She took every opportunity to train Bodie with the simple commands and manners like the videos had shown her. He would be going to his first live class next week, and she would get more of an idea what they should tackle. He sat, earning him a few treats.

She had been concentrating on not letting him jump on people. That was paramount at the moment. He got so excited he couldn't control himself.

Whenever she raised her voice and said, "No, Bodie," he looked dejected. His sweet face and eyes were enough to melt anybody's heart. She wanted him to understand there would be no jumping. Dogs that did that irritated her.

After training was over, she led the dogs back to the deck for hydration. Andy gave each of them a thorough petting, even getting down in the grass and letting them scramble over him. "Miss Lily, I have to get home. Thank you for the cookies. And for letting me play with Fritz and Bodie."

"Come by anytime, Andy. We love to see you." She followed him to the gate and waved goodbye.

She turned to the dogs and said, "How about we fix your dinner?" Bodie already understood what that meant. The two furry friends scampered upstairs and beat her to the door.

Fritz was trained to rest after he ate, and Bodie mimicked him and followed his big brother to the bed in the living area. Lily wasn't hungry but snatched a cookie from the plate before she put them back in the container.

She made a pot of tea and caught up on emails and wasted some time on social media. While she was catching up on the news in Virginia, Fritz bolted to the deck door, with Bodie loping after him. "The girls must be home."

A few minutes later the intercom sounded. "Lily, are you home? It's Abby. We brought back pizzas and wanted to invite you to join us."

Lily mulled the decision for a few minutes and said, "How nice of you. I'll be down in a few."

She looked at the two dogs and scrunched her nose. "I'm not sure

I can handle listening to these women for long." She attached their leashes and took them outside, doing her best to avoid the fire pit area where they were gathered. Once the dogs were handled, she put them out on the deck. She filled a tumbler with iced tea and joined the group.

Abby had saved her a chair next to hers. She took a piece of pizza and her seat. "Did you enjoy your spa treatments?"

The gaggle of voices overwhelmed Lily. They gushed over their time at the spa and thanked Lily for the recommendation. Even the two quiet women were animated. "I've never felt this relaxed in my life," said Carrie.

"The ladies were all so nice. I haven't had a pedicure in forever and love my toes." Pam wiggled them in her sandals and smiled.

Lily eyed the six sets of toes. "They all look wonderful. I'm glad you had a good time."

"So, what's your story, Lily?" asked Sherry. "You've got this gorgeous place, and you're alone? No husband?"

"She probably had the good sense to get rid of him," said Barbie, with a cynical laugh. The others, except for Abby, joined in the laughter.

Lily took a deep breath. "I'm a widow. My husband was a police officer who was killed in the line of duty last year."

For the first time since the group had arrived, there was complete silence. Wide eyes above gaping mouths, stared at Lily. Abby's eyes narrowed into daggers as she drilled them into Barbie.

Amy was the first to recover from the shock. "Oh, I am so sorry." She looked at Barbie, imploring her to speak.

"Yes, Lily. I apologize. Totally uncalled for. I had no idea and shouldn't have been so flippant. I'm very sorry for your loss."

All of the others murmured their condolences. "It's easy to take things and people for granted until they're gone. I'd give anything to have him back." She glanced at Abby. "Grief is a complicated voyage. Abby and I were discussing that fact earlier."

She took a sip from her glass and continued. "We concluded it's best not to judge others on the topic of loss. Everyone travels through the darkness at their own pace. It's a long journey. An emotional one. I don't think the wounds from loss ever heal. Not completely."

The women nodded in agreement. Fussing and cooing to each other about how hard it is to lose those you love. "Well, you've done a fantastic job with this place," Amy said, as she gestured to the cottages. "I admire your strength."

Lily nodded and said, "I didn't plan to share my story. I wouldn't have, normally." She looked at Barbie and smiled. "It's not a happy topic."

"Of course," said Sherry. "We should have never assumed or even asked. It was in poor taste."

Lily took another bite of her pizza and directed the conversation to safer themes. "Are you all going to the Fourth of July Festival?"

The group breathed a collective sigh of relief. Amy spoke for them and explained they planned to attend the festival and spend time along the waterfront. "I can't wait to see the fireworks. I'm sure they'll be spectacular."

Lily listened to them chat about their Friday plans until there was a lull in the conversation. "Thanks so much for the pizza, ladies. I hope you enjoy the rest of your evening."

She gave them a wave as she walked toward the house. They chimed in with well-mannered replies. Barbie laid it on a tad too thick, complimenting the yard and the new lights and going on about how much she liked the cottages. Lily smiled, remembering they were guests and accepted them with grace, as she continued to the stairs.

Bodie and Fritz were asleep. Lily herded them downstairs to make sure they were set for the evening, before locking the door and calling it a night. They hunkered down in her bedroom, and as she got ready for bed, she thought about her plans with Cyndy tomorrow. She noticed her smile in the mirror. She was looking forward to spending time with someone she liked and could call a friend.

Thursday morning, Bodie joined them for his first beach experience. He followed Fritz as they took the path from the property that led to the shoreline. He trampled through the beach grass and got distracted a few times, but they made it in time for the morning show. The sun dazzled with a brilliant gold that glinted across the water.

As the water moved, the morning light twinkled and shimmered. Bright flashes, like starbursts, flickered above the water. The view was magical.

She kept hold of the leashes so the dogs wouldn't jump into the water. With such a perfect background, she couldn't help but want a photo. She found a smaller log and wrestled it, while holding the dogs, closer to the shore. She positioned the dogs and used her phone to capture several shots.

She scanned through them and saw two that weren't a disaster. She texted one of them to Kevin with wishes for a good day. As she started to put her phone back in her pocket, she flicked through her contacts and texted Mac the same photo showcasing Bodie's first beach day.

They walked along the water, and she smiled at Bodie's smaller paw prints next to Fritz's. As the foamy waves reached him, he growled at them and lifted his legs to escape. Fritz cocked his head, looking at him like he was crazy.

A tear leaked from Lily's eye as she laughed at the antics. Memories of Fritz when Gary brought him home flooded her mind. "Come on boys. Let's get home." She stressed "home" several times on their way, hoping Bodie would learn what it meant.

They hurried past the cottages and inspected the yard before going upstairs. After their exercise and breakfast, the dogs were content to rest at their spot near the door, where they could see outside.

The intercom sounded as Lily was making a pot of tea. The women had left early, and Abby stayed behind. She asked permission to borrow one of the bikes in the rack on the side of the house. "Sure, have fun," said Lily.

Lily made quick work of straightening the cottages and tossing dirty towels into the washer. She hurried upstairs and jumped in the shower. Lily emerged from the bathroom and eyed her closet, looking for something to wear to lunch instead of her usual jeans and t-shirt. The choices were sparse. She settled on white pants and a black tank with embroidery around the neckline. "I really need to buy some new clothes," she muttered.

Her phone chimed, and she saw a reply from Mac. *Great photo. See you all tomorrow!*

By the time she finished getting ready, drank the rest of her tea, and reviewed reservations, it was time to head to the Busy Bee. She took the dogs for a quick break outside before putting them in the enclosure. She refilled their water bowls and made sure the utility room door was shut, so Bodie couldn't sneak in and wreak havoc. They each received a tiny treat to compensate them for their imprisonment. "I'll be back soon, boys."

She found Cyndy sitting at an umbrella table outside. She greeted Lily with a warm hug. "Isn't it perfect weather for eating al fresco?"

"It is. Love the breeze off the bay." They made their choices, and the waitress brought them iced teas.

"So, how's the innkeeper life?"

"I'm trying to get a routine going. So far, so good. These six guests leave Saturday, and I've got new folks coming in on Saturday and Sunday." She ran a finger along the condensation of her glass. "I'm not as busy as I expected but still feel a bit anchored to the place. I feel guilty when I leave."

"I'm sure you'll get over it. You can't be there all the time. As long as you are there to welcome them and tell them goodbye when they leave, that's what's important."

She nodded. "It makes sense. Just seems weird. At least I know I'll have plenty of time to work with Bodie. I was worried about that."

"You'll get a groove soon. It's good that you decided to send them to town for breakfast. That gets them moving and on the road."

Lily rolled her eyes. "More than thankful after engaging with the guests last night. Some of them are like mean girls from high school on steroids. They invited me to join them by the fire pit for pizza last night."

Over their yummy salads and sandwiches, Lily entertained her with stories from the week. After recounting last night's significant foot-in-mouth moment, she added, "Abby's a sweet girl, and I feel for her. The three loudmouths don't let the two quiet ones speak, so who knows about them. I can't say I'll be sorry to see their tail lights."

"It's sort of interesting to meet all these new and different people. They'll all have a story. You'll get a tiny glimpse of them while they're there."

"Tomorrow night I'm doing the first wine and beer evening by the fire pit. Hopefully, most of them won't be home and will be enjoying the fireworks."

Cyndy had been busy at the store with loads of tourists in town, which always made her business brisk. "I've been working late almost every night. Drinking far too much wine when I get home and doing little else."

"I need to find some less casual clothes. Any recommendations?" asked Lily.

"Oh, I love Plum Crazy. She's got some unique clothes. Upstairs Closet is another one I like to browse." Cyndy gave her directions to both of them. "I wish I had time to go with you this afternoon, but I've got to get back to work."

Lily grabbed the check before Cyndy noticed it. "My treat. You can get it next time."

They finished their tea, and Lily headed down the sidewalk in the direction of the clothing boutiques Cyndy recommended. "See you tomorrow," hollered Cyndy, as she turned the other direction.

The breeze carried the scent of salt, and Lily took a deep breath. She took in the charming businesses that lined the streets. Huge pots of colorful flowers outfitted with small American flags decorated corners on the downtown blocks. Vivid blooms dripped from baskets hanging on old-fashioned street lamps. Together with the red, white, and blue banners, flags waving in the breeze in front of almost every business, and posters advertising the festival, there was a definite festive vibe in the heart of Driftwood Bay.

Plum Crazy had a sale going on to celebrate the birth of America. A pleasant woman greeted Lily when she came through the door and offered to help her. "I'm just going to browse a bit."

After searching through the racks, she fell in love with a blue silk sleeveless dress. She shook her head when she looked at it again. "I don't need a dress," she muttered.

She selected several things to try on, and the helpful clerk ushered her into an oversized dressing room. She discarded several picks but found three blouses and a pair of pants she liked. The blue dress winked at her from the hanger. She slipped it on and looked in the mirror.

She hadn't worn a dress in a long time. The soft fabric was cut in a simple line with a slight drape on one side, like a lazy ruffle, and an asymmetric hem. The color was called moonstone blue. She looked at the price, and her eyes widened. It had been on a sale rack. She did the math in her head and turned to admire the dress.

She added it to the items she was purchasing and made her way to the counter. The saleswoman chatted as she took care to wrap each piece of clothing with tissue and place them in a bag. She offered to leave the dress on a hanger and slipped plastic over it.

Lily forked over her credit card and winced when she signed the slip. Even on sale, the items cost more than she spent on jeans and t-shirts for the season. Lily thanked the woman and carried her new purchases out the door. She made her way up the stairs of an old brick building to the aptly named, Upstairs Closet.

Signs with fireworks advertised a sale on everything. A woman dressed in an outfit with a beautiful silvery gray duster greeted her. The shop was tiny but overflowing with one-of-a-kind clothing. Lily had never worn a long duster but loved how it looked over black pants and a tank on the saleswoman.

She gravitated to the rack that held them and chose one in a gorgeous watery color that reminded her of sea glass. A nearby hook held several tanks in similar colors. She selected one that matched the duster. The woman offered to put them in a dressing room, along with the bag and dress Lily was carrying.

After looking in every nook and cranny of the shop, Lily found several summery tops and another pair of pants, plus a long jacket she liked. It was a sheer white fabric with short sleeves and looked great on the mannequin.

Much to her dismay, all the items fit, and she liked them. She added up the prices and sucked in a breath. "Wow," she whispered. She toyed with the idea of putting something back, but then heard Gary's voice in her head. She had never been one to shop or spend much on herself. He had always encouraged her to do that. She had plenty of money from Uncle Leo, and the cottages were set to be profitable.

She shook her head and quit thinking, hauling the whole lot over to the counter. The woman complimented her on her choices as she rang up the sale. The woman gave her the total and told her to pick out a necklace and earrings set as a gift.

Lily looked at the case and pondered her choices. She didn't wear much jewelry and steered clear of the large pieces and giant colored beads. She was drawn to a simple silver necklace with three circles and matching hoop earrings.

The woman wrapped them up with a smile and handed Lily another large bag. She added the duster and long jacket to Lily's dress and wrapped them together.

Time had gotten away from her. A wave of guilt washed over her. She tossed her purchases in the backseat and steered for home. Once she had her packages inside, she hurried downstairs to check on the dogs. She found Abby had returned and was inside the enclosure with them.

She laughed at the sight of the dogs romping on top of her. "That's quite the picture."

Abby turned and smiled. "They saw me when I got back and looked so sad, I just had to come and play." She shaded her eyes and added, "You look nice all dressed up."

"Oh, just something besides my jeans. I went to lunch with a friend and did some shopping. I'm glad you were here to keep them occupied."

"I didn't want to let them out without having their leashes, so thought we'd just play in here."

"I appreciate that. Fritz would behave, but Bodie is an unknown at this point." She turned and said, "I'll grab them and rescue you from the attack."

After clipping on their leashes, Abby offered to walk them around the yard. Lily got to work making sure the beverage station was refilled with fresh water and iced tea. She put out a plate of treats and invited Abby to join her in a glass in the shade.

As they watched the dogs run around the yard, Lily asked, "Did you decide to go to the festival tomorrow?"

Abby nodded. "It sounds like fun. I'm going to go. I may not stay with them through the fireworks, but I'll go for part of the day." She patted her pocket with her phone. "I've got my rideshare app on my phone in case I need to bail."

"After spending time with them the other night, I can see why you were reluctant to come with them. It's like signing up to be tortured."

"You would think I would have learned by now."

They heard the noise of a vehicle in the drive, followed by the slamming of doors, and the yammering of voices. "They're baaaack," said Lily, with a sly smile.

Chapter 15

Friday morning, Lily rose early to make sure the dogs enjoyed some exercise at the beach. She took them the long way home, through the park. It was quiet and serene, with only the sound of a few sprinklers running.

Once they arrived home and ate their breakfast, she slipped into the shower to get ready for her outing. She chose one of her new blouses and paired it with jeans and her new earrings and necklace.

From her table on the deck, she saw the six women leaving together and waved goodbye. She finished her cup of tea and led the dogs to the yard. They played ball and fetch and then did some leash training and commands with Bodie. "Tuesday is your first day of training. That should be fun, huh?" she said, rubbing the pup's head.

She kept her eye on the time and led the tired dogs upstairs for water and rest. They lounged in the cool shade while she filled their outdoor bowls with fresh water, making sure there was enough for Sherlock.

She trudged back upstairs and discovered the dogs at the front door, announcing the arrival of guests. She hollered through the door to meet her at the side gate. She wasn't quite ready for a rambunctious furry get-together in her somewhat clean house.

The dogs beat her downstairs and were at the gate waiting. As soon as the opening was large enough, Sherlock shot through it.

Bodie was overexcited and kept hopping between the two big dogs. The three dashed across the yard, tufts of golden fur flying. Mac laughed and said, "Wow, that's quite the welcome committee."

"How are you? Come on in. Do you want something to drink before we leave?"

"Iced tea sounds great. We can watch the show from the deck."

She led the way and retrieved their teas. She took a chair and let out a breath. "Whew, I've been running with those two hooligans all morning. I was trying to tire them out so they'd be calm."

He winked as he finished a swallow. "Seems like they recharge much quicker than we do. It'll be good for them to exercise before we go." He let out a long sigh.

"Tough week, huh?"

"Short weeks are always longer. You know how that works?"

She laughed and rolled her eyes. "Boy, do I. It seems like each time there was a Monday holiday, Tuesday was pure chaos, and by the end of the week, it felt like two."

He raised his glass and clinked it with hers. "Amen. Everybody was squeezing in all the problems of a six-day week into four. I'm off until Monday, thank goodness." He pointed to the dogs rolling in the grass. "How goes your first batch of guests?"

Her eyes widened, and she smirked. "Well, they're…interesting. One of them has taken to the dogs. She lost her golden retriever not long ago and is still grieving. She's happiest playing with Fritz and Bodie. Three of her gal pals are over the top pretentious and annoying, and the other two barely say a word. Strange group."

"It takes all kinds, I guess. How does it compare to the career you left?"

"Hmm. Similar in that you have to smile and make nice with staff and politicians and cater to their needs." She paused in thought and said, "It's really not that bad. I don't have to interact that much.

I made the mistake of accepting their invitation to share some pizza with them the other night. The chatty ones were making glib comments about me probably having dumped my husband. They were all smiles and laughing until I told them he died. Could have heard the proverbial pin drop."

He grimaced. "They sound obnoxious."

She took a sip and said, "They are."

"We should probably get going. Shall we marshal the beasts?"

She pocketed a few treats, and they made their way down. The dogs had settled into a quiet pile. They pranced over when they were called and followed Lily to the enclosure. She distracted them with treats while Mac locked the gate. "Be good boys. We'll be back soon," she said.

Lily led him through the downstairs and made sure the utility room area was ready, should they decide to come indoors. She shut the door to the room and said, "This is the common area for guests. I don't expect them to be home while we're away, but you never know."

She led the way up the stairs and deadbolted the door. "Let me lock the deck door, and then we're ready to go."

She slipped some money and her cell phone into her pocket and met Mac at the front door. "Is Cyndy meeting us there?"

"Yea, she had some things to do at the shop." He held the door for her as she got into his SUV.

They chatted about the dogs on their way to Fort Walden. He found a parking spot that wasn't too far away from the entrance and checked his cell phone. He tapped a few keys and slid it back into his pocket. "Cyndy is just leaving. I told her we were here and would meet her at the root beer float booth."

The grounds were teeming with people, and kids were running everywhere. They snaked through the crowd with Mac leading the way. He surprised her when they were moving through lines of people and he stretched his hand behind him reaching for hers.

She accepted his hand. He held it in a firm grip and yelled, "I don't want to lose you."

She let him clear the way, and they passed by the games and kid-friendly vendors to a less congested crowd of adults hovering around a beer garden and several vendors. The root beer float tent was behind the beer garden. Mac led Lily to the line and said, "I'll find us a place to sit. The beer garden is best, otherwise we'll be run over by kids." He handed her two tokens. "You've got to have these to get them. They won't sell them, only give them away for a token."

She wrinkled her brow but agreed. She stood in line watching people, morphing into her old job duties. Looking for anyone that didn't belong or was acting out of the ordinary. She inched forward as the line moved.

She reached the window and presented her tokens. A friendly white-haired man with a bushy mustache handed her two plastic cups. "There you go, young lady. Enjoy!"

She smiled and thanked him, turning to find Mac. She skirted the main entrance to the beer tent and went through the back side. She saw him waving his arm, and she maneuvered through the tables. He took the cups and set them on the table, before pulling out her chair. A gentleman. She had begun to think they were extinct.

They dug into the thick vanilla ice cream covered with homemade root beer. "Delicious," she said, taking another bite.

"I hate to tell you, but it's probably the best thing you'll eat today." He laughed as he scooped more ice cream from his cup. "They have a lot of fair type food. I usually stick with the giant hot dogs. They're not bad."

"How'd you get the tokens for the floats?"

"Oh, it's through the service clubs in town. They give them to donors and use it as a fundraiser. They don't like to mess with cash, so it's become sort of a novelty booth. People clamor to donate so they can get the free floats. They always run out."

"Marketing genius."

"Born from laziness." He laughed and said, "Oh, there's Cyndy. She knows where to find me." He waved, and she made her way to them, stopping to visit and chat with everyone on her route through the crowd.

"I'll go get her float," he offered. "It'll take her that long to get here with all her chitchat."

Lily watched as Mac greeted people with a smile or a handshake but didn't linger. His sister, on the other hand, pulled up a chair at most of the tables and visited and laughed with everyone. She could have been the mayor.

As he predicted, he beat her back to the table with her float. She looked over at them once, and he held the float up and put it to his mouth, teasing her. She cut her conversation short and made a beeline for them.

"Don't you dare, Jack. I've been waiting all day for one of these." She swiped the cup from him and took her first sip, followed by a spoonful of ice cream. "Ah, just like I remembered."

"Are you ladies up for a game of miniature golf?" asked Mac. "I must warn you; I'm a scratch golfer." He winked and laughed.

"Oh, we're up to it," said his sister, rolling her eyes. She finished off her float and led the way to the golf course set up on a huge grassy lawn. Mac paid the fees for all three of them, while they picked out their colored putters and balls.

As they approached the first hole, Lily saw Andy and Wade leaning against their work truck. She gave a wave, and Andy came running over to them.

He explained they had helped build and set up the course this morning. "How's Bodie and Fritz?"

Lily signed to him that they were home playing with Sherlock.

His eyes enlarged, and he smiled at Mac. "Aww, Sherlock is the best." He turned and looked at his dad. "We're going to get our root beer floats."

"The course looks wonderful, Andy. You did a great job on it," said Lily, as she signed.

"It's a fun project. We like to help out."

It was Lily's turn, so she said her goodbyes and told Andy to come and visit soon. She turned her attention to the bright green AstroTurf and sent her ball whirring down the fairway. It hit the obstacle and launched across the open area, right into the plastic cup. "Hole in one," she shouted.

Mac was keeping score and shook his head. He turned to his sister and said, "I think we've been snookered."

"Probably just beginner's luck," said Lily, grinning.

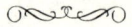

After lots of teasing and laughing, they finished their game. Lily won, Mac came in second, and Cyndy was last. "Loser buys lunch," said Mac, sounding like a taunting brother.

"I've lost every year since this festival started. Why should this year be any different?" Cyndy shrugged and smiled at Lily. "I'm glad you whooped him," she whispered.

Cyndy paid for their lunch at the hot dog shack, and they found a recently vacated table under a shady tree. Mac went to retrieve their drinks.

"I meant to tell you, I love the blouse. I take it you had some luck shopping yesterday?"

"Far too much luck, I'm afraid. I found some great things at both stores. I came away with several blouses with this funky hemline. I like them."

"It looks lovely on you. That teal is terrific with your coloring."

Mac interrupted when he arrived with a tray of drinks. "You gals snagged a great table. Here you go," he said, passing around the cups.

"I haven't had a hot dog in years," said Lily. She took a bite of hers, dressed in onions, mustard, and relish. "Quite good."

"This is my yearly treat. I steer clear of them for the most part," said Mac.

"So, tonight is my first wine and beer evening for the guests. I'm thinking it will be a giant bust since they'll be enjoying the festival activities and fireworks. Would you two be interested in coming?"

Mac nodded. "Sure, I don't have any plans this evening."

Cyndy wiped her mouth with a napkin and said, "I'd love to, but I'm going to a friend's house to enjoy the fireworks tonight. Jack will have to keep you company on his own."

Lily looked at her plate and hesitated for a moment. "Sure, the dogs would love to have Sherlock stay and play tonight. What time are the fireworks? I'll need to make sure the dogs are inside by then."

Mac agreed with a nod. "Not until it's really dark. It will be after nine, for sure."

"I'm making a cheese board with a bit of fruit and veggies. Will that do you for dinner?"

"After all this junk, that sounds marvelous," said Mac.

Lily looked up to see Jeff and Donna Evans looking for a table. "Hey," she said, as she waved her arm.

Jeff spotted her and led Donna in their direction. "Wow, it's a busy one today," he said.

"We're almost done, so feel free to take the table," offered Lily. Mac moved from his seat and offered it to Jeff, while Donna slid into the empty chair at the table.

"Thank you. How are you all doing today?" asked the Chief of Police.

"Mostly visiting and eating. So, all in all a good day," said Cyndy, with an infectious laugh.

Lily looked around the table. "I'm sure you all know each other, right?"

The foursome nodded. "Dr. Mac is the best vet in town and Cyndy here," Jeff looked at his wife, "has the best gift shop my wife has ever seen." Cyndy nodded and smiled as she took her first bite. "And believe me, she's seen 'em all," said Jeff, flinching before the expected smack on the arm from his wife.

"Cyndy helped me decorate the cottages, and I agree. She's the best."

"Lily, I need to talk to you about a project you may be able to help us with," said Donna. "When's a good time to stop by?"

"Does Sunday work? I've got people coming and going tomorrow, but Sunday or even Monday works for me. Just stop by whenever it's convenient."

"Wonderful. I'll call you before I head over."

Lily and Cyndy both stood and gathered up the boxes and napkins from the table. "Enjoy the rest of your day," said Cyndy. "And Jeff, don't forget I keep a hint list at the store, and I know Donna's name is on it. Stop by, and I can help you with a gift or get you out of trouble."

Jeff shook his head and smiled at her. "I can see why you're so successful."

They said their goodbyes and took a walk through the vendor booths. Lots of talented artists showcased their creations, as well as several specialty food purveyors. Clothing and jewelry booths were plentiful, as were those selling fresh flowers and produce.

Lily couldn't resist the baskets of fresh berries and bought some strawberries and marionberries. Children competed in three-legged races, egg-and-spoon races, and corn hole. Horseshoe pits were filled with adults. Table tennis and badminton were popular with all ages.

"Anyone want to play a game?" asked Mac.

Cyndy shrugged. "Not really, but I'll watch you two. Go sign up for badminton, and I'll sit right here," she pointed to a vacant chair with a good view of the grassy area serving as the court.

Lily surveyed the players. "I'll try. I haven't played since I was in high school."

"I seem to remember getting hoodwinked at golf today. I won't be fooled twice," said Mac, hurrying to the table to add their names to the list.

Lily read the rules posted near the table and studied several players to refresh her memory. She and Mac were called to a court and given their equipment. Each game ended when a player scored twenty-one, and Lily won the first game. They both laughed when they heard Cyndy hollering from the sidelines.

Mac paid closer attention in the second game and won it. Cyndy clapped but wasn't as excited as she had been when Lily won. It all came down to the third and final game of the match.

They ended up neck in neck. They had drawn the attention of bystanders. The crowd chanted, "Lily. Lily. Lily." Cyndy was laughing as she egged them on with her hands. The first one to gain a two-point lead would win. Lily scored the first point. The next serve from Mac arrived inches from the net. Lily had to run and lunge to try to send it back over the net.

The crowd gasped when she made her move. She stretched and the racket connected with the rubber nose of the shuttle. It sailed back over the net and landed on Mac's side. She won. The crowd and Cyndy went wild.

Lily shrugged and laughed. Mac met her at the net. "That was impressive. You sure you haven't been practicing in secret all week?"

Mac guided her through the crowd of well-wishers to collect Cyndy, who was still whooping and hollering. "Let's go, bigmouth," he said, his tone full of fun.

They made their way through the booths, and Mac stopped at the local ice cream vendor Lily knew and loved. "I think the winner deserves a treat. How about it?" he asked her.

"I never refuse ice cream." She ordered lemon buttermilk with marionberries, and Mac chose peach cobbler.

Cyndy gave them each a hug goodbye as she waited for her mocha chunk cone. "I need to run to get to my friend's place. I had a terrific time. Let me know when you can squeeze in lunch," she said to Lily.

"I will. I'm glad I came; it was lots of fun."

"See you Sunday," said Mac, giving her a quick peck on the cheek.

The two took a slow stroll through the park and back to Mac's car. "We try to have dinner once a week. She's cooking on Sunday. It's nice to relax and talk to each other when we're not rushed."

"You're lucky to have her so close." She licked her cone before it had a chance to drip. "I'm not close to my sister. She's younger and lives in Texas." She caught another trickle of lemon ice cream. "In fact, I haven't talked to her since Gary's funeral."

"We are lucky to have each other. We've grown closer with Mom and Dad gone. As much as we harass each other, we do love each other. Cyndy is close to my daughter, which has been a godsend over the years."

"I've never been able to rely on Wendy for support. She's self-absorbed, to say the least. Our relationship took a dive after my parents died. Apparently, they were the only thing we had in common."

"Nobody said family was easy," said Mac, as he opened the door for her.

The dogs were beyond ecstatic to see their owners. They spent over an hour playing with them in the yard. Mac gave her some tips on making Bodie listen. She worked with the dog on the leash, while he watched and provided coaching.

"We're going to our first class on Tuesday."

"They have terrific trainers. You'll see huge changes as Bodie goes through the program."

Sherlock and Fritz lounged in the grass and watched the action, content to let Bodie get schooled while they napped. When Lily ran out of treats, she said, "I better get to work on my appetizer spread." She glanced at the cottages. "I doubt they'll be here, but if I don't do it, they'll show up."

"I'll stay out here with the dogs a bit longer. Give you some space to work. Do you need anything done out here?"

"If you're serious, you could make sure the fire pit is clean and arrange the chairs and side tables near it. I've got to get the beer and wine downstairs, and I'll need a table for the cheese board. I appreciate the help."

She made for the house and left him to deal with the setup and the dogs. She checked the computer and took another look at the spread she was trying to replicate. She cut up enough veggies and cheeses to cover tonight and tomorrow. After placing cheeses and meats around the wooden board, she added different kinds of crackers, grapes, and a few of the strawberries she picked up at the festival. Next came slices of cucumber and grape tomatoes. She used her aunt's small glass bowls and placed nuts, olives, and pickles on the board. The last touch was a container of heavy duty wooden picks.

As she sampled a few bites, she murmured, "Yummy." After wrapping it in plastic wrap, she stuck it in the pantry fridge. She heard the clomp of footsteps on the deck stairs and saw Mac at the door.

"Ah, you're just in time to help cart some beer and wine downstairs. I don't leave it down there. Don't want to tempt the guests." She showed him the fridge, and he selected a handful of bottles. He added a bottle of red and one of white and set off for downstairs.

She fed the dogs their dinner, including their guest, and they stretched out on the deck, with Bodie between the two big dogs. After checking to make sure she had everything, she retrieved the cheeseboard and joined Mac, who was sitting at the fire pit.

"That looks like a professional did it," he said, eyeing the display of snacks. "I grabbed a beer; did you want a glass of wine?"

"Nah, I think I'll stick with iced tea for now."

"One beer is my limit. I don't like to drink at all if I'm driving, but figure I'll be here long enough, it should metabolize." He helped himself to a cracker and loaded it with meat and cheese. "I'll grab your tea," he said, as he walked back to the house.

"Thanks, you don't have to do that." She noticed he had added the plates and napkins to the table. She murmured, "Thorough and a gentleman."

He handed her the frosted glass and pulled out the chair next to his. "It's a tranquil spot. Nice to sit and soak it all in."

"I agree. I love the sound of the waves. I've found my time here and down at the beach to be therapeutic."

"There are some interesting studies to back that up." He told her about articles he had read touting the healing powers of the ocean. "It's used often in psychological therapy. Sitting or walking on the beach and staring at the ocean forces you to be in the moment. It's multi-sensory stimulation at its best. Smell and taste the salt, feel the grains of sand, watch and hear the waves break, and let the breeze touch your face."

"I never thought of it, but you're right. I notice its power. It can erase what's right in front of you in the sand in seconds. Then it can rush in and build a whole new formation of sand the next time it arrives. The power to give and the power to take away. It makes me realize there is something way greater than me." She reached for a wooden pick, speared several items from the cheese board, and added them to her plate.

"It's long been known as a healing element, physically and spiritually. Healing more than cuts and skin conditions. It's where the roots of naturopathy were born. I feel a strong connection when I sit and watch the water. It's calming and makes me feel at peace."

She nodded as she sipped her tea. "I agree. A total sense of calm, even when the tide is raging. I feel a strong connection to Gary there."

"There is definitely something that draws humans to the sea. It may not be totally explainable, but it's undeniable." He loaded another cracker with cheese and veggies. "I can relate to what you're saying. I spent a good amount of time watching the waves after I lost Jill. It was cathartic."

Daylight was drifting away, with soft lavender rays announcing the arrival of dusk. The lights strung overhead came to life. "Ah, I love that," she said, admiring them. "Makes for a picture-perfect spot."

She drained her tea and said, "The dogs will need a break in the yard by now, and I think I'll grab a glass of white wine," she said.

"You sit," he said, placing his hand on her arm. "I'll do it." He took the last swig from his bottle and added, "Looks like your guests won't be joining us." He turned on the fire pit. and golden flames flickered in the shiny rocks.

She leaned her head back and watched the fire. "I hope they don't come back. It's nice here without having to entertain them or listen to their nonsensical chatter. Abby is the only one I thought might be here. Hopefully, that means she's enjoying herself. They were all interested in the fireworks."

"We'll get the three musketeers in the house by nine. I always recommend putting them in their crate for fireworks. It helps them feel safe."

"I don't think I have Fritz's crate."

"We'll figure something out." He hurried to the deck to complete the nightly ritual.

She gazed at the vivid sky, with the sun beginning its descent into the ocean. The blues and golds in the heavens matched the dancing flames in the colored glass of the fire. "Gorgeous," she whispered.

Chapter 17

Mac returned with the three dogs and a glass of wine for Lily. Over the next hour, they watched the colors change in the sky as it darkened. "Well, we probably better head indoors before it gets any later," said Lily, gathering the cheese board.

"I'll give the dogs one last run around the yard and turn off the fire pit. Meet you upstairs."

She left the beer and wine downstairs since tomorrow she'd be featuring an encore presentation. The ladies would be gone by ten, so the chance of them drinking all her booze was minimal. She wrapped the appetizers and put everything in the fridge.

"Fritz's crate," she grumbled. "I'm sure it's not here. I would remember moving it."

As she pondered the crate situation, Mac arrived with the dogs. "So, if you don't have a crate, we can huddle in a closet with them. The important thing is to have a small space, so they don't get frantic. If they're in a nest-like environment, they'll be calmer."

"There's my closet. It's not small, but better than all this open space. I usually hold him on my lap."

"Let's try the closet. We can bring Bodie's crate, and he can use it if he needs to."

She led him to the master suite and the oversized closet. "Well, there's plenty of room for all of us," he said with a laugh. "And an orchestra." He ushered the dogs inside and grabbed Fritz's fluffy bed on the way to the closet. "Seriously, it's a good spot. The lack of windows is helpful."

"Means we'll miss seeing them," said Lily.

"They stream the display live. We can watch on my phone." He positioned the bed and told Fritz and Sherlock to lie down. Bodie followed and scrunched in between them. "You sit here next to Fritz, and I'll sit on the other side. We'll make our own miniature fort."

They hunkered down in the near dark, with the only illumination coming from a dim nightlight. Lily petted Fritz and Bodie. "It's like a dog slumber party," she said with a laugh. She continued to talk to the dogs in a soft and soothing voice, telling them how smart and good they were.

Mac tapped his phone and after a few minutes turned it so she could see the screen. "Looks like they're going to start in less than a minute."

He positioned the phone on Fritz's bed behind the dogs, so they wouldn't get distracted by it. "No sound, of course," he said, glancing down at the furry trio. Lily repositioned herself onto her stomach with her arm stretched across the dogs and her head resting against the soft dog bed.

She felt Fritz tense at the faint thud of a firework launching. She had to strain to hear it but knew the dogs heard much more. She continued to stroke and comfort them, telling them everything was okay.

Mac's phone screen lit up with a beautiful fountain of color. A few more thumps sounded, followed by twinkling lights showcased on the screen. This went on for about fifteen minutes.

All three dogs' ears perked up each time the weak thud of a launch sounded. They didn't run or struggle but were far from relaxed. She kept the weight of her arm over them.

Lily's phone, which was on the floor behind the bed, came to life. A text message from Kevin flashed on the screen. *Happy early birthday, Mom. Have a great weekend. I'll call you Sunday.*

She couldn't reach it to turn it off. "It's your birthday?" asked Mac.

"On Sunday. Kevin believes in celebrating the entire weekend, actually the whole month if he can get away with it."

"Well, you can't spend your birthday working. Why don't you join us for dinner on Sunday? It's not much, but beats you sitting at home eating leftover cheese and crackers."

"Oh, you don't need to worry about it, really."

"It'll be easier if you just say yes. Once I tell Cyndy, I can't be held responsible for her actions. You could have a singing telegram in the form of a male stripper at your house Sunday morning. She's been known to pull some epic pranks."

"I don't want to make a big deal out of it. It's just a birthday."

He picked up the phone, realizing the fireworks had ended. "Don't make me call her."

She laughed and grabbed the phone. "Okay, I surrender. You win."

"Bring the beasts with you. Cyndy has a great yard, and Sherlock goes with me. Does four o'clock work?"

"Of course. Thank you," she said, feeling the sting of grateful tears in her eyes.

Saturday morning, Lily took the dogs to the beach and thought of Mac's words as she sought solace in gazing at the moving waters. She concentrated on the smell of salt and licked her lips to taste it. She plunged her fingers into the coarse grains of sand and listened as the waves crashed the beach.

Tomorrow she would be forty-nine. She never imagined she would be on the other side of the country, without Gary, and missing Kevin on her birthday. She never thought she'd leave Virginia. So many unexpected tomorrows.

A few months ago, she wouldn't have dreamed she would be celebrating her birthday with new friends, in a place that held tender childhood memories. A place she trusted would begin to heal her broken heart.

She grinned as the dogs stretched on their leashes to reach the water. She stood and guided them away from the temptation. "Come on guys; we need to get home."

She fed the dogs and hurried to get ready for the busy day. The six women would be checking out soon, and Lily had to welcome six new guests that afternoon. The maids were coming to clean all the cottages. She'd have enough laundry to keep her busy until bedtime.

She led the dogs to the deck and left them there while she went downstairs to prep for the day. The women wandered out of their cottages, two by two. Amy saw her and waved, "We're heading out, Lily. Thank you for a wonderful stay. It's been so much fun."

"Glad you enjoyed it here. Hope to see you again." She pasted a happy smile on her face as she delivered the lie.

The other women all waved and muttered their thanks. Abby lingered and asked, "Do you mind if I say goodbye to your dogs?"

"Of course not. Come on up to the deck. I've got them penned in up there so they stay out of my hair while I get the cottages ready." She led the way upstairs and found the dogs waiting at the door.

Abby sat on the deck, much like she did when she first met them, and let them cover her with kisses as she nuzzled them. Tails wagged as she told them they were beautiful and sweet.

Amy's horn honked, broadcasting impatience. Abby stood, fresh tears on her face. "Thanks, Lily. For everything. I'm glad I came and appreciate you listening." She rushed to Lily and embraced her before hurrying down the stairs.

"Safe travels," hollered Lily.

———

To get a head start on the laundry and dishes, Lily gathered the dirty towels and glasses from each room. She found an envelope on the dresser in Amy's cottage. Lily's name was written in curly script across the front of it.

She added it to the basket of towels and toted it all to the house. She started a load in the washer and filled a glass with iced tea. Inside the envelope was a pretty card and five, crisp, hundred-dollar bills. Amy had penned her thanks and another apology for the insensitive comments. She suggested Lily treat herself to a day of pampering at the spa, with her compliments.

Lily's eyes widened in surprise as she fingered the money. "I just might do that, Awesome Amy."

———

The housekeepers arrived, and within two hours, the cottages were sparkling clean with fresh linens. Lily ran the glasses and vases through the dishwasher and had a bite of lunch while it ran. The dogs accompanied her in the yard while she selected some colorful blooms for the cottages.

Her never-ending commitment to safety and security nagged at her to change the code on the gate each time all the guests vacated the property. She found the instructions in her desk drawer and marched to the gate. After two tries, she had it reset.

She had prepared the guest folios in advance and had them ready for the new arrivals. She added the new gate code to their information and threw in another load of laundry while she folded towels.

The dogs meandered around the yard and chose a shady spot on the concrete next to the house to relax. She let them nap while she straightened the common area and found a small box that fit in the fridge for toting the beer and wine. She wouldn't have Mac around to help her tonight.

She herded the dogs upstairs before three o'clock, so as not to overwhelm the new guests. She had just sat down with her tea when the doorbell rang. She answered and found a cheerful young man holding a huge bouquet of flowers.

"Lily Reed?" he asked.

"That's me." She signed his clipboard and took the vase. Gorgeous pink roses were nestled in between lavender, purple, blue, and fuchsia flowers. It looked like an entire flower garden. She opened the card and saw they were from Kevin. *Sorry, I'm not there. Happy Birthday, Mom. Love you!*

She placed them on the granite island counter in the kitchen and stood to admire them. Her phone chimed announcing movement at the side of the house. She scanned the camera and saw a car in the driveway.

She hurried downstairs and opened the gate. She waved at the two women getting out of the sedan. "Hello. I'm Lily. Are you checking in?"

The younger woman replied. "Yes, I'm Kelly, and this is my mom, Alice."

The frail woman she introduced gave Lily a weak smile. She leaned against the car for support. "Lovely to meet you," said Lily. "Let me help you with your luggage."

A look of relief came over Kelly. "That would be great." She set two wheeled bags in front of Lily. "I'll help Mom navigate."

Lily led the way and carried the bags until she got to the sidewalk where they would roll. It took Alice a long time to reach the doorway. In anticipation of her being worn out from the walk, Lily had pulled out one of the sturdier wooden chairs by the table.

Once Alice was seated, she offered her a glass of water or tea. "Water would be wonderful," said the woman in a voice so soft it could have been a whisper.

While Alice rested and sipped her water, Kelly filled out the registration forms, and Lily ran her credit card. "So, we've got you scheduled to leave on next Sunday, correct?"

"Yes, that's right." She smiled at her mom and said, "You doing okay, Mom?"

Alice nodded and took another drink. She gazed out the window and smiled. "It's pretty here."

Lily finished the paperwork and gave Kelly the folio and keys. "I'll walk you down to the cottage and show you around. Tonight, we've got complimentary appetizers with beer and wine by the fire pit. It's lovely here in the evenings, so I hope you'll join us."

"Sounds terrific. We're tired from the drive, so it would be great to lay low and relax." She glanced at her mother. "I'm going to get our luggage stowed, and then I'll come back for you."

The woman nodded and watched as Lily and Kelly followed the path through the yard to the second cottage. Lily showed her inside and placed the luggage in the bedroom. "Oh, it's so beautiful." The young woman's eyes roamed around the rooms. "Looks peaceful. My mom has terminal cancer." Her voice cracked. "She decided to stop treatments and take a trip to enjoy the little time she's got left."

"I'm so very sorry, Kelly. If there is anything I can do to make the stay more comfortable for her, please don't hesitate to ask. I usually recommend a walk to the beach, but you could drive to it and have a much safer and shorter walk. There's also a lovely park not far down the road."

"Sounds terrific. Mom wants to sit on the beach. I'm just not sure she has the strength."

"If you need my help, I can go with you."

Tears flooded the woman's eyes as she nodded. "I appreciate that. I'll let you know," she whispered, as she dabbed a tissue under her eyes. She took a deep breath and let it out. "I just need a moment. I don't want her to see me crying."

"I understand. You get organized, and I'll go chat with your mom. I'm expecting some more guests, so I'll be up at the house for a while."

Lily found Alice sitting in the same position. "Would you like some iced tea? Kelly is getting things organized in the cottage, so we have a few minutes."

"That sounds wonderful," said the woman, in a weak voice.

"Are you much for puzzles? I'm happy to start one with you while we wait."

A spark flashed in her watery eyes. "I always loved doing puzzles. When Kelly was a youngster, we did them all the time."

Lily placed a fresh glass of tea on the table and then helped her make her way there, holding the chair while she sat down. She pulled a box from the bookshelves and showed it to Alice. "This one is pretty. Shall we give it a go?"

"It's gorgeous," she said, eyeing the photo of a sandy beach scene with scatterings of sea glass.

"Sort of matches our theme here, right?" Lily smiled as she unboxed it and piled the pieces closer to Alice. She balanced the box against the ledge for reference.

Alice reached for the pieces and said, "We need to find all the edges first. This one is going to be hard." She grinned and started separating the pile.

They hadn't made much progress when a young couple appeared at the doorway. Lily hurried to greet them. "Hello and welcome. I'm Lily."

The man extended his hand. "I'm Joe, and this is my wife, Lisa." He stepped aside, and his wife greeted Lily with a warm smile, her hand on her pregnant tummy.

"Your place is beautiful," said the woman.

"Let's get you settled in your cottage." She went about the registration and payment process and invited them to the gathering at the fire pit. "Your breakfast vouchers are in here," she said, handing him the folio. "I'll walk you down to the cottage."

On the way, Lisa said, "This is our last trip before our baby girl arrives. We wanted to squeeze in one more getaway before we get too busy."

After Lily gave them the lay of the land, she pointed out the trail along the bluff to the beach and let them know about the intercom at the back of the house and the common area open for their use. "Enjoy your stay and let me know if you need anything."

She met Kelly as she was returning to the house. "I've got your mom doing a puzzle. She seems to be content there." She made sure Kelly understood about breakfast, the gate security code, and the intercom.

"I think I'll join her on the puzzle for a bit and then see if I can get her to take a nap before we join you for appetizers." She went through the door and slid into the chair across from her mom.

Lily went outside and walked to the gate just as another car pulled in and parked. A woman and a teenage girl emerged from the SUV. "You must be Lily?" said the woman. "I'm Nora, and this is my daughter, Brianna."

"Bree, Mom. Geez," said the girl, her voice full of contempt.

Lily nodded and said, "Yes, I'm Lily, pleased to meet both of you. Do you need any help with your luggage?"

"We've got it. We don't have much," said Nora.

A sullen look matched Bree's slow movement as she ambled along the walkway. It was clear she wasn't overjoyed to be here. She plopped down on one of the benches alongside the house. "I'll wait here," she announced.

As Nora filled out her paperwork, she said, "Chief Evans recommended your cottage. I'm interviewing with the police on Monday." She handed her the form and added, "He told me you're retired law enforcement."

"Yes, this is quite the new career for me. I wish you the best on your interview. That's exciting."

She glanced at her daughter. "One of us is excited. Bree, not so much. She doesn't want to leave her friends and school. We're here early to explore the town, and I'm hoping she warms to the idea."

"It's a beautiful place with a friendly community. She'll fall in love with the beach." Lily gave her spiel about the property, breakfast, and tonight's gathering. She handed Nora all the information and introduced her to Alice and Kelly on their way out the door.

When Lily led them into the cottage, she noticed Bree's eyes perk up as she glanced around the rooms. Lily did her best to talk up the beach and the waterfront. Her eyes sparkled as she thought of another advantage. "I've got a golden retriever, Fritz, and a new puppy, Bodie. We usually go to the beach each morning, and they love it."

"You have two dogs?" Bree's interest was piqued.

"I'm fostering the puppy. He's in training to be a hearing dog, so I'll have him for just under two years."

"Oh, mom, I want a dog. That would be so cool."

Nora smiled and said, "Let's see what happens, and then we'll talk about it. We can look for a place with a yard, so we're prepared for one."

"Can I play with your dogs?" asked the girl, all smiles.

"Sure." She pointed at the house. "They're keeping watch on the deck, but I'll be bringing them down once I get everyone settled. There's a rather frail guest up at the house, and I want to wait until she's in her cottage. I don't want them bugging her. They think everyone loves them."

Nora and Bree both laughed. "Well, let's get unpacked. We'll see you in a bit for refreshments."

Lily plodded back to the house, glad everyone had arrived. She saw her two fluffy observers looking down at her, tails wagging faster the closer she came. She poked her head into the public room and saw Kelly helping Alice from her chair.

"Need any extra help?" asked Lily.

"I think we've got it. Mom is hooked on your puzzle, so we know what we'll be doing each evening." Kelly smiled and held her mom's arm. "We're going to take a nap."

Lily collected the paperwork and hurried upstairs. With the guests in their cottages, she let the dogs roam the yard. Their noses were in overdrive as they scrutinized every blade of grass and followed the new scents of the strangers.

After they had run and played, Lily finished the last of the laundry and led them upstairs. She nibbled on a few bites while she refreshed her cheeseboard and gazed at her birthday flowers. She sent Kevin a quick text to thank him when she finished her work.

Once the dogs were fed, she joined them on the deck for a few minutes of relaxation with a cup of tea. She caught movement out of the corner of her eye. Bree stomped down the pathway from her cottage. "Hmm. Mothers and daughters can be complicated, and we've got a full house of them." She petted Fritz's ears, "Maybe you can work your magic on Bree tonight."

Chapter 18

The guests gathered and helped themselves to beverages. Lily made sure there was a selection of sodas for Bree. Alice looked refreshed and a bit stronger. Once they were all settled, Lily said, "I've got two dogs who are over-the-top friendly and have a hard time respecting personal space, but Bree wants to play with them, so I'm going to let them join us in the yard tonight. Just don't feed them any snacks, please."

Nora smiled and mouthed a *thank-you* to Lily, who dashed upstairs and returned with the two of them on their leashes. She let the dogs sniff each person, so they'd calm down and lose interest.

"Come on, Bree, I'll let you walk them around for a bit." Lily motioned her to join them and led them away from the fire pit. She showed her the boundaries and told her if she tired of them, to put them in their enclosure.

The girl beamed when she took their leads. She petted them and talked to them before taking off to explore. Lily returned to the guests and poured herself a splash of wine.

"These snacks are delicious," said Joe. "We've got dinner reservations on the waterfront tonight. I need to stop snacking, or I won't be hungry."

The others murmured their agreement. "This is dinner," said Nora with a laugh. The group carried on an easy conversation, explaining where they were from and what they were doing in Driftwood Bay.

Neither Kelly nor Alice mentioned the illness. They framed their trip as a mother-daughter escape. They lived outside of Seattle and enjoyed the small-town atmosphere and slower pace in Driftwood Bay. It had been a place where they had vacationed many years ago.

When Nora told the group about her interview, they all wished her luck and wanted to know more about her police career. She and Bree lived in a small town in the eastern part of Oregon. She shared a few humorous stories about escapades with criminal mischief in the rural setting she described as a bit like Mayberry.

"It's our first baby. A girl. She's due in two months, and we're just trying to have one last trip as a couple," said Lisa. Joe shared he worked in the technology sector, and they lived east of Seattle.

"We're going to visit Olympic National Park." Joe glanced at his wife's midsection. "As much as she can handle, anyway."

"It's well worth the trip. My son and I visited last month. Stunning views of the mountains and beaches. Absolutely gorgeous. Bree might like that if you have the time," Lily suggested.

Nora nodded. "It's on our list. It will have to be a quick day trip. If I feel good about the interview, I want to try to find a place to live, so I'm ready to move if I get the job."

Alice, who was sitting next to her, patted Nora's hand. "I have a good feeling. I think you'll get the job. Then you'll have all the time in the world to explore the park." She glanced at her daughter. "Kelly and her dad and I came one year long ago. It remains one of my favorite trips."

As the sky grew darker, the lights illuminated the yard. "Oh, that is lovely," said Alice. "Seems like a party, doesn't it?" She gripped her daughter's hand.

Joe and Lisa excused themselves to get to their dinner reservation.

Bree walked by the group with the two dogs, their tongues hanging out of their mouths. They were ready for a break. Lily offered to take them and gave them the command to lie down next to her chair.

They settled into the grass, and Bree loaded a plate with snacks and grabbed a soda. "They are so sweet. I think I want a golden retriever, for sure, Mom."

"They are wonderful dogs." Nora smiled at her daughter and glanced at the dogs, who were behaving like highly trained royalty at the moment.

Lily saw the strain in Nora's eyes. She understood not wanting to have a conflict with Bree in front of strangers. The woman had a full plate. A stressful job interview, hunting for a new house, moving, a rebellious daughter, and now a fight over a new pet.

After finishing her last sip of wine, Lily said, "If you do end up here, I'm friends with a local vet. Maybe you could volunteer at his office and walk the dogs and play with them. Then you'd get a better idea of what other breeds you might like and how to care for them."

Nora's eyes brightened. "That's a great idea. Doesn't that sound good, Bree?"

The girl nodded with enthusiasm, not understanding she'd been tricked by two older, experienced moms. Dogs were work, not a toy or novelty. She suspected Bree needed to see the other side of having a pet, not only the fun part.

Alice brought her hand to her mouth to cover a yawn. "Well, ladies, this has been a delight. I'm afraid I need to turn in and call it a night."

"Yes, thank you so much for the food and conversation," added her daughter. "I'm glad we're here through next weekend."

Nora offered to go with Kelly to help Alice navigate the pathway in the dark. While she was away, Bree's cell phone rang, and she hurried to answer it and ran across the yard to their cottage.

When Nora returned, she said, "Call from one of her girlfriends. She'll be on the phone until it runs out of battery." She picked up her empty glass and filled it again.

After a long swallow, she rested her head against the back of the chair and said, "I needed this tonight. It's been a long day. Listening to Bree complain all the way here has me at the end of my rope. She's either belligerent or silent. Not much in between these days. Tonight, with the dogs, was the cheeriest I've seen her."

"Dogs have a way of bringing out the best in us." Lily bent and rubbed Fritz's back.

Nora glanced over her shoulder and said, "Your idea about her volunteering was brilliant. I don't think I can deal with one more thing right now, and that satisfied her. I hope."

They chatted while Nora finished her wine. She talked about the upcoming interview and asked Lily for advice. "I don't know Chief Evans that well. I know he moved here from California and likes the small-town vibe of Driftwood. His wife is the librarian. They're both very active in the community." She paused and said, "The best advice I've ever received is, to be honest and be yourself. That way you don't have to worry about pretense. I'm sure you'll do well."

"I'm planning to let Bree stay here Monday morning. I don't need the hassle she could give me right before I go in for the interview. Is that okay?"

"Sure. I'll be around in the morning. The dogs and I will keep her occupied."

"She's not an early riser, so you may not even see her," Nora said with a smirk.

She polished off the wine in her glass. "Thanks for this, Lily. It's the best evening I've had in a long time."

She stood and added, "Can I help you clean any of this up?"

"No, it's easy. See you tomorrow. Have a good night." Lily urged the sleeping dogs to their feet and took them on one more constitutional before depositing them on Fritz's bed.

She dashed back to the yard and collected glasses and what was left of the cheeseboard, before dousing the fire pit. It didn't take her long to straighten things and lock up downstairs.

She loaded the dishes into the dishwasher and collapsed into bed. The soft snores coming from Fritz's bed, along with the social interaction and conversations tonight, made for a smooth transition to sleep. The wine didn't hurt either.

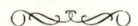

The morning of Lily's birthday, she got up early and collected the boys for an early jaunt to the beach. The yard and cottages were quiet. They arrived at her favorite spot in time for her to see the dawn of her forty-ninth year peek over the horizon.

She worked to focus her thoughts on the present. She thought of things for which she was thankful. Kevin's flowers were marvelous. She'd have fun with Mac and Cyndy tonight. The weather in Driftwood Bay was idyllic. The beach was free therapy. She loved Fritz and Bodie, who made her smile every day.

Tears rolled down her cheeks as she continued to gaze across the expanse of blue. Gary's absence weighed heavy on her heart. Her thoughts drifted to prior birthdays. Gary had always made a point of making her feel special and loved. Flowers, notes stuck on her steering wheel, dinners, trips, texts and funny videos, cakes, and treats. Nothing over the top, but he always made it a celebration.

Missing him came in waves, like the ones she was watching curl into the shoreline. Today, the waves surging inside her were powerful. She gasped for breath as the grief overtook her.

Fritz leaned against her and put his head across her lap. Bodie stood watch, edging closer to her. Her body shuddered with sobs.

Sometimes happy memories were the hardest to bear.

She bent and touched her head to Fritz. "You are such a good friend, Fritzie. I don't know how I would survive without you." She reached for Bodie. "You too, my new furfriend."

She practiced long, deep breaths and focused on everything she could see and touch. Grounding herself in the present. Distancing her thoughts from the past. "Let's go home, boys. I think we'll go into town for an early breakfast to celebrate my birthday."

Sand sprayed behind the dogs as they ran ahead of her. She hurried to keep up with them and secured their leashes. They arrived at the yard, and there was still no sign of activity from the cottages. It was before seven, so she didn't expect anyone to be outside.

She hurried to the house and made sure her hair was presentable. She loaded the dogs in her car and drove through the quiet Sunday streets. Muffins and More had dog-friendly tables on their deck, and she chose one with a perfect view. As she cradled her warm chai tea latte, she noticed the gray clouds in the sky. "Could mean rain, boys."

They were busy chewing on their homemade dog treats and couldn't have cared less. She splurged on a hearty scramble breakfast, with yummy potatoes, and homemade toast with fresh marionberry jam.

The only thing missing was her husband.

Determined to focus on today, she shook off the melancholy thoughts and concentrated on the passersby. Driftwood was friendly and full of smiling faces. Folks greeted her and several stopped to admire the dogs.

Her waitress approached with a plate of sample bites of a fresh maple-walnut cinnamon roll, still warm. Resistance was pointless. It was her birthday after all. Accepting the giant sample, she savored the combination of tastes that reminded her of one of her favorite flavors of ice cream.

She paid the check and gathered the leashes. As they made their way down the sidewalk, the staff at the market was setting up their sidewalk display with buckets of fresh flowers. She stopped and sniffed several.

One of the young men working handed her a pink rose. "For you," he said.

"Well, thank you. That's very kind of you."

"Have a good day," he waved, as she continued to the car. She brought the blossom to her nose and inhaled.

Once they arrived at the house, she put the new rose in a skinny vase and hurried downstairs to check on the guests. Joe and Lisa were on their way to their car and waved.

Nora was standing in the doorway of her cottage, pleading with Bree to hurry. Lily walked by the path and said, "Good morning. Are you heading out?"

She rolled her eyes. "Trying to."

She walked around the end of the last cottage and heard voices. She made her way behind them and saw Alice and Kelly sitting on the patio, having coffee. "Hello there. How are you two this morning?"

"Wonderful. We were just admiring the beautiful view. We're going to head into town for breakfast," said Kelly. "Thought we'd take a quick tour of the town and check out some of the landmarks, maybe try the park."

"It looks like it might rain. There are some umbrellas in the cupboard if you need any." She gestured to the house. "I'll leave them out for you. I'm going to be at a friend's house this evening, so if you need anything, you have my cell phone number."

"We'll be fine. We're going to tackle more of that puzzle this evening," said Alice.

"I'm going to get started on my cleaning routine. Talk to you ladies later."

Lily was getting more efficient at her cottage chores. By the time she reached Kelly's, she and Alice had left for the day. After a quick freshening, she dumped a load of towels in the washer before hurrying upstairs to shower.

While she was finishing the laundry, Kevin called for a video chat. She carried the phone upstairs so she could show him the flowers. He caught her up on his work and the happenings in Richmond.

"I had my first progress meeting with my professor. He said I received glowing reviews from my supervisors. He told me how glad he was I took the internship and that he thinks it will help my career."

"That's terrific, Kevin. I'm so glad it's going well. You sound happy."

"I am. I miss you, but really like the work and the people. So, what are you doing for your birthday, Mom?"

"I took the dogs to breakfast this morning. It was huge, so I'm skipping lunch. Tonight, Cyndy invited me to her place for dinner. She and her brother, Mac, he's the vet I told you about, included me when they found out it was my birthday."

"Oh, that's great. She seems like a fun person."

"I spent the Fourth of July with them at the festival. It was a great day, and they had delicious root beer floats."

"A bunch of us went to the baseball game and watched the fireworks."

Her screen showed an incoming call from Donna Evans. "I should run, I've got a call coming in. Bodie and I start training Tuesday, so I'll have a report next weekend."

They said their goodbyes, and she hurried to answer the call, apologizing for the delay. Donna asked if it was a good time for her and Jeff to stop by for a few minutes.

"Perfect timing. All the guests are gone, and I'm free until later this afternoon."

"We're at the Bean and Leaf. What can we bring you?"

"Hmm. I love their peach iced tea, but you don't need to bring me anything."

"After you hear what we have to say, you might rethink that." Donna chuckled and added, "Consider it a bribe."

Chapter 19

Lily frowned, talking to the dogs, as she put together a plate of cookies and took it outside to the deck. "I wonder what they're up to?" Fritz and Bodie perked their ears up but offered no answers.

"She probably wants me to volunteer for a library project. I'm not sure I have time for that right now." Fritz's tail thumped against the decking.

The dogs rushed to the door at the sound of the doorbell. She herded them to the deck before answering it. Donna presented her with the tea, and she and Jeff stepped inside, each holding a cup from the Bean and Leaf.

"I've got some cookies out on the deck. Thought we could chat out there. We can close the roof panels if it starts to rain."

They followed her through the house, greeted the dogs with pets and scratches, and settled into chairs around the table. Lily took a sip of the tea and said, "Thanks for this. So, you've got me curious."

Donna looked at her husband, and he gestured for her to speak. "Well, it's about a young woman, Melanie, I met through the library. She's been hanging around there this summer. Pretty quiet and keeps to herself. Uses our computers and reads. It's taken me this long to break through her wall."

She took a sip of her coffee and reached for a cookie, nibbling a bite. "Anyway, she's had a tough time of it. She came here from Oak

Harbor. Her mom's sister used to live here, and she remembered visiting as a child."

"Her dad was in the military and died in a training operation in the Middle East when she was around fourteen. Her mom took it hard and struggled. A little over a year later, the mom committed suicide. Mel, she likes to be called that, got caught up in the system. She's almost nineteen now," Jeff clarified.

"Right, right. Sorry, I'm a little discombobulated," said Donna. "That's when her life took a downward spiral. Her mom had spent the death benefits she received, so no savings. Mel was left in a military house that her mom had to vacate."

"The military gives surviving spouses a year to move, and she didn't," added Jeff.

"What a horrible story. Where do I come in?" asked Lily.

Donna glanced at Jeff. "Here's the thing. Mel is really trying to make a go of it. She's been doing some volunteer work for me. She's bright and well read. I think books have been her escape since her dad died. She needs a mentor in her life, and a purpose. A job, something."

"I've checked into her story and background. She's never done anything criminal. She's staying in a shelter." He shook his head. "It's no place for a young woman."

"We've been trying to come up with ideas on how best to help her. She's proud, won't take handouts. I started bringing snacks and lunches to the library and told her all of the volunteers could help themselves, as a perk for volunteering. That's the only way she'll take something."

Jeff cleared his throat. "We know it's an enormous request. Our idea was to see if we could get you two together. She could work and do chores around here for room and board. That way she'd have a safe place to live and feel useful and productive."

"She could have some normalcy in her life and a chance at a real future," added Donna.

Lily's eyes widened. "Wow, that's heartbreaking. I sympathize, believe me. Let me think about it. This is all so new to me," she waved her hands across the deck. "I'm a bit nervous about taking on something else. I need this business to work."

Donna nodded as she chewed on the rest of her cookie. "You wouldn't be on your own. We're not trying to shove her off on you. Just hoping to find something that will work for her. If she could get some work experience and stability, I think she'd thrive. I'm talking to Driftwood Community College now and hoping we can find a scholarship for her."

"How about this? I meet her, and that will give us both a chance to see if it's a possibility. My main concern, at this point, is can I trust her around here?"

Jeff nodded. "I get it. I told Donna the same thing. I've stopped by the library and interacted with her… as much as she'll cooperate. She's quiet. She doesn't freak out when she sees a uniform or act guilty. She doesn't try to leave, just says very little."

"She's like that with everyone. She shelves books for me and does a few other background duties. She's too timid to work with the patrons," Donna further explained.

"If you decide to do this, I think the best way is to appeal to her, like she'd be helping you. She's averse to charity. I don't know her whole story, but I think she's kept herself alive with odd cash jobs here and there."

"I've got training with Bodie on Tuesday. That's the day the housekeepers come and do all the cleaning in the cottages, so it's my least busy day. I'll leave it up to you to figure out how to introduce us, but I can stop by the library after I run him home. Should be around noon."

Donna smiled and let out her breath. "That would be wonderful, Lily. Just wonderful."

Jeff eyed the cottages below. "You've got this place looking top-notch. You've met Nora, I assume?"

"Yes, she and her daughter, Bree. They're exploring the area today. I like her."

"We interview tomorrow, so it will be an exciting day."

Donna gathered her purse and said, "We don't want to keep you. We'll get out of your hair. Thanks again for being willing to meet Mel. I hope you two get along."

Lily led them into the kitchen and tossed their empty cups. "Oh, my, those are gorgeous flowers." Donna stuck her nose in the midst of the blooms.

"Thanks, they're from my son. For my birthday."

"When was your birthday?" she asked.

"Oh, it's today."

"Oh, my goodness. I'm so sorry we bothered you on your birthday," she said, with an embarrassed look.

"It's fine. I'm the one who said Sunday worked. It's just another day."

"Hope you do something fun and treat yourself," said Donna. She followed Jeff to the door.

Lily watched as they walked down the pathway. Jeff turned and said, "I almost forgot. We've got a shoot scheduled in two weeks. Did you get the email? You're welcome to tag along and get in some practice. Happy to pick you up early."

"I did get it. I've just been too busy to figure it out. Sounds good. I'll be in touch when I firm up my schedule here."

She watched them drive away, her brain in a fog. She sat back down in front of her peach tea, amazed that she could actually be considering adding another thing to the chaos in her life.

She turned to pet Bodie, snuggled next to Fritz on their cushion. "You were definitely a good idea. I'm not sure I can handle a wayward teenager with so many problems."

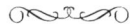

The threatening clouds of the morning let loose on Driftwood Bay in the mid-afternoon. The fresh scent of rain drifted inside through the open windows. Lily inhaled and smiled. She got the roof panels closed before the deck got soaked.

Kelly and Alice had returned to their cottage as Jeff and Donna were leaving the driveway. She was relieved to know they weren't out and about in this weather, with Alice so unsteady on her feet.

She collected two bottles of wine to take to Cyndy's and put a note on the door downstairs to let the guests know to call her cell phone, should they require assistance. She eyed the collection of puzzles. After selecting one, she grabbed an umbrella and hurried down the path to Kelly's cottage.

Kelly answered her knock and Lily said, "I figured with this rainstorm, your mom might not want to walk down to the house. I thought I'd deliver a puzzle to keep you two busy while you're stuck indoors."

Kelly motioned her inside and said, "Thank you. That's thoughtful. We were enjoying watching the rain from in here, but a puzzle sounds great. We have some leftovers for dinner, so I think we're set."

Alice waved and smiled from her seat in the living area. "I'm going out for a few hours, but you've got my cell number if you need anything."

Lily turned and wished them a pleasant evening before dashing back to the house with her umbrella. She shook it off and stashed it in Gary's truck, along with the wine.

After a quick change of clothes into one of her new outfits and a couple of adjustments to her hair, she loaded the dogs into the backseat of the truck. Cyndy's house, a gorgeous Victorian, was a few blocks off Bay Street. She saw Mac's car in the driveway and pulled in behind it.

Before she could decide to unload the dogs or check in with Cyndy first, Mac appeared from a gate behind the house. He was carrying an umbrella and approached the driver's door. "Hey, Lily. You can bring the dogs through back here. We've got a covered porch area where they can stay out of the rain."

He offered to take the leashes and gave her the umbrella. She gathered the wine and the folded umbrella she'd brought with her. She steadied the umbrella over both of them as they followed the hurried pace of the dogs.

Once they greeted Sherlock and chased each other a bit, they settled onto rugs on the porch. "We've got a nice summer storm going on," said Mac, eyeing the sky.

He stood the umbrellas at the back door and held it open. "Come on inside. They'll be fine out here. It's totally fenced. Sherlock spends time here, and we've never had a breach."

She smiled and went through the door. Cyndy was in the kitchen at the stove. A delicious aroma filled the house. "Oh, my, something smells out of this world," said Lily.

Cyndy turned and greeted her with a long hug. "So happy you're here. I decided with our drizzly day, a nice comforting meal of pork roast, mashed potatoes, and applesauce would hit the spot."

"It smells heavenly." She put the bottles of wine on the counter. "My contribution. Thanks so much for inviting me."

Cyndy waved her hand. "Of course. You need a celebration on your special day."

"Is there anything I can do to help?"

"Not a thing. Pour yourself a glass of wine and visit with Mac. There are some snacks set up in the other room."

Mac held a bottle of wine so she could see it. "Would you like some?"

"I think I'll pass for now. I might have a few sips with dinner."

"Iced tea?" He offered, retrieving a pitcher from the fridge.

She smiled and nodded. He grabbed a beer for himself and handed her a tall glass of tea with slices of orange floating in it. She took a sip as she followed him through the large kitchen. "Mmm, this is tasty."

"Cyndy gets all the compliments tonight. She's a wonderful cook and hostess." He offered her a chair in a sitting room. Lily admired the traditional furnishings she always associated with vintage homes, combined with more modern pieces.

"This is some house. It's like Cyndy's store on steroids," Lily said, taking another sip of tea.

"She's talented. My only skills are in medicine, not decorating. I've learned to cook a little, with Cyndy's help."

"I'm no cook. As a matter of fact, I'm no decorator. I guess my talent was in my career. Hopefully, being a good mom."

"I have no doubt." He set his bottle on a coaster. "You look nice today."

Her cheeks colored. "Thanks, I went on a shopping spree and thought I'd wear something besides a t-shirt and jeans in honor of the occasion."

"It's quite becoming," he raised his bottle in a toast. A tray of crab puffs sat on the table between them. He popped one in his mouth and offered her a napkin and one of her own.

She selected one and bit into it. "Delicious."

Footsteps sounded on the wooden floor, and Cyndy appeared, carrying a full glass of wine. "Whew, I'm ready for a break."

She sat on the velvet settee, bringing the glass to her lips and taking a long swallow. "So, what's new at Glass Beach Cottage?"

"I've got some lovely guests this week." She went on to give them a brief overview of the occupants. "I have to share what happened today. Jeff and Donna Evans asked if they could drop by and talk. I figured she wanted me to volunteer at the library."

The brother and sister nodded in agreement. "She's always hitting up folks for help," said Cyndy.

"Well, turns out, they want me to consider inviting a nineteen-year-old young woman to help at the cottages in exchange for room and board. She's had a tough life with her dad dying, and then her mom committed suicide when she was just fifteen. She's been scraping by, living in a shelter. Donna met her through the library. The girl, Mel, spends much of her day there, it sounds like."

"Wow," Cyndy's eyebrows rose. "That's quite a favor, don't you think?"

Mac nodded. "At least Jeff has the resources to check her out, make sure she's not a lunatic or criminal." He looked over at Lily, "She's not, right?"

She chuckled and said, "No, he's looked into her background. I told them I would meet her and see if I thought it would work. I'm just a bit reluctant."

"I can't criticize them for asking. Look what I did to you with Bodie?" Mac winked.

"True," she said, giving a nod. "This one requires a bit more thought."

"I don't think they'd ask you if they felt it was risky. They're both level-headed and community-minded," said Cyndy.

"I got that feeling. They also said they are going to be involved with Mel. Donna is trying to get her a scholarship to your community college. It sounds like the girl needs a stable routine. A purpose, I think Donna said."

"It's heartbreaking to think of a young woman living in a shelter. If you end up involved and there is anything I can do, let me know. She could volunteer at the clinic if she likes animals," said Mac.

"Funny you should mention that. I sort of already volunteered you for another project." She explained about Nora and her possible job in Driftwood Bay. "Her daughter, Bree, wants a dog, and Nora can't deal with one more thing at the moment. I told Bree I knew you and might be able to get her involved with helping with the dogs. She needs to learn how much work is involved."

"She might get her fix without having to have a dog of her own," said Cyndy.

"Exactly. Not sure Nora will get the job, but she seems capable to me. So, you may end up having a young woman ask you if she can volunteer to walk the dogs."

"That's easy. I can handle that. I like to have animal lovers stay with the dogs when they're undergoing surgery and coming out of surgery. They do better if someone is there touching and talking to them."

Lily nodded. "Makes sense. It's easier when you have a friend by your side."

The conversation turned to the house. Cyndy offered Lily a tour and asked Mac to keep an eye on dinner. He took his beer and disappeared to check on the dogs and make sure nothing burned.

Cyndy led Lily up the beautiful staircase and showed her the many bedrooms. Each had a color theme and incorporated hues of the primary color in all the furnishings and décor. Cyndy's bedroom was done in shades of white and cream with a few accents in soft greens.

"It looks so relaxing and inviting. I love it," said Lily, admiring the charming accent pieces.

The bedroom was huge, and Cyndy explained she had taken

three rooms to make her private sanctuary, which included an alcove that served as her office, along with a separate reading nook and a small library.

The bathrooms, like the front entrance surrounding the staircase, used the traditional black and white tile popular in Victorian homes. They made their way downstairs, and she showed her the other rooms, all done in rich colors, incorporating the traditional wood and velvet with more contemporary pieces. One of them reminded Lily of a peacock with the deep jewel tones Cyndy had used. The mix of old and new worked well and gave it a more casual feel than other Victorians Lily had seen.

"I envy your talents. It's just a stunning home."

Cyndy shrugged and smiled. "It's just what I love to do. I'm fortunate to live here. It's my happy place."

They wandered through to the kitchen, which Lily took the time to notice. A massive granite topped island dominated the space. All the cabinets were white, save for the cabinets under the island. They were a gorgeous color somewhere between lilac and lavender. White was the dominant color everywhere, with the exception of a bit of subtle green. Stainless appliances and beautiful wooden floors rounded out the space.

Cyndy lifted the lids of the pans on the stovetop and opened a wall oven to check progress. "We're almost ready. I'm sure Mac is out on the porch. Go on and join him. I'll call you when I've got things ready to serve."

Lily made her way through the back door and found Mac on the wicker couch, petting the dogs and talking to them. When they saw her, they ditched him and ran to greet her.

She led them over to the seating area and chose the rocking chair. "This is some house. I love it."

"It suits Cyndy. I'm not much on all the smaller rooms in these old houses. They're neat and all, but I like more modern living spaces. When you visit my house, you'll see what I mean. At first, we tried living out at the old farmhouse with the clinic, but it became a hassle. I could never get away from work. Within five years we moved into a different place in town."

He took the last swallow from his beer. "After Jill died, I bought a new place. Trying to escape the memories. I still live there and love the house."

"I can relate to running from memories. I ran about three thousand miles."

Cyndy's voice carried from the kitchen. "Dinner's ready you two."

"I fed the dogs, so no need to worry about them. They can rest out here, and then we'll give them a walk when we're done. Hopefully, the rain lets up a bit," said Mac, holding the door open for Lily.

They ate in Cyndy's elegant dining room. Lily raved about the meal. "I haven't had something this delicious in years."

"You've outdone yourself, Cyn. Terrific biscuits," said Mac, as he added butter to another one.

"It's my pleasure. I enjoy cooking."

After the meal, Lily tried to help with the dishes, but Cyndy insisted she go outside and enjoy the porch. "I'm just going to do a few things, and I'll be out to join you."

The rain had diminished and was down to a soft sprinkle. Mac handed her the umbrella and said, "You're in charge of this, and I'll handle the herd."

She laughed and helped him get leashes on the three friends. She steadied the umbrella over both of them as they went through the gate and down the sidewalk. Lily took a deep breath, savoring the fresh, clean smell in the air.

"Beautiful night," he said, adjusting the pace of the dogs to slow them.

"I love it after it rains. Everything looks new again. It's like a fresh start."

"We don't get many summer showers. We're in the rain shadow here, only getting about half as much rain as Seattle."

"Well, I'll think of it as a birthday treat then."

They walked several blocks, admiring houses and yards, chatting like old friends. When they returned, Mac toweled the dogs dry, and they settled on the rugs on the porch, tired from the exercise.

They found Cyndy in the kitchen in front of a beautiful cake adorned with strawberries. She lit the sparkler on top of it. Tears filled Lily's eyes as she listened to them sing "Happy Birthday" to her. Cyndy presented her with a beautiful silver chain and a sea glass pendant wrapped in silver wire. It was cornflower blue. Lily held it to her heart. "You don't know what this means to me, Cyndy. I had a similar pendant that my aunt made for me but lost it years ago."

Mac's gift bag contained a heavy silver frame with golden retrievers and the word "WOOF" engraved in it. He offered to hook her new chain around her neck. "There you go," he said, securing the clasp.

She stayed much longer than she had planned, but couldn't tear herself away from the conversation and companionship. She yawned for the third time and said, "I've got to get going. I can't tell you what tonight has meant to me. It's been lovely."

Cyndy hugged her and retrieved a box of leftovers for her. Mac carried her gifts, along with Cyndy's care package, to the truck. The rain had stopped, leaving wet streets and a few puddles. She dodged the wet patches and got the dogs in their seat.

Mac helped her secure them in the back. "Glad you joined us tonight. I hope your first birthday in Driftwood Bay was a happy one."

She slipped into the driver's seat. She looked into his gentle eyes and smiled. "It really was. Thanks to you and Cyndy."

He shut the door and waved as she backed out of the driveway. On the way home, she looked in the mirror, seeing Fritz looking back at her. "We had a great day, didn't we, Fritzie?"

What had started as a birthday she dreaded had been transformed into a fun day filled with new memories and new friends.

Chapter 20

All traces of rain had disappeared by Monday's sunrise. Lily spent the morning visiting with her guests, wishing Nora good luck on her interview, and getting her chores done. She had finished lunch on the deck and was playing with the dogs when the doorbell rang.

She found Wade when she opened the door and waved to Andy, who was standing next to their work truck. "Hey, Lily. Andy has something for you. Want to come and check it out?" He motioned her to follow him.

Andy's smile filled his face. "Miss Lily, I wanted to build Fritz and Bodie a nice dog house. We just got it finished yesterday." He removed a tarp, and Lily gasped with surprise.

A miniature cottage stood before her. It looked identical to the original guesthouses. "It's wonderful, Andy! I love it and so will the boys."

Wade positioned the truck as close to the gate as possible. He and Andy hoisted the posh dog house across the yard and to the dogs' enclosure. Lily watched as they positioned it. "Oh, it even has a cute little porch."

Andy beamed with pride as she complimented all the details he had incorporated into the design. "Let's see what the dogs think," said Lily, as she hurried upstairs.

Fritz and Bodie greeted Wade and Andy with lots of tail wagging. They sniffed out their new addition and wandered inside. It was roomy enough for both of them, with room to spare for Bodie's growth. Trimmed in white to match the main house and covered in the same siding as the cottages.

"It will protect them from bad weather if they have to be outside. I was thinking of them yesterday with all the rain," said Andy.

Lily signed her thanks and how much she loved the dog house. Andy sat on the grass near the new house, and the dogs crawled all over him, happy to see their friend. He laughed as the dogs licked him and vied for his attention.

Wade smiled as he watched his son. "You know, we never considered a dog for him. We really should have. I sure hope this works out with Bodie. He's already brought Andy so much joy."

"Andy deserves it. He's a wonderful young man."

"Hi Lily," said Bree, who was on the path to the house. "What's going on?"

She motioned the young woman over to them. "Andy and Wade just delivered a surprise for the boys."

"Wow, that's so cute," said Bree.

Lily introduced her to Wade and Andy, signing to him, so Bree would know he couldn't hear. "We've got to get a move on. Come on Andy," Wade said.

Andy scratched both of the dogs' backs before he stood. "See you later, Lily. Nice to meet you, Bree."

Lily walked them around front to their truck. "I can't thank you enough for the kind gift. I really do love it."

Andy hugged her and said, "It was fun. We put it together while we were building the golf course. Just used some leftovers from your project. I'm glad you like it."

They waved as they drove down the street. Lily started to turn when she saw Nora's car pull in on the other side of the house. She waited and hollered, "We're out back."

Lily found Bree in the enclosure with the dogs. "Your mom's here."

"Good, I'm starving."

Nora's heels clicked on the sidewalk as she approached them with an enormous smile. "Sorry I'm so late. They included a tour after the interview."

"Can we go get something to eat?" asked Bree, in a whiny voice.

"Just let me change my clothes."

"How do you think it went?" asked Lily.

Nora's eyes sparkled. "I feel really good about it. The interview board seemed nice. I saw them nod several times after I answered, which I take as a good sign. Chief Evans comes across as professional, but down-to-earth."

"Mooooom," Bree grumbled as she extended the word.

Nora nodded and hurried toward the cottage. "I'll be right back."

Lily resisted the urge she had to tell Bree to back off and give her mom a touch of support. It was none of her business. Instead, she tried to distract her. "Do you want to take the boys on a quick walk around the yard while you wait for your mom?"

"Sure," she said, taking the leashes from Lily and attaching them. Lily watched her talking to them as she guided them around the perimeter. They were on the other side of the yard when Nora emerged dressed in jeans and a t-shirt.

She met Lily at the back door and said, "Sorry again for being late and for you having to put up with Bree complaining."

"She just came out of the cottage right before you got here. It's no problem."

The dogs ran to Lily, making Bree hurry after them. She arrived, smiling and laughing. Nora turned to face Lily and whispered, "Maybe we do need a dog."

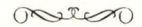

As soon as the maids arrived on Tuesday, Lily left with Bodie. Fritz looked sad and confused as she told him to stay upstairs. "We'll be right back, Fritzie. It's okay."

They arrived at the training facility, situated on a large parcel of land about ten miles from town. She knew from reading about the facility that they had all types of classes for dogs, not only service animals.

Bodie's nose was in overdrive as she led him to the main building and followed the signs to his class. She was greeted by a cheerful man named Matt, who bent and chatted with Bodie while he petted him.

He reviewed the paperwork Mac had provided relative to Bodie's health and vaccination records, along with his acceptance into the hearing dog training program. "Looks like we're all set. Martha, the trainer, will be with you shortly."

Lily had time to peruse their brochures on different training classes and their agility program while she waited. A middle-aged woman, dressed in khaki shorts with pockets all over them, a t-shirt, and a matching vest with even more pockets, approached Lily.

"You must be Lily. Mac told me you were kind enough to foster at the last minute. I'm so happy to meet you and Bodie," she said, shaking Lily's hand. She went on to explain that she would be assessing Bodie and then working with Lily each week on skills and training games. Bodie would also practice socializing with other dogs at the center when he came for training each week.

Martha let Bodie off his leash and encouraged him to run around the open space. Toys were scattered around the room, and Bodie hurried to get a ball. Martha called him, and he responded to his name. She gave him the command to come, and he looked at her but kept searching for toys.

She continued to administer her pop quiz to gauge the areas she needed to focus on for training purposes. He didn't jump on her, and sat when he was told, but had no idea what *wait* meant. When she used the down command, he got it right two out of three times.

She grabbed a few toys and played with him and praised him for his performance. Her pockets held treats and toys, and she used them whenever Bodie did something right and said "Good boy, Bodie," dozens of times.

She attached his leash and led him around the room, nodding as she told Lily, "He's a good walker, not much tugging."

After a few more commands and a couple of treats, Martha returned the leash to Lily. "So, you saw where he excelled and where he needs a bit more work. This week, concentrate on the essential puppy commands. He needs to respond to his name, always. Learning *sit*, *down*, and *wait* are the ones we want to master at this stage. Give him treats when he does well and ignore it when he messes up."

She continued to explain that she wanted Lily to expose him to new places. "Once he masters the commands at home, take him to the park or around the neighborhood, where he'll have more distractions and work on them there."

Martha continued to explain about the group training and interaction. Bodie would be playing with other puppies in the program each week and doing some one-on-one with Martha as she sees fit. "We'll increase the complexity of the commands and what we ask the pups to do each week."

Lily explained that he had a big brother in Fritz at home and that he's exposed to a variety of people who are guests at the cottages. Martha nodded, "That's excellent. We like to make sure the dogs stay calm and aren't afraid of new situations. Take him for rides, expose him to noises while you are with him, so he learns new things aren't so scary."

Lily thanked Martha and loaded Bodie into the truck. As she

made the trip home, she glanced in the mirror at his sweet face, with his cute pink tongue protruding from his mouth. "You were such a good dog at class. You are so smart."

Once home, they rescued Fritz from solitary confinement, and the two took off running around the yard. She let them burn off some energy while she grabbed a snack. Questions tumbled through her mind as she got ready to go to the library. Was she nuts to think she could take on a wayward teenager?

She promised the dogs she'd be home soon, and made sure they had fresh water and some toys stashed inside their new house, before leaving for her chance encounter with Mel.

The original building, built in the 1910's, stood several blocks off the main street of Driftwood Bay. The white building with a red tile roof had the hallmark symmetry of a Carnegie library. The beautiful building was a testament to the Renaissance Revival style, popular at the time it was built. A large, more modern addition was tucked in behind it.

Lily climbed the steps to the entrance and looked around the space, hoping to see Donna. She walked past the shelves of books and the comfy reading spaces scattered around the main floor. She followed the signs for the offices and spotted Donna's name on a plate outside a door.

Donna's face brightened from behind her desk piled with papers and books. "Lily, so glad you came. I wasn't sure whether we'd scared you off."

"No, no. I committed to coming and meeting Mel. No guarantees at this point."

"I understand. I'm going to say you're thinking about volunteering at the library and I wanted to pair you with Mel, so she could tell you about her experience and what she enjoys." Donna led her away from the office and back to the main building.

"She's working on putting away some books." They found Mel in the stacks. Donna led the way. "Mel, this is Lily, the woman I told you about that is thinking about volunteering."

The young woman, with long dark brown hair, turned. Her expression didn't change. "Okay," she said, adding nothing more.

Lily approached her and extended her hand. "Nice to meet you, Mel."

Mel looked at her for several moments and then offered a weak handshake. "These are books I picked up from the bins. All the books get checked in on a conveyor belt. I'll show you."

Lily nodded, taking in the girl's uneven hair, fuzzy with split ends. She was all business. No chit chat. The first word that came to Lily's mind was *harsh*. Mel had hardened eyes, much older than her nineteen years. A face devoid of emotion. Blank.

Mel was slim, so much so that the bones of her spine were evident through her thin shirt. Her shoes had seen better days. Lily's heart ached for the girl.

"Do you enjoy volunteering here?" asked Lily.

Mel nodded. "I like books and the quiet. Miss Donna is nice and so are the others. I like helping out."

"What's your favorite book?"

A glimmer of light shone in her eyes. "Oh, wow. I read so much, it's hard to say." She rattled off several titles unfamiliar to Lily, and a few classics she recognized. "I like mysteries and Jane Austen type books. I'm reading a new one Donna recommended now."

She showed Lily the spine of the book she was shelving. "Do you know how the system works?"

Lily thought back to her mother's life's work and her explaining the Dewey Decimal System. "It's been several years, but I know fiction is categorized by the author's last name and non-fiction uses the decimal system."

Mel nodded her approval, a hint of surprise on her face. "That's right. Just make sure you put the books back on the shelf in the right order."

"I like to separate the fiction and non-fiction and do one section at a time," said the young woman. Lily helped her finish the cart full of books and asked her a few questions when they reached the non-fiction stacks. She could tell it made Mel feel valuable to share her knowledge.

Lily moved her purse with her as they walked among the shelves. "You'll want to lock your purse up in Donna's office if you volunteer." She lowered her voice, "Sometimes there are some undesirables that hang out in here. Some of them would steal from you in a heartbeat."

"Smart advice. Thanks for the tip."

Other than talking about books and her duties, Mel didn't offer much conversation. As they worked, Lily said, "I'm new to Driftwood Bay. Just moved here in May. My dog, Fritz, and I that is. Have you lived here long?"

"No, just a few months."

"I like it here. The people are nice. Beautiful weather and location."

"I haven't been many places, except for the library."

"My son came to visit last month, so we toured around the area and went to the Olympic National Park. It's quite stunning."

"Oh, yeah, Donna gave me a book about it. I loved the rainforest photos."

"Could I treat you to a snack at the café next door? I'm getting hungry and would like to thank you for sharing about the library."

"Oh, I don't know. I need to finish another cart of books."

"I'll help you. We can do it together, and then I insist," Lily said with a smile.

A tiny movement in Mel's lips hinted at the beginning of a smile. "I guess that would be okay."

Lily took the fiction books and separated them by last name to make her job in the stacks quicker. Mel took the smaller cart of nonfiction. Lily finished and sent Donna a quick text to tell her she was taking Mel to the café.

The two met up at the doorway leading behind the circulation desk, each wheeling an empty cart. "Only staff and volunteers are allowed back here," said Mel, giving the door a push.

She showed Lily the check-in system. Patrons or librarians could place books or other materials on a belt, and a computer would read the electronic chip in the book and check in the item. Then the belt would dump them all into a bin at the end.

"Volunteers need to check the bin several times a day and then put the items on a cart to shelve." With admiration in her voice, Mel said, "You were smart to separate your books by last name. Most of the volunteers spend all their time running their carts back and forth."

"Just being efficient," said Lily. "Shall we head to the café?" Lily led the way out the side door, and they walked down the street to a cute book themed café. They had a small selection of baked treats and a limited variety of sandwiches, along with soups and salads.

Lily wasn't hungry but felt the overwhelming need to feed the skinny young woman. They looked over the menu and Lily said, "What sounds good to you?"

"Anything, really. I'm not picky."

"Sandwich with soup or salad, and something sweet? You order whatever you'd like. Will you drink tea, I'll get a pot?"

"Sure, I like tea." Mel studied the chalkboard menu but didn't voice her order. She looked at Lily and said, "You choose. It doesn't matter to me."

Lily asked the woman at the register if they could get a pot of Earl Grey and two of the blackberry scones to start. "We'll decide on our sandwiches while we wait for the tea. Will that work?"

The cheerful waitress nodded and promised to bring it to their table. Mel chose a corner spot, and Lily took a seat with her back to the wall. "So, what sounds better, turkey, roast beef, egg salad?"

"I'll eat anything."

Lily gave up and ordered a turkey and egg salad, plus a soup and a salad. She would see which one Lily gravitated to when they arrived. Mel watched Lily pour her tea and add a pinch of sugar and a bit of cream.

She did the same with her cup. She took a sip and said, "Mmm, this is good. I wasn't sure what Earl Grey was. I've read it in books, but never had it. I just have plain old tea."

"It's nice to change things up once in a while," said Lily.

"How old is your son?"

Lily explained Kevin was in college in Virginia and had planned to visit over the entire summer, but he got a fantastic internship and had to leave early.

"Where's your husband?"

Lily inhaled and said, "He was killed last year. He was a police officer, as was I. I retired in May and moved out here when I inherited my uncle's house and the cottages he and my aunt rented out to guests. It's nice, right above the beach."

"So, you moved all the way out here and run it by yourself?"

The waitress arrived and placed their lunch in the middle of the table. Plates covered the entire surface. Lily noticed Mel eyeballing the delicious array of food.

Lily moved to the sandwiches and said, "How about we have half of each?" The soup was a hearty potato and cheese. She moved that closer to Mel. "How about the soup? I'll take the salad."

Mel dug into the soup and ate with gusto. "This is good."

"Back to my new business. Yes, I run it. I have help with some things, but I'm the only one there on a daily basis."

"Did they find who killed your husband?"

Lily swallowed hard and nodded. "Yes, thank goodness." The waitress came to check on them, and Lily asked for a carryout container.

She put her half of the turkey sandwich in it and most of her salad. She nibbled her scone and drank her tea while Mel finished her lunch. "Did you work with your husband?" asked the young woman, sliding her empty plate to the side.

"No, not in the same department. My work was with the Virginia Division of Capitol Police. I worked to protect the Capitol Building, governor, and the grounds around those areas."

"That would be an interesting job. I like learning about the history of the capitols. They are all so unique and full of interesting features. There's a great book on them at the library. I like working there for the same reason. It's a cool building."

Lily agreed and finished her cup while Mel ate her scone. Lily paid the check and gave Mel the container of leftovers. "You go ahead and take this home. I've got enough leftovers for dinner already."

Mel hesitated, like a wary rabbit sensing a trap. "Are you sure?"

"Positive. Have it for your dinner."

"Thank you," said Mel, gathering the box, while Lily stood and retrieved her purse.

"I appreciate you telling me more about your volunteer work. If I can find the time, I'd like to help. I volunteered to foster a puppy for the hearing dog program, so he keeps me busy."

"Wow, you have two dogs?"

Ah, a topic that evokes emotion. "Yes, they're a lot of fun, and a lot of work, but I love them." As they walked back in the direction of the library, she added, "Maybe someday you can come and visit them. I could show you the beach."

She shrugged. "Maybe. I keep pretty busy at the library."

Lily left the young woman at the door and said, "Nice meeting you, Mel. See you later."

The girl lifted a hand in a wave before disappearing inside the building.

Chapter 21

When Lily arrived home, she freed the dogs. She spent some time working with Bodie on commands. Fritz watched the action from his spot on the grass. The puppy sat when told and repeated it dozens of times. He was also responding to the down command.

In the midst of training, Kelly and Alice returned to their cottage. Lily put Bodie's leash on so he wouldn't startle Alice. "Hello there. Are you two enjoying your day?"

"Yes, dear. It's been lovely."

Kelly added, "Time for our afternoon break and maybe a nap." She steadied her mother as they entered the cottage.

Lily herded the dogs upstairs to the deck. She texted Kevin a note and asked him to call her when he got off work. She wanted to discuss Mel.

Nora and Bree came through the yard while Lily was contemplating the young girl she met today. They waved as they passed in front of the deck. Bree said, "Can I play with the dogs?"

"Sure, they'd love it. We'll be right down."

She and Nora sat in chairs along the house and watched Bree run and play with her furry pals. "When will you know about the job?" asked Lily.

"Should hear something tomorrow." She crossed her fingers. "It's driving me batty waiting."

"I had an interesting day today." She explained about Mel and Jeff and Donna's idea. "She's a complicated young girl. Part of me wants to help her. The mom part of me. The other part of me is ringing warning bells. I don't think she would be easy."

"She's a teenager. Who said anything about easy?" Nora waved her hand toward Bree. "She can be such a beast."

"I worry most about the impact on the business. Guests aren't going to tolerate much. I want them to have a good experience so I can build my business."

"I understand the concern. It's a tough choice. Maybe a trial period is a good idea?"

"I was thinking along the same lines. She'd have to stay in one of the bedrooms down here. That's probably a good thing. She'll feel more independent."

Lily pondered. "I keep thinking if that was my daughter, I'd want someone to give her a chance. I can't imagine her life in the shelter. I'm sure that's why she spends all her time at the library."

"You might find you enjoy the company. As much as Bree tests my patience, she can also be a true joy. Sometimes she even acts like she likes me." Nora gave Lily a wry smile.

"Kevin was easy. I think boys are a bit easier for moms than daughters."

"It's more complicated with the divorce. She blames me or maybe resents me. That's part of this whole moving drama. I think she thinks her dad will eventually return to us, and if we move, the possibility will diminish."

"Speaking of moving here, I did talk to my vet friend, and he's willing to have Bree volunteer."

Nora's eyes brightened. "That's terrific. She would really enjoy that."

"Did you have any luck finding a house?"

"I was thinking about renting at first, but there isn't much available, and the prices are ridiculous. I found one small house. I wanted to find something close to town in a safe neighborhood, so I wouldn't worry about Bree when I'm working."

"I don't know much about the real estate market here."

"It's tough to find something affordable. This house is smaller than I wanted but in the right area and in my price range. It'll be a good starter for us. Just two bedrooms, but two bathrooms. It's only about three years old, so like new."

Lily nodded. "Did Bree like it?"

Nora shrugged. "Hard to tell. She's negative about the whole idea." Bree walked toward them with the dogs following her.

She plopped into a chair and sighed. "I'm tired now." Her phone chimed from her pocket. She dug it out, excitement filling her face. She hurried away to answer it.

"She's addicted to that phone."

"I don't think she's alone," said Lily, pointing to hers. "It seems like we rely on them for everything now."

Nora stood and said, "I'm going to wait for her in the cottage. I'll keep you posted on the job."

After checking the downstairs and making sure a plate of cookies was set out for the guests, Lily herded the dogs upstairs. While she was considering what to have for dinner, her cell phone rang. Mac's name appeared.

"Hey, Lily. Just checking to see how our new student did on his first day of school."

She chatted with him and gave him the details on Bodie's performance. "I'm struggling with the wait command."

He chuckled and said, "Puppies aren't known for their waiting skills. Why don't you bring him over to my house one night this week? We can work on it together, and I'll make dinner."

"That sounds great. I could use some pointers."

They agreed on Thursday, and then he asked about her meeting with Mel at the library.

She gave him the highlights. "I'm sure Donna will be calling to see what I think. I'm torn. I think I would feel worse if I didn't try than if I give it a go and it doesn't work."

"I tend to agree. Sounds like she could use a good influence and some stability."

"I'm going to run it by Kevin and see how he feels before I decide."

"Smart idea. One I wouldn't have considered. Probably why my relationship with Missy isn't the best."

"I was just visiting with Nora. We decided daughters are harder."

"I'll agree with that one. I shouldn't say that. It really wasn't Missy's fault. I'm the one who's to blame."

"All we can do is our best. You're probably too hard on yourself. It's difficult to watch our kids suffer, especially when we're grieving ourselves."

"I try not to spend too much time thinking. It doesn't end well when I reflect. I do better when I'm busy."

"I've been there." Lily saw the dogs looking at their bowls and remembered she hadn't fed them. "I better get going. The dogs are giving me their pleading look. They're hungry."

"See you Thursday," said Mac.

She disconnected and went about measuring out the food. Her thoughts drifted to Mac. "He's such a nice guy. I feel like I've known him forever," she mumbled as she placed the bowls in front of her hungry boys. "It's nice to have someone to talk to. Someone who understands all too well."

Lily waved to Joe and Lisa as they were leaving for dinner. They were the most active of her guests and spent most of their time away from the cottage. She checked on her email and saw a cancellation for the weekend. She frowned and then saw the couple had a family emergency.

Kevin had encouraged her to have a strict no refund policy during the high season. She knew he was right, but she felt for the couple. They had intended to stay three nights. She replied to their email and let them know if she was able to rebook the cottage with another guest, she wouldn't charge them the whole fee, only the nights she wasn't able to book.

She cringed and hit the button. It seemed harsh, but she was full almost every night, and booked on weekends. She hoped a last-minute traveler would book it and save the couple some money. She collected the mail and found a letter from the Pentagon Memorial. She had attended the annual ceremony each year since her mother's death.

This September, it would mean a flight and a lot more time. When Kevin helped her set up the calendar software for reservations, he had blocked out the time around September 11th so she would be free to travel. She knew she had to go. For her mom. For Kevin. She searched online for available times. She booked a flight and hotel that would allow her to spend the weekend with Kevin, attend the ceremony, and fly out the following day.

After she caught up on the computer, she scrambled some eggs for dinner. Mel's situation dominated her thoughts as she tried to watch television while waiting for Kevin to call. She kept dozing off, exhausted from the mental gymnastics of the day.

Close to nine, her phone sounded. She smiled and said, "Hey, Kev. Thanks for calling." She shared the highlights of her dilemma with him. They discussed the pros and cons of having Mel at the house.

"If you're sure she's not a con artist or someone that will steal, I think it's worth a try. I can't imagine losing both my parents and having nothing. Nowhere to go. It would be awful."

Her heart warmed listening to the kindness in his voice. He had always been a compassionate child. "I think you're right. I'll sleep on it and call Donna tomorrow. We'll have to see if Mel is willing to try it."

"I booked my flights for Grandma's memorial." She gave him the itinerary, and he promised to pick her up at the airport.

"It will be good to see you. We'll do something fun that weekend," said Kevin, before he wished her goodnight.

She ran her fingers across the invitation to the memorial, lingering over the embossed seal. Memories flooded her mind. Losing her mother had been devastating. Then her dad so soon after. Now Gary was gone. It was so easy to slip into despair.

She imagined feeling all that as a teenager and made up her mind that she'd invite Mel to stay. She knew what being alone could do to a person.

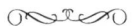

Wednesday morning while she was doing her cottage chores, Donna called. She wanted to know what Lily thought after meeting Mel.

"I've mulled it around and would like to give a try. I need you to understand that if it doesn't work, or having her around impacts my business in a negative way, you'll have to find a different solution."

Donna's voice was full of gratitude. She promised to talk to Mel and present the opportunity as a way to help Lily, hoping Mel wouldn't sniff out the underlying charity.

"One other problem. I'm going to be out of town in September for a few days. I won't have any guests and would prefer she not be here all alone. So, we'll need to think of something creative for that period."

"Got it. I'll work on a solution for that. If I can get her in school, that will be around the time it starts." She planned to talk to Mel today and would let Lily know as soon as she had an answer.

Lily was carting the dirty towels to the house when Nora and Bree came around the corner. Nora was beaming with excitement. Bree looked furious. Lily could guess the news.

"I got the job," she said. "Chief Evans just called me."

"Congratulations. That's terrific news." Lily looked at Bree's pouty face. "Did your mom tell you I talked to my friend the vet and he said he'd be glad to have you volunteer at his clinic?"

Lily saw the flash in her eye. Bree almost smiled but caught herself. "Oh, joy," she said, her voice laden with sarcasm.

"Brianna Marie," said Nora, in a voice Lily was sure she reserved for suspects who were less than cooperative. "That is no way to talk to Lily. She's been nothing but kind to you. You've communicated your disapproval at every opportunity. I've got it. Lily doesn't need your attitude."

Bree's eyes widened in shock.

Good for Nora. Bree needs a wakeup call. Lily picked up the basket of towels to continue to the washer.

"I'm sorry, Lily. I shouldn't have been so rude. Thank you for talking to your friend." She turned and gave her mother a nasty look, with a head tilt mastered only by teenaged girls, and stomped to the cottage.

"I pray for patience each day," said Nora. "I'm not going to let her spoil my happiness. I hate to ask, as it probably won't work, but is there any way we could extend our stay through Saturday?"

"As luck would have it, I just had a cancellation for the weekend, so yes, it will work. I'll run in and book it right now."

She popped the towels in and hurried upstairs to change the reservation system, happy the couple would only pay a one-night penalty, at most. She joined Nora downstairs in a celebratory glass of iced tea and a cookie, the dogs at their feet.

"I talked to the realtor and am signing an offer on the house. He thinks he can have an answer back by Saturday."

"When do you start here?"

"Chief Evans was flexible. He told me to coordinate what I needed to do back home and with Bree. The sooner, the better, for him, but he's giving me a bit of leeway to get settled. I'll need to get Bree enrolled in school, and I'd like to be in the house before starting."

"You should go by the library and talk to his wife, Donna. She might be able to give you more ideas for Bree."

Nora smiled. "Chief Evans made the same suggestion. There's only one high school, so that makes it simple. I just hope Bree can meet some nice kids and has an easy adjustment."

"She just needs to find something she's interested in and enjoys. She seems to like the beach and dogs, so there's something. I'm sure she'll adjust. Kids are resilient."

Nora nodded. "She just has to punish me first." She hung her head. "I better go check on her and see if we can do something she would enjoy while we're here." Lily watched the woman as she made her way across the yard, shoulders slumped, dread conveyed with every slow step she took.

Lily's heart ached for the woman. She should be celebrating and basking in the joy of a new job and a new life, not fearing the wrath of a sullen teenager. "Furkids are easier, right boys?" Fritz and Bodie raised their heads and thumped their tails against the patio.

Thursday morning, Donna called and asked if she and Mel could stop by the house. "How about you two come for lunch. We can sit outside on the deck."

Donna asked if she could bring anything, and Lily suggested dessert since she was close to several good bakeries downtown. Lily hurried to the market as soon as she finished the cottages. She gathered the ingredients for her chicken salad, some fresh bread, tortillas, fruit, and chips and salsa. Paper-wrapped bouquets of flowers stood in buckets by the door. She added one to her basket of provisions.

Once home, she put together the chicken salad and stuck it in the fridge. One of her aunt's pretty glass bowls made the perfect container for the fresh fruit she had chopped. The store-bought salsa looked much better in her aunt's glass seashell bowls. The chips went in a huge wooden bowl. She gathered place settings and made sure the table was set.

Bodie and Fritz sat on their ottoman watching her frenzied movements as she rushed to get everything ready. She remembered the flowers, trimmed them, and stuck them in a vase, which she added to the table. Iced tea was already made. She looked at the clock. "Five minutes to spare," she said, nibbling an errant chip.

She left the dogs on the deck and went outside to greet her guests when they arrived. Minutes later, Donna's car pulled in the driveway. Lily waved, hoping to disguise how jumpy she felt.

Donna smiled as she came around the car. Mel got out, remaining expressionless, her eyes darting around the yard and house. She wore the same pants she had worn when Lily met her at the library, paired with the same type of shirt, in a different color. "Welcome, come on inside. I've got lunch ready."

Lily waited for Mel and said, "Glad you could come. How are you today?"

"Okay, I guess. Your house is huge," said the young woman, as she stepped inside.

"It belonged to my aunt and uncle. He died several months ago and left it to me in his will. I'm sure Donna explained there are three guest cottages in back."

Mel nodded, taking in every inch of the living area as Donna led the way through the kitchen. Both dogs bolted from the ottoman and rushed to greet the newcomers.

Lily watched, intent on gauging Mel's reaction to the dogs. She was timid and tensed as they wiggled against her legs. "They're friendly. You can just reach down and pet them. They'll calm down," said Lily.

Lily moved closer and put a hand on Fritz's head. "See, he's a sweetie. This is Fritz." She used her hand movement and said, "Sit, Bodie, sit." The dog obeyed and sat next to Fritz, his tail moving at warp speed.

Lily urged Mel's hand to the dog, and when she petted Fritz's head, Lily detected an actual smile on her face. She bent closer to reach Bodie, and he licked her several times. "Oh, oh," she said, looking at her hand.

"It's okay. Sort of his way of kissing your cheek," said Lily. "You can wash your hands before we eat. There's soap right by the kitchen sink, and paper towels."

Mel turned and went inside. Lily got the dogs back on the ottoman and sat in the chair closest to them. She gave Donna an inquiring look across the table.

She shrugged. "She hasn't said yes, but she hasn't said no."

Mel returned and took the chair next to Donna. "I'm not known for my cooking skills," said Lily. "Just simple chicken salad. You can make a wrap or a sandwich," she passed Mel the bowl and pointed to the bread and tortillas.

They passed food and Donna said, "So, Lily, I told Mel you had been looking for someone who could help out around here in exchange for room and board."

"Yes, what do you think of that idea, Mel?"

She took a bite of her sandwich and moved her shoulders toward her ears. "Well, when we're done I'll give you a tour, and you can ask some questions."

Lily chattered on about training Bodie and how much time that was going to take, explaining he'd already been to his first class. Donna steered the conversation to the library and books.

Mel's interest piqued, and she talked about a new book she just checked out at the library. Lily remembered she liked Jane Austen. "Have you ever watched *Downton Abbey* on television?"

"No, I've seen it at the library. The shel—uh, where I live, we don't have access to a DVD player.

"I've got the whole series. If you decide to try out this arrangement, we could watch it. I've also got quite a collection of my mom's books." Mel's eyes flickered with curiosity at Lily's mention of books. "I told Donna, I'm interested in trying out this idea. You and me. If it doesn't work for either one of us, we could go our separate ways. Sort of a trial to see if we like it."

Mel didn't say anything, but her head moved in an almost imperceptible nod. Donna waited for everyone to finish eating and said, "How about we take a tour, and then we can try the desserts I brought?"

Lily let the dogs lead the way down the stairs, and then they got involved sniffing and exploring and left the three women alone. Lily showed Mel the common area and explained how it worked. "If you decide to join me, this will be your room."

She led her to the guest bedroom that was decorated in shades of purple and lavender. "You have your own bathroom right next door."

"Wow, this is nice down here, Lily. It's like having your own apartment." Donna's enthusiasm matched her wide smile.

Mel's eyes widened when she gazed at the large bed and the tiled oversized shower in the bathroom. "It's really pretty."

"Let's take a walk out to the cottages. I'll explain what you would be doing to help." Lily led the way and knew Nora and Bree were out for the day. She took a key from her pocket and opened the door. Both Donna and Mel gasped. "It's gorgeous," said Donna.

Mel didn't say anything, but surveyed the area, admiring several of the beach-themed items Cyndy had added. "We clean up the cottages each day, straighten the bedding, take away dirty towels and replace them, replenish the toiletries, just give everything a good once over and take care of any messes."

She went on to explain the laundry process and the housekeeping service she contracted for checkouts and every third day of a consecutive stay. "If you come aboard, I'll eventually transfer the third-day bedding changes to you. The housekeepers would continue to do the heavy cleaning when guests leave."

Mel nodded her understanding. "You'd have to keep the downstairs common area clean and, of course, clean your room and bathroom." She explained about the Friday and Saturday night gatherings around the fire pit. "I'd have you help me get that ready, and you are welcome to join in the social hour."

"I'll provide a stocked fridge and pantry, and you're free to eat whatever you like. I'm not much of a cook but can make a few things. I bake treats and freeze them, so there are always cookies available downstairs. You can help me with that task every few weeks."

Lily looked around the yard as they came out of the cottage. "That's about it. I have a yard service do the yard work. I'll probably have you help me with the dogs occasionally." She led them to the trail that ran along the bluff. "There's the killer view I love."

Mel shaded her eyes and looked out at the ocean. "It's beautiful."

"I take the dogs down to the beach most mornings, early, just as the sun is coming up. It's a quiet time, and they get some exercise."

Donna led the way back to the house. "Well, what do you think, Mel?"

"I'd still work at the library, right?" she asked.

"Of course," said Donna, nodding.

"You would be done with the cottage chores on most days by eleven or so. If you have to change the bedding, it will take longer, but not much. I've got bicycles the guests use and would be happy to let you choose one for yourself. You could ride it to and from the library as long as the weather is decent."

Donna nodded. "That would work. If the weather is bad, we'll work out something, or you could take the bus. You'll have to make sure all your work is done before you leave, no matter how long it takes. The library is open until eight, so there's no hurry."

Lily called to the dogs, and they came running. She motioned them up the stairs. The ladies followed, and Donna retrieved her pastry box. "I couldn't decide, so chose a variety of yummy looking things."

Mel chose a piece of decadent chocolate cake with wide chocolate curls decorating the thick frosting. Donna took the carrot cake with thick cream cheese frosting. Lily decided on a slice of vanilla caramel cake wrapped with caramel buttercream frosting and chocolate ganache.

"This is delicious," said Lily. "Thanks for bringing them. I haven't tried any of their cakes."

Mel had eaten every speck of her lunch and did the same with her dessert. She pushed her plate away and sat back in her chair.

"Well," said Donna. "What do you think? Are you willing to give it a try?"

Chapter 22

After a long pause and a walk around the yard with the dogs, Mel announced her decision. "I'll give it a try, but like you said, if it doesn't work, I'll be free to quit."

With her face expressionless, it was difficult for Lily to tell if she was happy about her choice. Donna, on the other hand, had a smile that wouldn't stop.

"That's terrific, Mel. Could you come over Friday after your work at the library? I'm sure Donna can give you a ride and transport your things. I only have one new arrival on Friday, so I won't be swamped."

Donna's head bobbed with excitement. "Of course, I'm happy to give you a lift."

"Okay," said Mel. That was it, no emotion.

"Well, we better get back to the library. Thanks so much for having us over," said Donna.

Lily walked them through the gate and to Donna's car. She watched as the two drove away. Donna waved, and Mel stared out the window.

"I hope I didn't just make a huge mistake," mumbled Lily.

◦◦◦

After cleaning up the leftovers from lunch and stashing the rest of the bakery treats in the fridge, she checked her computer. No additional reservations came in for Sunday. The chance of someone booking a one-night stay was slim.

She wrote an email to the couple who canceled and told them she was able to book their cottage for two of the three nights, so she would only be charging their card for one, as per her cancellation policy. She wished them well and invited them to Glass Beach Cottage in the future, providing them with a small discount coupon to use on their next booking.

She fed the dogs their dinner early so they'd be ready to go to Mac's. While they rested, she stocked Mel's bathroom with shampoo, toothpaste, and other basics. She wasn't sure what she had and didn't want her to be without some staples.

She found Alice and Kelly at the table working on their puzzle, snacking on cookies. "Hello there. How was your day?"

"It's been great. We took a drive through part of the park today. It was gorgeous," said Kelly.

Alice placed her hand on her daughter's arm. "This has been a wonderful trip. I'm so glad we did this." She paused and added, "I wanted to do something special with Kelly before it's too late."

"It's been a rough couple of years," said Kelly. "This has been heavenly to be somewhere so beautiful and relaxing. We've spent so much time in hospitals and doctor's offices, so when Mom decided she'd had enough, she was determined to make some happy memories." A tear fell down her cheek. "For both of us."

Lily's throat tightened as she watched the pair. "I'm glad you decided to visit here. It's wonderful that you'll have memories of this special time together." Lily glanced around the room and out the window. "I have such fond memories of my aunt and uncle and this place. It's my own cozy haven. Those memories are such a comfort to me now."

All three women had tears in their eyes. Lily fixed them glasses of iced tea and brought them a few more cookies. "Enjoy the rest of the day. I'm taking the dogs and will be going out for a few hours."

She left them to their puzzle and went upstairs. The dogs were excited to go for a ride in the truck. She made a quick stop at a store in town, stashed some bags in the front seat, and steadied the box of leftover pastries she was contributing to the meal. She glanced at her scribbled notes and set off out of town, following Mac's directions. He lived about five miles west of downtown on the coast with a view of Victoria.

She took the last turn and found the driveway. Her eyes widened when she got her first look at the enormous Cape Cod style home. Sherlock and Mac were outside, waiting for them.

Mac waved and helped her unload the dogs. Sherlock and Bodie wiggled and waggled as they touched noses. Mac said, "Come on up to the house. I've got a fenced yard we can leave the dogs in to play."

She followed him around the back of the house, which was crowded with floor to ceiling windows and glass French doors, affording what she suspected were million-dollar views. He opened the gate and led the dogs into the grassy area. "Okay, boys, you guys burn off some energy, and then we'll work on some training."

He detoured to a fenced pasture area. He pointed at two llamas inside the fence. That's Margo and Coco.

"Oh, they look so sweet and soft."

"They're lots of fun. It all started with Margo. She was sick, and her owners didn't want to pay for treatment. They wanted to put her down. I asked if I could have her instead, and the rest is history. Except, I had to find her a friend."

He guided Lily back to a set of stairs that led to a beautiful deck off the kitchen and dining area. "Hope you like burgers. Decided to keep it simple and enjoy this beautiful weather."

"Love them. I brought some extra bakery treats from Donna and Mel's visit today."

"Oh, great. I'm anxious to hear how that went."

She couldn't help gawking at the gorgeous home. A modern kitchen with black granite counters, stainless appliances, and pendulum lighting was flanked by a cozy upholstered window seat that would be perfect for reading. Gleaming wood floors below a gorgeous tongue and groove ceiling with open beam construction, gave it a woodsy feel.

The views were stunning. The magnificent blue waters could be seen from every room. "Your home is gorgeous. Incredible views."

"I'll give you a quick tour," he offered.

She followed him as he walked from the dining area, past a large brick hearth with a wood stove and built-in bookshelves across from it. He gestured to a step down into a living room with windows along the walls. "It's an open design, so no huge separation of space."

"The master suite and one bedroom is upstairs. Two more guest rooms are on the lower level." He shimmied up the stairs and showed her into an enormous master bedroom with huge windows along the back wall. A gorgeous bathroom completed the space. A door connected to a home office, with a desk, computer, and tons of books. "This was Missy's bedroom, but I converted it to my office space after she left."

They walked past another bathroom, and she followed him downstairs to the lowest level. "This is sort of the family room or den area." It was outfitted with a large television and comfortable chairs. "Two guest bedrooms down here and a bathroom they share."

"There's another powder room off the kitchen upstairs. I'll show you the flagstone patio that's off the kitchen's back door." He led her outside from the lower level, and they spied on the dogs, who were still romping on the grassy area.

"You're so secluded out here. Almost by yourself."

"I've got just over four acres. I bought this place, like I said, after Jill died. I overcompensated, as they say. Trying to give Missy everything. Had a horse for her out here, always had dogs. I wanted us to have a refuge, away from all the memories. A new start."

He stopped and looked across the grounds. "It's too big for one person, but I like it here and don't want to move. It's an escape from work. From the world."

They walked around the house, and he led her to a small shaded patio on the side of the kitchen. It was nestled among glossy green shrubbery and adorned with pots overflowing with flowers and herbs. It didn't have the jaw-dropping views of the ocean. Instead, it offered a cozy space and the inviting scent of the flowers and rosemary. A small bubbling fountain decorated the center of the irregular shaped flagstone surface.

"It's tranquil here. A quiet space for solitude," said Lily.

He nodded. "I often have coffee here in the morning."

He led her through the side door of the kitchen. "Now we're back where we started." He moved to the refrigerator. "I've got iced tea, wine, beer, water?"

"Iced tea would be great."

He fixed two glasses and said, "Let's see if we can work with Bodie for a few minutes and then I'll get the grill started."

The dogs were flopped on each other in a pile in the shade. As soon as they heard their owners, they jumped to attention. Lily sat on the grass with Sherlock and Fritz while she watched Mac's technique with Bodie.

He practiced the words Bodie excelled at first, giving him treats. After several rounds of success, he took him to the gate on the far end of the grassy area, toward the front of the house. Mac put his hand on the latch and Bodie wiggled with excitement. "Wait," he said.

He started to open the latch, and Bodie lunged forward. "Oops," said Mac, taking his hand from the latch. He kept doing the same thing over and over, until Bodie understood he had to stop and wait.

Once he did that Mac opened the gate, giving him the command to wait. It took several more tries before Bodie would stop and not move until Mac said, "Okay, let's go."

He brought Bodie back to Lily and said, "I'm not a professional dog trainer, but have used that technique for years. You just have to keep practicing. Take him to different doors, gates, stairs, whatever. Just be consistent and use the same words. *Wait, oops,* and *okay, let's go.*"

"No treat on the *oops*, right?"

He nodded, "That's right. Reward him when he's correct and no treat when he gets an *oops*." He turned and whistled at Sherlock. The three dogs followed them back around the yard and to the stairs.

He motioned them into the house and said, "I'll get the grill started. I've got watermelon and some twice baked potatoes I picked up at the market."

She helped him in the kitchen and set the outdoor table. They enjoyed the meal as the sun began to set. She gave him the rundown on Mel's visit and expressed her doubts. "I guess we'll see what happens in the coming weeks. She's impossible to read."

The soft pinks in the sky over the water glowed as the sun sank deeper. "She's probably learned not to trust and to put up a wall. Sounds like she hasn't been given too many reasons to count on people."

Lily gazed across the water and said, "You're right. I'm sure she's learned not to give too much away. Trying to protect herself."

The dogs were lounging on the deck. "It's a perfect evening," said Mac.

She opened the box and gave Mac first choice on dessert. He

took the lemon cake with a meringue frosting. She opted for the strawberry and cream cake.

He took a bite and groaned. "Wow, I could get used to this. Burgers, cake, and good company."

Lily found it difficult to tear herself away from the view from Mac's deck. She stayed later than she planned, causing her to oversleep on Friday. She hurried to get ready, knowing Joe and Lisa were checking out and expected to get an early start.

She fed the dogs and said, "Sorry, guys, no beach this morning. We'll go tomorrow."

She hurried down the stairs when she saw Joe lugging their bags across the yard. Lisa emerged from the cottage and asked Lily if she would take their picture in front of the door.

Lily captured several shots for them and handed the phone back to Lisa. "For our scrapbook." She patted her midsection and said, "We'll be back when she's old enough to appreciate the beauty of this area."

"I look forward to it. I'm glad you enjoyed your stay." She made sure all their paperwork was in order and walked them to the side of the house. "Safe travels."

While Lily was having breakfast on the deck, Nora and Bree opened their door and waved goodbye. "See you tonight at the fire pit," said Nora.

The housekeepers arrived as Alice and Kelly were leaving for the day. They made quick work of turning over the vacant cottage and changing all the linens in the other two. They left behind a mound of laundry.

Lily spent the next several hours traipsing up and down the stairs to get all of it washed and dried. She used up her pocketful of treats training Bodie at the kitchen door and the back stairs.

He was improving each time. She took him in the yard and tried the command without a door, just using hand gestures and her voice to make him wait. He stopped and looked at her with his head tilted. She practiced this with him around the yard, and by the afternoon, he was obeying each time she told him to wait.

When the laundry was done, she started on the evening snack presentation. It had much of the same ingredients as last week, but she had picked up a couple of different cheeses and fancy olives at the market. As soon as she finished slicing and arranging, her phone chimed.

"Must be the new guests," she said, leaving the dogs on the deck.

She found an older man and woman unloading their car. "Hello, you must be Mr. and Mrs. Jensen."

The woman with beautiful gray hair smiled. "We're Mike and Louise."

"Welcome. Your cottage is ready, and we'll get you checked in." Lily offered to carry one of her bags and led the way to the house.

"Oh, my, it's even prettier than I remember," said Louise.

"You stayed here before?" asked Lily.

She smiled at her husband. "We spent our honeymoon here. We came here a few times over the years. It's our fortieth anniversary, so we thought it would be fun to return."

"To the scene of the crime," said Mike, with a long laugh.

"How wonderful. Happy Anniversary. You probably knew my Aunt Maggie and Uncle Leo?"

"Yes, they were wonderful. We always enjoyed visiting with them. We were sorry to hear about Leo's passing." The smile faded from Louise's lips.

"But thrilled to have the place stay in the family. It looks like you've done a bit of work. The cottages look brand new," said Mike.

"They've just been refurbished. I'll get this paperwork done and take you down to show you." She went about the registration process and made sure they knew about snacks tonight, as well as the amenities in the common area.

She guided them to their cottage and listened with a sense of pride when they complimented the décor and all her work. "It's just lovely, Lily. Better than before, even," said Louise.

On her way back to the house, her phone rang. Donna was calling to see if it was a good time to deliver Mel. "Sure, I've got my work done, so I'll be free for a bit."

Within minutes the doorbell rang. Mel and Donna stood before her, each holding a small box. "Come on in," said Lily.

"We'll get you settled in downstairs, and then it will almost be time for appetizers with the guests." Mel followed her downstairs, took the box from Donna, and disappeared into her room.

Lily shrugged. "Is she okay?"

"I think so. Just nervous, I think," said Donna. "As I said, she's a quiet one. A bit on the cautious side." She turned to leave and said, "The library is open seven days a week, so she usually spends time volunteering and reading on the weekend."

Lily nodded. "Got it. She won't be so busy she can't continue. She'll have plenty of time."

Donna wandered down the hall and said, "Goodbye, Mel. I'll see you at the library on Monday."

The young woman came out of the room and said, "Okay. I'll finish those magazines this weekend."

Lily led Donna through the yard and out the gate. "Wish me luck," she said.

She decided to leave Mel alone and let her decompress and get acclimated. She had everything ready for the guests, so she had time to relax. She made sure the door was open at the top of the stairs, so

Mel wouldn't feel locked out and sat down with a book.

She had leftover chicken salad that would have to do for dinner tonight. She set the offerings on the outdoor table and called down the stairs for Mel. No reply.

She gave up on trying to yell and went down to find her. She was on her bed, reading a book. "Hey, I've got some stuff set out for dinner. Come on up."

She put her book down and followed Lily up to the deck. "It's not much, just what we had the other day for lunch."

Mel made a plate and began to eat, as the dogs watched from their perch atop their cushion. Lily tried to make small talk while they shared a meal, but didn't get much more than one-word replies.

"Do you have enough light in your room for reading?"

"I think so." Mel ate and gazed across the yard, signaling she wasn't in the mood to chat.

"Would you like to join us for snacks tonight? We've got some really nice guests today. Even a teenage girl. Her mother just got a job, so she'll be moving here."

She shrugged with noncommitment.

Lily finished the awkward meal and went about cleaning up the mess. After exercising the dogs and letting them play in the yard, she contained them on the deck. She retrieved the snacks and hauled the beverages out to the fire pit.

The cottage doors opened, and guests trickled across the yard to join the gathering. Lily introduced Mike and Louise to the others. They chatted with each other, and Nora shared her good news about moving to Driftwood Bay.

Lily excused herself to check on Mel. When she walked by the desk area, she noticed the bags she had picked up at the second-hand store were sitting there. The day she met Mel, Lily stopped at the store and picked out some clothes and shoes that looked almost new.

She asked the clerks to set aside anything that might fit, based on her guesstimate of sizes.

She took the bags with her and marched into Mel's room. Her door was open, and she was on the bed reading again. "Hey, Mel, what's with this?" She held the bags higher.

Mel moved her eyes over the top of her book. "I don't need your pity or charity."

"This is just some stuff I cleaned out of here when I moved in. Old clothes left from guests, lost and found stuff, extra clothes for people who needed them. My aunt always had a stash." Lily lied as she explained. "I was storing them in your closet." She looked at the two bags full of clothes. "You're welcome to anything you like. I'm just going to donate them when I get around to it."

"Well, I don't need any clothes."

"Well, then you won't mind if they continue to be stored here. Looks like you have plenty of room for them." She tossed them in the closet, taking note of one pair of pants and three identical shirts, two blue and one green, hanging in the huge closet.

Lily left without a word, shaking her head. "We're out at the fire pit," she hollered from the hallway. "Come join us or don't, up to you."

Her heart ached for the young girl, but she wasn't going to walk on eggshells and coax her on a continual basis. "Better she learns now," muttered Lily, as she walked to join the others. "Just like Bodie, she needs a bit of training."

Chapter 23

On Saturday morning, Lily gathered the dogs and went downstairs to unlock the back door. She tiptoed to Mel's room. She hadn't seen her since she returned the bags of clothes to her closet last night.

She gave the door a soft knock and said, "We're going to the beach if you want to join us." She waited a few minutes, but there was no reply.

"Come on boys," she said, leading them outside. Once they got to her favorite spot, she sat on her log and let the dogs off their leashes. It was time for them to get a bath anyway.

As the sun greeted her, she took a deep breath and let it out slowly. She did that several times while she watched the dogs splash each other in the water. She looked across the water and said, "So, do you think I messed up? She's not easy, that's for sure. I just couldn't stand by and do nothing."

A ray of light caught the soft ripples on the water and flashed in her eyes. She smiled and said, "Glad to see you agree."

She chased the dogs along the shore and then attached their leashes and led them back to the house. Knowing she would need a shower after she washed the dogs, she left them in their enclosure and gathered their bath supplies. As she was rinsing them, Mel came out the back door.

Her hair was wet from a shower, and she wore the same pants

and one of the shirts from her closet. "We missed you at the beach this morning. I knocked, but you must have been asleep or ignoring me."

"I didn't feel like going."

"We go most mornings. If you want to join, just be out here by six. I won't bother you again."

Mel sat on a chair and watched as Lily made sure all traces of soap were rinsed from each dog. Fritz was a model bather. Bodie was not. He fidgeted and tried to bite the water from the sprayer. Lily ended up drenched when he grabbed the hose in his mouth.

She used old towels and got them as dry as she could before sticking them back in their enclosure. She cleaned the tub she used and wiped everything down before storing the supplies in the utility room.

As she came outside, she waved to Nora and Bree. The teenager spotted Mel and came bounding over to the house. "Hi, I'm Bree. Are you staying here?"

Mel looked at Lily. "Mel is staying here and helping me out. I'm showing her the ropes this morning."

Nora and Bree smiled and told her how pleased they were to meet her. Nora didn't let on that she knew anything about Mel's story. She rambled on about their upcoming move and asked if Mel was in school. "No, I'm almost nineteen. I work at the library."

Nora carried the conversation, with Mel contributing little. The two left for breakfast and promised to be back in time for the social hour at the fire pit. Before Lily could go upstairs to shower, Mike and Louise made an appearance. They, too, were headed to breakfast.

They greeted Mel on their way out. She murmured a quiet reply. Lily looked down at her clothes covered in dirt and mud. "I'm going to run and grab a shower, and then we'll get started on the cottages."

She texted Mac when she got to her bedroom and invited him to join the social hour tonight. She wanted him to meet Bree and discuss her volunteering when she moved to Driftwood Bay. She returned within fifteen minutes and found Mel sitting with Alice at the puzzle table. They were working on it while Kelly savored another cup of coffee. "Good morning," said Lily.

Alice looked up and smiled. "Just doing my favorite thing with your new helper."

Kelly lifted her mug in a greeting. "Needed a bit more coffee this morning before we head out for breakfast."

"Well, we've got to get our chores done. I'm giving Mel her first lesson today."

"See you tonight. Looking forward to spending another evening visiting," said Kelly.

Lily showed Mel where to find the cleaning supplies and fresh towels. She had her observe what she did in the first cottage, and then Lily watched Mel complete the other two. Lily showed her the handy checklist she used to make sure she didn't forget anything.

Mel did a good job and followed instructions well. Lily praised her and encouraged her excellent work and attention to detail. Mel's expression didn't change. There was no joy or happiness in what she did, even at the library. She was dutiful, not cheerful.

"I'm going to head to the library if you don't need me for anything else."

"Sure, let me show you the bikes, and you can choose one." She led her around the side of the house and showed her the choices.

Mel surveyed the group and chose a vintage beach cruiser in blue. It had a sturdy basket on the front and a matching blue helmet. "I think there's a backpack in those bags in your closet, if that would be easier for you."

A trace of interest flickered in her eyes. Lily didn't push it and turned her attention to the bike. "The combo on the lock is the same as the house number. Easy to remember. Just make sure and lock it at the library."

Mel nodded. "Oh, I will. I wouldn't trust it unlocked. Someone would steal it for sure." She ran her hand over the frame. "It's a nice bike."

"I'll be upstairs, just let me know when you leave. You know the way, right?"

"Um, I think so." Lily gave her the most direct route out of the neighborhood, which involved only two turns.

Mel nodded. "Thanks for letting me use the bike, Lily."

"You're welcome." Lily checked on the dogs, who were still damp. She let them up on the deck to continue drying. After she made a shopping list, she did some work on the computer, paying no attention to Mel.

She caught movement out the window and saw Mel coming through the kitchen door. "I'm going to take off. The library closes at five, so I'll be back then." Lily noticed the backpack strapped on her when she turned to leave and smiled.

"See you when you get here. Tonight's another evening with the guests, so I'll be down there if I'm not in the house."

She nodded and hurried down the stairs. Lily shook her head. She sent an email to a psychologist she knew in Virginia, looking for advice on how to communicate with Mel and create some trust.

After giving the dogs a break on the grass, she left them in the enclosure while she went to the market. She gathered everything on her list and loaded it in her car. As she was opening her door, she saw the sign for the bakery. She remembered how much Mel had enjoyed the chocolate cake.

She dashed across the sidewalk and selected a few chocolatey treats. Yes, she was stooping to the level of bribery.

Once home, she pronounced the dogs dry, gave them a thorough brushing, and let them scamper in the yard. She worked with Bodie on his new command and reinforced all the old ones. He performed like a champ.

She checked her computer while the dogs lounged on the deck, recuperating from all their work. Her friend had replied. She perused the lengthy response, nodding as she read it. She recommended professional help for Mel. Her behaviors were common in adolescents who had lost a parent. Depression, emotional insecurity, inability to trust, closing herself off, and not taking the risk of developing relationships, were all common in those who lost parents.

Lily read the summary paragraph, and guilt washed over her for how irritated she had been with Mel. *Her lack of a support system in the form of her mother, who had a hard time coping with the father's death, and a system that failed her after her mother's suicide make it easy to understand why she would be reluctant to form relationships. She escapes in her duties at the library and now with you. She is protecting herself from future injuries by remaining unattached. She needs time and for you to prove you are trustworthy, but most of all, she needs professional help. You also might try sharing your story of the loss of your parents. She needs to see people surviving and leading a productive life after a tragic event.*

Her friend included some doctors in the area who might be able to help. Lily sent Donna an email to inquire about support programs or services for Mel. She added the names her friend had provided.

"I need to be patient," Lily coached herself. "There was a tiny breakthrough with the bike today, so maybe there's hope."

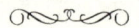

Mac arrived with Sherlock soon after Mel returned from the library. She chose one of the bakery treats for a snack and went straight to her room. Her only comment when Lily asked her how her day went was, "Fine."

Lily took a deep breath and carried the refreshed snack board to the backyard. Mac took care of igniting the fire pit and had corralled all three dogs in their enclosure. When he saw Lily, he said, "Where did you get the cool dog house that matches your cottages?"

"Andy. He wanted to make sure the dogs had shelter in bad weather. He's going to be a great dog parent."

Nora and Bree were the first out of their cottage and joined Mac and Lily. The others followed them within minutes. Lily introduced Mac to everyone and made a point of telling him about Bree's interest in dogs.

With great patience, he answered her questions and then took her to meet Sherlock. Once they were gone, Nora said, "Thank you so much for doing that. It will give her something to look forward to in our move."

Mike and Louise reminisced about their other trips to Glass Beach Cottage and entertained the group with stories. They couldn't linger long, as they had plans for a special dinner in town.

While Alice and Kelly were visiting with Nora, Mac and Bree returned, along with Mel. Lily couldn't believe her eyes. Mel was wearing clothes from the bag she had left in her closet. Jeans with a lavender shirt and sandals. Bree was chattering about how much she wanted a dog at their new house.

Lily stood and walked over to Mel. "Ladies, this is Mel. She's come on board to help me out around here."

Everyone introduced themselves, and Mel gave them polite nods and murmured a greeting. Lily offered her a chair between Alice and Mac.

The snacks were a hit, and as the night wore on, almost everything was devoured. Mac shared some of his memories of growing up in Driftwood Bay. Before they left, Mike and Lou remarked about the bond they had formed with Lily's aunt and uncle over their years of visits.

Lily noticed Alice and Mel engaged in a long conversation. Nora told them the buyers had accepted her offer on the house. Bree's attitude about the move wasn't as cynical as it had been. She was infatuated with the idea of working at Mac's clinic and had toured the high school and liked it.

As Lily watched the easy conversation and the connections form among her guests, she smiled. The soft lights illuminated the beautiful yard, the restored and inviting cottages, the house that held cherished memories, her furry best friends lounging on the deck, and the laughter and smiles of new friends and strangers who were transforming into friends. This was it. This was what she had envisioned when she decided to leave her old life. Returning to Glass Beach Cottage and the inviting beach haven she remembered with such fondness, had been her best decision.

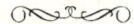

The next morning, Nora and Bree got an early start and assured Lily they would be in touch when they settled in Driftwood Bay. Mike and Louise lingered over their coffee, promising when they left to come back next year.

Alice and Kelly were the last to leave on Sunday. With tears in their eyes, they both hugged Lily. "We had a wonderful trip. I'm so glad we came, and I enjoyed meeting you," said Alice. "Your aunt and uncle would be so pleased to see this place revitalized and thriving."

Mel came from her bedroom, dressed in a casual pair of exercise pants and a new t-shirt from the stash of clothes in her closet. Alice gripped her hand and put her arm around the young girl. "You two make quite a team. I think you're lucky to have each other." The old woman gave Mel a wink.

"I'm collecting moments, and I've got a whole trunk full from this special trip with Kelly. It's so easy to get caught up in all the day-to-day parts of living. Time goes by so fast, but it's the moments that matter. Those memories you make that will be with you forever."

Tears were running down Lily's face as she and Mel waved goodbye to them. Lily let the dogs out, and Mel sat on the grass with them. "I'm sorry I was so rude about the clothes," she said. "I could use some new ones, so thanks for letting me have them."

"I'm glad you found some things you like. I loved that shirt you wore last night."

"I liked Alice. She reminded me of my grandma."

"She's a lovable lady. It's been a bittersweet trip for them. She knows it's probably her last trip."

Mel nodded. "She told me she's dying. She's not scared. She's just worried about her daughter and her grandkids."

"It's not easy losing our parents. My mom died in the plane crash at the Pentagon on 9/11, and my dad passed just a few months later. I was numb for months. I still miss them. I didn't get to say goodbye to either of them. Gone in a heartbeat."

Mel stared across the yard in thought.

"When my husband was killed, I wasn't sure I'd survive it. Without my son and Fritz, I probably wouldn't have. I couldn't do it by myself. It's tempting to withdraw. I still struggle with that, but I've found new friends here who make me feel better."

Mel plucked at the grass, but listened as Lily continued. "I think it's natural when you lose those you love, those most important in your life, to shut yourself off. I mean, why risk having your heart shattered again, right? It feels safer to take care of yourself and not let anyone get too close. In the long run, it's much harder. I knew I had to take care of Kevin and help him, but Fritz is the one who helped me the most. He comforted me and sensed when I was sad or most vulnerable. He didn't have to say a word. He was just there, no matter what."

"People aren't always like that though," said Mel.

Lily nodded. "You're right. Some of them aren't sincere. They're not real friends. I'm picky about who I let into my life. The problem is, if you paint everyone with the same brush and don't trust anyone, you'll miss out. You'll never have a chance at the true happiness that comes from close relationships."

Mel stroked Fritz's fur as she listened to Lily. "Alice said sort of the same thing. She told me she knew I could trust you. She thinks we met for a reason."

Lily smiled. "I think Alice is a wise woman."

Lily heard a noise at the side of the house and saw the housekeepers arriving in the driveway. "Well, we get a break from cleaning today, but we'll have loads and loads of laundry."

After letting them know all the guests had checked out, Lily gestured to Mel. "Come on in, and we'll have breakfast."

Mel stopped downstairs and brought a book with her. As she was scrambling eggs, Lily took note of Mel. The book was the perfect defense. She didn't have to engage with anyone. It kept her from having to make eye contact. Lily suspected it made her feel less alone, as she escaped into the world created by the author.

After adding the warmed leftover pastries to the eggs, she brought their plates to the island. As they ate, Lily shared that her mother had been a librarian.

Mel's eyes moved from her book. "Did you have tons of books at your house?"

"Oh, yes. My dad was a teacher, so between the two of them, our house was filled with books. I have quite a few books here in the house. You're welcome to borrow any of them."

When they finished, Mel offered to handle the dishes. Lily

showed her where to find everything and opened the dishwasher. She left her to it and took the dogs to the deck.

Her cell rang. She looked at the screen and said, "Hey, Mac."

"Hope I'm not disturbing you. We didn't get a chance to talk much last night, but I told Mel about my llamas, and it seemed to spark her interest. I thought you two might want to come this afternoon or evening to visit them. Sherlock would love for you to bring the dogs, and we'll have a picnic."

"Oh, wow, that's nice of you to offer. Her freeze out has begun to thaw a bit. Thanks to Alice and you, I'm sure. She even thanked me for the clothes."

"Lots of trauma at a young and vulnerable age. An age when a girl needs her mom. Believe me, I know. Maybe we can build on that small crack and get her interested in some new things."

"Well, I've got two checking in today and a bunch of laundry. It will be close to four before we could be there."

"No rush. Whenever you get here is fine. I've got everything we need."

"I've got some leftovers I can bring for a small snack plate. I can pick something up at the store if you need anything else."

"Not necessary. The snacks will be terrific. See you when you get here."

Mel came through the door as Lily disconnected. "Is the laundry ready?"

"I'm sure there's enough for the first load." Lily made for the stairs, and the dogs followed. On the way to the cottages, Lily said, "Mac called and invited us out to his place. He wanted you to see his llamas, and he said we could have a picnic."

"I've never seen a llama in person." Lily detected a trace of excitement in Mel's voice.

"We'll go after our arrivals this afternoon. That should give us time to get all this laundry done."

In between loads, Lily worked with Bodie on his training words.

Mel played with the dogs and read her book. She also cleaned and refilled the beverage dispensers downstairs and made sure everything was restocked and ready for the week.

A few minutes before three, two couples arrived. They were in town for a family reunion and would be spending most of their time with family. Lily gave them a quick tour of the downstairs and made sure they knew the gate code.

Lily gathered the remaining snacks from the fridge and pantry and threw on a clean shirt. She went downstairs to fold the last load and tapped on Mel's partially open door. Lily saw Mel sitting on her bed, reading, and noticed she had also changed her shirt.

Lily glanced at the closet and saw all the clothes from the bags had been hung on hangers. The room was neat and orderly, but at least it looked like she might stay. "I'm ready to head out," she said. "I just need to load the dogs, and we can hit the road."

Mel left the book on the nightstand and followed her upstairs. She locked the deadbolt and grabbed the bag of food. Fritz hung his head out of the window as they drove through town.

As they made their way, Mel said, "I'm sorry you lost your parents and your husband. I lost both of my parents, so I know how you feel."

"Thanks, Mel. I'm also sorry for your loss. I know it would be much harder to lose them at your age."

"What you said about trusting other people was right. After my mom died, I had to go live with other people. They were only nice when the social workers were there to check. I lived with four different families. The social workers told me they would take care of me and help me. It was all lies."

"I know you have no reason to believe me, but you can count on me," said Lily, making the last turn to Mac's. "Glass Beach Cottage is my haven. It can be yours too."

As she steered down the driveway, the dogs' tails wagged with enthusiasm. Mel's head moved back and forth, taking in the large area. "Wow, he's got some place."

"It's gorgeous. You'll enjoy it here. Beautiful views and lots of space," said Lily, turning off the engine.

Mac appeared with Sherlock at his side. He opened Lily's door. "Hello, ladies. I'll take the dogs. Go ahead and stash your food in the kitchen. Mel can come with me down to the pasture."

She watched as he walked with Mel, the furry companions romping and playing as they followed. She found a large plate in a cupboard and took the time to cut and arrange the food, giving Mac a bit of time alone with Mel.

She spied them at the fence, petting the llamas. She saw the three dogs were in the grassy area, too busy playing to take notice of her presence. She continued past them to the pasture. "So, what do you think of them, Mel?"

When she turned, a genuine smile filled her face. "I love them. They're so soft." Mac grinned as he watched her talk to Margo and Coco.

"Let's see how Bodie does on his commands," he suggested. "We'll be just over there with the dogs."

As he walked with Lily, he whispered, "She seems a bit more relaxed today. Wants to know all about llamas. I predict she'll be researching them at the library tomorrow."

"That's the first time I've seen her smile. Thank you for taking the time with her."

He held the gate for Lily. "I think it will be worth it." The dogs rushed to them, and he gave them lots of attention and a good run around the perimeter before tackling Bodie. Lily sat with Sherlock and Fritz to watch.

Bodie didn't miss a beat. He had a hard time being still when

Mac asked him to wait the first time, but persevered and didn't go through the gate until Mac gave him the command. Mac tested him several times, but he didn't falter.

He brought him back through the gate and said, "He's improved. Good boy, Bodie." He gave the other dogs a few treats and said, "Let's see if we can tear her away from the llamas to eat."

They left the dogs to play and retrieved Mel, with the promise she could come back to the pasture after dinner. Mac put them to work setting the table, filling glasses, and adding Lily's snack tray to the spread. He retrieved a stack of containers from the fridge and hauled them outside.

"We've got sandwiches, lots of salads, watermelon, and a special dessert for later." They passed around the food while they chatted. Everything llama dominated the conversation.

Lily offered to clean up the mess while Mac and Mel retrieved the dogs. With all the windows along the back of the house, she never lost sight of the pair. They made a detour at the pasture and leaned against the fence. Margo and Coco made their way across to them.

When she finished tidying the kitchen, Mel and Mac were still petting the sweet animals. She could tell Mac was explaining something to Mel and showing her Coco's ears. Lily strolled out to the edge of the property, where several feet below, the waves crashed into the shore. There wasn't any easy access to the skinny ribbon of sand that made up the beach on this part of the coast.

What the property lacked in beach access, it made up for by delivering jaw-dropping views of the pristine water, distant land masses, and the rugged coastline as it wrapped around the peninsula.

Soft golden light filtered out from the clouds as the sun moved closer to the edge of the horizon. A wooden deck anchored above the bluff held two Adirondack chairs. She slipped into one, leaning back to soak in the panoramic views.

She let out a long breath, gazed across to the fenced area and saw Mel and Mac playing with the dogs and smiled. The sound of the waves coming ashore and the gentle breeze made for a flawless summer evening.

She closed her eyes and concentrated on the sound of the sea and the smell of salt, grass, and pine trees. She practiced deep breathing and relaxed. A whiff of Gary's aftershave tickled her nose. The breeze ruffled her blouse, and she swore she heard his voice. "Goodbye, Lily. I love you. Live your life and be happy."

She felt a tear slide out of her eye. She looked at the chair, but it was empty. The water below rippled and glistened as the light touched it. Soft footsteps made her take her eyes off the vista.

Mac stepped onto the deck. "You've got the best seat in the house," he said.

"It's incredible. I could sit here for hours." She wiped the tears from her face.

"You okay?"

"I will be."

The sphere of bright light kissed the dark water, and the blue transformed into liquid gold. A wide band of brilliant light glittered across the water, connecting to the shore. "It never gets old," he said. "Watching the day say goodbye as it slips into the sea."

He stood and offered her his hand. She took it and stepped down from the deck. As they followed the illuminated path of stepping stones, he squeezed her hand in a firm grip. "And then in the morning, the sun appears again and promises us another chance."

ACKNOWLEDGEMENTS

The idea for a new women's fiction series came to me this summer. My research for this story focused on the training of hearing service dogs. I am so impressed by all the programs offered for those who need these wonderful dogs. If you have such a program in your area, I encourage you to visit and learn more about how you can support them. I hope you enjoyed the beginning of Lily's story. I have plans for two more books in my Glass Beach Cottage Series but will be writing another murder mystery first.

My early readers are always willing to critique my work and provide such useful feedback for improvements. I'm grateful for Theresa and Tami, who were kind enough to read the earliest drafts and my team for reading the early release copies.

Elizabeth Mackey was able to design the perfect cover based on my rambling of ideas. She is a joy to work with and hit a home run with her ideas for this series. Many thanks to my editors, Connie and Jaime. They both do a fabulous job and I enjoy working with them. Jason and Marina at Polgarus deliver expert formatting and are always pleasant and accommodating.

I'm grateful for the support and encouragement of my friends and family as I continue to pursue my dream of writing. I appreciate all of the readers who have taken the time to provide a review on Amazon. These reviews are especially important in promoting future books, so if you enjoy my novels, please consider leaving a positive review. Follow this link to my author page and select a book to leave your review at www.amazon.com/author/tammylgrace. I also encourage you to follow me on Amazon, and you'll be the first to know about new releases.

Remember to visit my website at http://www.tammylgrace.com and join my mailing list for my exclusive group of readers. I've also got a fun Book Buddies Facebook Group. That's the best place to find me and get a chance to participate in my giveaways. Join my Facebook group at www.facebook.com/groups/AuthorTammyLGraceBookBuddies/ and keep in touch—I'd love to hear from you.

From the Author

Thank you for reading BEACH HAVEN the first book in my Glass Beach Cottage Series. You'll need to read this series in order, as the stories build on each other. If you're a new reader and enjoy women's fiction, you'll want to try my Hometown Harbor Series, filled with the complex relationships of friendship and family. Set in the picturesque San Juan Islands in Washington, you'll escape with a close-knit group of friends and their interwoven lives filled with both challenges and joys. Each book in the series focuses on a different woman and her journey of self-discovery. Be sure and download the free novella, HOMETOWN HARBOR: THE BEGINNING. It's a prequel to FINDING HOME that I know you'll enjoy.

For mystery lovers, I write a series that features a lovable private detective, Coop, and his faithful golden retriever, Gus. If you like whodunits that will keep you guessing until the end, you'll enjoy the Cooper Harrington Detective Novels. If you're a fan of Christmas stories, you'll want to read A SEASON FOR HOPE. It's my latest Christmas novella.

I'd love to send you my exclusive interview with the canine companions in the Hometown Harbor Series as a thank-you for joining my exclusive group of readers. Instructions and a link for signing up for my mailing list are included below. You'll also find questions for book club discussions at www.tammylgrace.com.

Enjoy this book?
You can make a big difference

Thanks again for reading my work and if you enjoy my novels, *I would be grateful if you would leave a review on Amazon*. Authors need reviews to help showcase their work and market it across other platforms. I'd like to be able to take out full-page ads in the newspaper, but I don't have the financial muscle of a big New York publisher. When it comes to getting attention for my work, reviews are some of the most powerful tools I have. You can help by sharing what you enjoyed with other readers.

If you enjoyed my books, please consider leaving a review

Hometown Harbor: The Beginning (FREE Prequel Novella)
Finding Home (Book 1)
Home Blooms (Book 2)
A Promise of Home (Book 3)
Pieces of Home (Book 4)
Finally Home (Book 5)
Killer Music: A Cooper Harrington Detective Novel (Book 1)
Deadly Connection: A Cooper Harrington Detective Novel (Book 2)
Dead Wrong: A Cooper Harrington Detective Novel (Book 3)
Beach Haven: Glass Beach Cottage Series (Book 1)

ABOUT THE AUTHOR

Tammy L. Grace is the award-winning author of the Cooper Harrington Detective Novels, the Hometown Harbor Series, and the Glass Beach Cottage Series. You'll find Tammy online at www.tammylgrace.com where you can join her mailing list and be part of her exclusive group of readers. Connect with Tammy on Facebook at www.facebook.com/tammylgrace.books or Instagram at @authortammylgrace.

Made in the USA
San Bernardino, CA
12 November 2018